THE GREEN SCREEN

a novel

Blake Madden

Cover Design: Shogo Ota
Edited & Formatted: Michelle Josette
Layout & Composition: Sarah Plein

www.mjbookeditor.com

For Annabelle, Isabelle, Liza, Toni and Darryl.

TABLE OF CONTENTS

1
NIGHT

"Home? What home? In a couple more hours, it ain't gonna be home anymore."

- Mikey, *The Goonies*

Floyd had always liked movies that take place over one day. "I've always liked movies that take place over one day," he began, taking a hit. He held the smoke and his next words in, passing the joint to his cohort. Thibault stared off into the distance and nodded silently while taking a hit of his own. Something rustled in the Dumpster behind them and they jumped, pausing their dialogue momentarily.

"*The Goonies*," Floyd continued after a moment, "takes place over one day. The *last* day." He pointed for emphasis, smoke still coming out of his mouth and nostrils.

They both shivered in the cold, underdressed as they were. Floyd wore Kate's coat, although it provided little warmth. It fit snug around his torso and had a mane that resembled a white feather boa. Thibault wore only a long sleeve t-shirt. He continually rubbed the back of his head where his shaggy, dirty blond hair sat just hours ago, before Kate's impromptu haircut. Outside the club, they could still hear the faint pulsing of the hard 140-bpm bass drum.

"It's the last day before these families have to move. This is the only home these kids have ever known, and it's their last day there. So they go on an adventure. With only one day left of life as you know it, wouldn't you? Every time they're ready to quit and go home, they remember that this day is all they have left, and so they press on."

He inhaled again, his second hit.

"And they fall just short . . . or so we think."

Floyd stepped to his left—his eyes glassy and full—and spread his hands out with a smile.

"There's that scene at the end on the beach: they're sitting in the sun, feeling exhausted, feeling defeated, but simultaneously happy and relieved to see their families, to see the light of day again and know they are safe.

"And it dawns on them: no matter what happens, they will never have another day like that one, another story like the one they just lived. They'll grow old, they'll go their separate ways, stop talking to each other. Chunk will lose weight and resent his cruel nickname. Mikey will become a drunk, reminiscing about the days when he was young and adventurous and the world was still full of promise. But that *one day* will live forever in crystal, unchanged. It's a complete story: a beginning, middle and end, compacted so that every thought, feeling, and emotion is amplified and accelerated, like some fever dream."

Another noise made them pause and look around the parking lot in all directions. Floyd continued at a lower volume.

"Even as they realize the preciousness of that singular experience in their lives, it's bittersweet. The sun shines on them, reminding them that the days move on without pause. As much as they want to hold on to that one day, time will keep washing it away.

"And wouldn't you know it—fate rewards those who live one day as if it is their last!" he said, throwing his hands into the air.

"The Goonies find some leftover treasure the Fratellis didn't get, buried in the bottom of Mouth's marble bag. Somehow they can all instantly appraise it as priceless— that's another conversation, mind you—and they realize they can save the town from the developers.

"And they all watch breathless as One-Eyed Willie's pirate ship sails off into the sunrise. THE SUNRISE! Do you hear? Not the sunset! It's a new day; another one has come, but that one is frozen, never to be repeated . . ."

He trailed off.

"*Ferris Bueller's Day Off*," mouthed Thibault, trying and failing to keep smoke in his mouth.

Floyd paused before his analysis, considering what to do with the joint he held again. One more hit would equal three, which would be one more than two, which would be going against his Uncle Paul's "Two Hit Rule". Paul explained it to him one summer in Maine. They sat around a fire inside a teepee his uncle built. Paul looked regal with purpose, his voice booming from his tan lips before he inhaled slowly.

"Floyd, wherever I am in the world, I only ever take two hits. That way, I never get so fucked up that I don't know what's going on."

Floyd almost never followed the two hit rule, but he liked

to think about it now and again, especially when something awful would happen to him after smoking too much. Still, Kate *did* roll this joint just for them. And they deserved at least one night of real fun, especially on the last day of school.

He took a deep hit, his third hit, and immediately began coughing violently, dropping the joint in the process. Thibault picked it back up and listened to him press on in between hacking and gasping.

"*Ferris* is a perfect example *cough cough* and one of my Top Five of all time by the way. *cough cough* Ferris knows his days are *cough cough* literally numbered *cough* so he decides he has to milk one last one *cough cough* perfectly."

After a minute, he finally mustered a deep, clean breath.

"He's got to live this last day right. He owes it to himself. He owes it to his best friend, who will never know what it is to live like this on his own. He owes it to his girlfriend. Down one road, they get married and grow old and boring together. Down another, Ferris goes off to college, he starts banging freshman girls two at a time, and they never see each other again. Either way, things are about to change big time. It's technically not the last day they'll all spend together, but it might as well be. They have to take it for all its worth."

A car sped by in the street and honked its horn. They both flinched.

"And isn't it fitting that his sister, Jeanie, who continually and stubbornly refuses to embrace the possibilities of a day fully lived—*she* gets busted, while Ferris gets off scot-free?"

Thibault passed him the joint again. Why stop now? It was the most he had enjoyed talking and the clearest his thoughts had felt in weeks.

"You hoping tomorrow is your one day like that?" Thibault asked, receiving the joint again.

Floyd shuttered briefly at the question, considering the arc of the last two years of his life in South Africa. Soon it would all be so much ancient history. But he did want that day. That ending. Something—anything—from his time here to look back on fondly. The thought brought a brief smile to his face and he answered sheepishly, almost dreamily.

"We'll see," he managed, as a figure approached them in the distance.

The figure didn't look much older than either of them. He wore cargo shorts and a black t-shirt, and was clearly headed right towards them.

"Oh shit," whispered Thibault.

"Get rid of it," whispered Floyd.

Thibault quickly flicked away the last of the joint, though neither of them knew exactly why yet. The sudden realization that they were woefully unprepared to deal with any unfamiliar or authoritarian force was motivation enough. A thick chemical-induced film had enveloped them, the horror and subsequent paralysis—*The Fear* as Hunter Thompson called it. Two hits, indeed.

"How's it, *chinas*???"

The stranger's voice was nasal, maybe even still teenaged. But it spoke with enough confidence and authority that the boys were cemented in tight-lipped fear. They may or may not have mumbled a reply.

The stranger worked fast. He poked and prodded them, patted and re-patted them, apparently searching for something. It was the dance of a snake charmer.

"What you gents doing out here, eh? Smoking *dagga*? Eh, *chinas*?"

The boys glanced at each other but said nothing, and the stranger continued patting them down while talking. They both silently hoped the other would find the strength and sense to take control of the situation, but neither of them felt qualified to do so.

"Come on, man! What you on about? You mustn't mess me around, you know! I'm a cop!"

It didn't make sense. Something didn't add up. Would it have made sense after only two hits?

"Uh . . . nothing, sir," Floyd still managed.

"Sir?" The stranger chuckled. "What's this?"

He was holding the sides of the great mane of Kate's coat, his face only inches from Floyd's.

"You a *moffie* or something?"

The stranger jammed his hands violently into Floyd's various pockets. Even as the fog lifted and the image taking shape became clearer and more terrifying, the boys' reactions were muted.

"And what's this?"

The stranger pulled out a can of Coke from Floyd's pants pocket. Floyd had carried it around since 7:15 that morning, planning to drink it that night in celebration of the last day of school and the second to last day of his life in South Africa. It was comically out of place now in the tense atmosphere. Indeed, even the stranger was amused by the artifact he held. He quickly shoved it back into Floyd's pocket, grinning a sinister, hollow grin at Thibault, who only looked at the ground.

"And *this*?"

The stranger held in his hand the 40 rand from Floyd's pocket, and all at once Floyd understood that this *should not* be happening.

He finally opened his mouth to raise a vocal protest, but no words came—only a flash and a sting.

And then the sky.

And the sound of fizz.

He realized he was on his back looking up. He sat up slowly, his face wet and still stinging. He looked over and there was Thibault on the ground, rolling around in a similar display of disorientation and futility. Floyd's can of Coke spun around between them, angrily spraying its fizz on them in its last gasps before impending death.

"What. Happened."

"We got mugged," Thibault managed. "You're covered in blood."

The words meant little. They formed no real answer to his question, itself a combination of other meaningless words. They were children again, babies even, unable to process the world around them and the fate that had befallen them. No explanation could accurately summarize the events that had just occurred, or educate them as to why they had occurred. The blur of the next hour proved no more informative.

"I'm so sorry," Kate said, aghast and near tears as she hugged her bloodied newborn nerd children. They said nothing.

"*Jassus*, what you guys doing just hanging 'round out there?" said the club's bouncer, examining the blood pouring from Floyd's nose onto his shirt. "Don't you know this is a bad neighborhood?"

No answer. No debate to be had. No sense to be found.

Other Afrikaans teens laughed and pointed in their direction from across the club as the two sat silent and motionless in the corner for the rest of the evening. Thibault wore sunglasses. Floyd stared straight ahead with the same vacant, glassy look he had perfected during the previous hour.

He thought of surprise endings in movies, the ones where the main characters look like they're going to be fine, but then something awful happens to them just before the movie ends. He had always hated those movies.

Neither he nor Thibault spoke to each other. The last clear thought he could remember was the discussion of the importance of a final, perfect day.

It was 1:15am.

It was officially his last day in South Africa.

2

MORNING

"You know, Billy...we blew it."

- Wyatt, *Easy Rider*

I'd say real life makes for a poor movie.

Things always end either too early or too late. The plots are convoluted. The characters are underdeveloped—just an unending string of meaningless cameos and bit players who stick around way too long without being remotely likable or interesting. The actors bumble their lines repeatedly; sometimes they can't come up with them at all. Heroes don't end up being particularly heroic. Then again, villains are never very 'super' either; they look and act just like normal people. There aren't really any Auric Goldfingers with lasers that will ever-so-slowly annihilate your balls. Mainly, there are just guys who sucker-punch you to get your 40 rand.

If anything, life is a straight-to-video movie, a sequel even. It comes out five years after the original, has no relation in quality or content to the original; it's just a hollow imitation of what it claims to be. It features either a Baldwin brother or Tom Berenger, just to try and convince you that it's a *real* movie. You're vaguely repulsed by it when you come across it in the video store, choosing to either openly mock it, or just feel sorry for the people you see on the cover. "Shit, I always thought Yasmine Bleeth was going places, but *this...*"

Since you're forced to watch, you stop trying to forget about how terrible it is, and start waiting for the scenes you can beat off to. *There's got to be somewhere in here where somebody gets naked, even for a tiny bit.* Some late-night Skinemax soft-core porn scene: people surrounded by candles, undulating wildly to smooth jazz. Some spark—*anything* to make you feel less alone and numb. Except *you're* never the one in the scene, you're just the guy watching the scene at 2am with his hand down his boxers, about to ruin one of his parents' handkerchiefs. And you only feel more alone and numb afterward. And you wonder to yourself: *What made me think this was going to be any good?*

It seems fair to ask that question now, to wonder what made me think my movie was going to be any good. Why should it end well? Did I see anything in my time here that told me I could pull off a happy ending, one that resonated with audiences and became an instant classic? Maybe the film was doomed from the opening credits.

The main character was thrown into the thick of things without any backstory, not knowing why he should care about the plot, the locale, the other players, not knowing how he could possibly make his story better, brighter, or at least better-acted. Flailing about under poor lighting and non-existent directing, grabbing desperately for a line that never came under constant darkness in the Dark Continent. Never quite knowing what to say.

And so I sit with Thibault by his swimming pool at 9 in the morning on a Saturday, one day removed from completing our Standard 8 school year, eight hours removed from being defeated by a non-super villain, neither of us quite knowing what to say. The sun beats down without joy or mercy, warming up all the bad feelings in me. We squint through it at each other, our faces made ugly by a dull, bitter anger. Thibault's mother has made us each eggs and bacon. They look like we feel: wretched. If you came across our movie in the video store, you would see us on the cover and solemnly shake your head in sympathy. Or openly mock us.

"Mmmph."

Thibault looks up from his chin in his hand.

"What was that?" he asks.

I must have tried to speak, but my mouth disobeyed out of contempt for the brain's recent track record.

"Sorry. I was just trying to say something but it didn't really come out right."

"What were you trying to say?"

"Nothing, really."

"I see."

In our heads, we're trying to figure out where it all went wrong. The events themselves are now only slightly blurry, and their evidence is plentiful. Thibault has a black eye. My head aches. My nostrils are lined with rings of dried blood; my shirt has been ruined by it. I know how we got here *literally*, I'm talking about where we've gone wrong *conceptually*.

"Your haircut looks good, at least," I say after another long silence.

Thibault instinctively reaches up to touch his hair, his fingers examining Kate's handiwork from yesterday. We can't remember now where the idea to cut Thibault's hair came from, probably from Kate herself.

"Think so, hey?" he asks, rubbing the back of his head again.

With his flowing grungy locks gone—and aside from the big shiner on his left eye—Thibault looks almost as clean-cut as when I first met him. Back then he was still an innocent, uncorrupted, bookish nerd, and I still thought I was a missionary of cool, bringing my religion to the great uneducated masses of the jungle.

Maybe that's what doomed this script from the beginning. I tried to play against type. The truth is we already know the script and we know our lines: we're the nerds, the comic relief. We're not cool, we don't get the girl; we don't win. The same youthful folly that our peers engage in without care seems to have drastic consequences for us. We cough up a lung after a single hit of pot while the guy next to us does two consecutive bong hits without blinking. We try on fashionable clothes but they never fit quite right. When we try to break from the script, the universe reminds us it's not a fan of improv.

It's like in *Revenge of the Nerds II: Nerds in Paradise*— the Nerds think they can let their guard down and trust the Alpha Betas; they think they can actually enter the realm of *cool*. And what happens? The Alpha Betas frame them for stealing a car and maroon them on a deserted island off the coast of Florida. Obviously, some similarities are lost in translation, but the basic premise is exactly the same: when nerds try to be anything other than nerds, bad things happen.

"Last day plans?" Thibault asks.

I look down at the swimming pool with a sudden urge to dive to the bottom of it.

"Only thing concrete is a goodbye dinner with Penelope. And . . . well I might go to that party."

"Seriously?"

"Well, yeah . . . there's some people there that . . . I mean *other* people, you know, not *those* people . . ."

Thibault rolls his eyes.

"But you know they will be there, too."

"I'll avoid them, like I've been doing for the last month."

"Wouldn't the best way to do that be not going at all?"

"I mean it's my last night, man . . . Haven't you ever seen *Dazed and Confused*? Say some goodbyes . . . just . . ." I trail off, giving up on completing a solid thought or defending myself.

More silence for a bit as we sizzle like Thibault's mom's bacon.

"Well, I dunno, goddammit. We can't just sit here in silence all morning, staring miserably into nothingness."

"But we're so good at it," Thibault counters.

"True. But I feel like we need to be men of action."

"That sounds unlike us. That sounds unlike you."

"I'll give you that it sounds like me to say we need to be men of action but not actually take action. That's why we need to actually be men of action instead of just saying we need to be."

"But isn't that what you've just done—talked about taking action while not actually taking it?"

"Well yes, but I would say merely even talking about taking action is taking more action than in the immediate past, in which literally no action of any kind was taken. I'm hoping we can build on this momentum, you see."

"Okay, what action shall we take? Shall we eat our eggs?"

"Not a chance. Sorry, I think I would puke."

"Mmmm."

"But we could feed them to the dog, or throw them in the pool, or bury them in a time capsule. That would be action."

"I can just bring them in and tell my mom you don't feel good."

"I don't."

"There you go. That's action."

"I suppose, a bit less revolutionary than we need, though."

"WELL WHAT THEN?"

I stand slowly and pace back and forth along the edge of the pool, as if preparing for a pre-war speech. I stoop down briefly to dip my hand in the pool. It feels terrific, cool but not cold. I briefly remember a scene—two lovers swimming together in a pool.

"I was thinking about this a lot last night, while I was not sleeping in your beanbag chair. I was contemplating my years of failure and inertia here, and how it's coming to a screeching, yet even more unspectacular halt. What can I tell people about my time here? What inspiring lessons will I have learned that I can pass on to the world?"

"Don't smoke *dagga* on the street in Randburg?"

"Among other things."

"Never let a guy wearing cargo shorts convince you that he's a cop?"

"Perhaps if you successfully teach the first lesson, you don't need to teach the second."

"Perhaps."

"But seriously, Thibault. I get on a plane for America tomorrow morning at 10:17am, which means I have to be at the airport at 8:17am, which means I have to leave my house with my mother by about 7:17am, which means I should probably be safe and sound in my home and ready to wake up for the airport by about 6:30am. Which all means I have less than 24 hours to put a final point on my time here, to heap one massive pile of shit into a box and wrap it up with a beautiful bow."

"Sounds like you need a perfect day."

"Exactly. The past is lost. The future is irrelevant. From where I stand now, with scabbed-over nostrils, a bloody shirt, and what I believe is the world's first hangover caused purely by shame, all I have left is today and how I approach it. I've got to grab it by the balls or the audience will be asking for its money back before the end credits have even finished rolling."

"Sounds great in theory. Have anything in mind?"

I pace some more, touching my index finger to my lips, as if trying to recall some ancient Latin phrase just on the tip of my tongue.

"Well. Admittedly, my judgment over time has proven to be iffy at best, and my ideas on occasion do backfire terribly."

"Admittedly."

"That said, I was thinking: there's a roadmap in place for this sort of thing already, one I've watched over and over again. A plan devised by one of the most charismatic, lovable, forward-thinking characters of cinema of the past twenty years. You mentioned it last night."

"You're talking about *Ferris Bueller's Day Off*?"

"I'm talking about a sequel."

"A sequel?"

"Err- A remake. Shot by shot."

"A remake. I don't get it."

"Here, I've made a list."

I remove a ratty, balled-up piece of tissue paper from my pocket. In between huge splotches of dried blood, I've managed to make some notes.

"*Jassus*," says Thibault, looking at the paper.

"Pickings were slim at four in the morning when I was making this. I didn't want to wake you to ask for something better."

"I wasn't really asleep anyway."

"You had your eyes closed."

"Yeah, but every time I came close to falling asleep, I would see a giant fist hurtling towards me."

"I know what you mean. Look here. This list is of the general plot points from the movie. I used vague language in describing them so they could be open for interpretation."

"What happened to a 'shot by shot' remake?"

"Remakes are generally a bad idea."

"It was your idea."

"As a general rule, my ideas are generally bad."

"You're not really answering the question."

"Look, it's not shot by shot, okay? We don't live anywhere near Chicago, I'm not Ferris, you're not Frye, and Mia Sara isn't going to hang out with me in a hot tub in her underwear. The magic of this movie comes from the idea of having a varied set of entertaining and attainable tasks, which, when pursued without fear and with full enthusiasm, create a domino effect of positive momentum, one that can't be stopped despite the interference of trespassing principals or the destruction of classic cars. In short, the world gets out of the way of a man with a plan."

Thibault contemplates this briefly.

"But it's not really your plan."

"That's the beauty. I'm taking it out of my hands. You remember the mid-term and final projects we had in Standard 7? We got a choice: either work within an assigned framework to make something, or conjure the whole thing up from scratch. I've never been good at the second type of project; my mind always freezes up trying to go in too many different directions at once. The end product is just unfinished noise. But the first way, people only think it has to be boring, but if you know the box and know what's in it, it's that much easier to break out of it.

"If you ask me to design my perfect day from scratch, I'll be stumped. I'll continue on with the same sad-sack behavior that has gotten me this far. Following someone else's plan for personal enjoyment seems counterintuitive, I know, but the constraints of the system will make us more creative as we work to satisfy them, as opposed to generating a plot from whole cloth. Again, if I were good at that, wouldn't I have done it already? I mean, I'm an American teen living in post-Apartheid South Africa; I've got a lot of material to work with there."

"Let me see this list," Thibault says begrudgingly. He fingers it delicately, attempting to avoid the bloodstained areas.

"The blood is all dry, Thibault."

"I still don't need to touch it."

He scans the list quickly. It reads:

Rescues his love from school.
Takes in a sporting event.
Visits the commodities exchange.
Takes in the sites from the highest point in town.
Takes in an afternoon of art appreciation.
Impersonates a VIP in order to gain access into an
 elite establishment.
Participates in a parade.
Inspires those around him.
Helps and is helped by friends to appreciate the joys
 of life.

Thibault scratches his head skeptically while reading, returning to fixate on the first line.

"*Rescues his love from school?*"

"Yes, well, I said it's open for interpretation, right? So in the movie, they literally go to school to sneak Ferris' girlfriend out of class. Obviously, the corollary here would be Kim and her living at Woodmere, but obviously as of seven days ago she is no longer my girlfriend, and I don't intend to pluck her from her house in some naively romantic gesture. Even in a town as backward as this, that sort of thing would probably land me in jail.

"In our case, it could mean I rescue my favorite Jimi Hendrix tape from Kim's clutches before I return to the States for good and her brief period of borrowing turns into a lifetime of undeserved ownership.

"Or maybe it's even more metaphorical, like the unresolved tension between Kim and I holds my love hostage from the rest of the world, and I have to confront her in some way in order to wrest it back."

"That's how you want to *start*? You think you're honestly ready to attempt that?"

"No, not really. But by committing to it as part of our movie script, I have no choice but to take the first step forward, read, and then react along the way. Each choice and each step obscures the road behind us, while new forks and detours open up ahead."

Thibault peruses the list again. He pulls it down from his eyes.

"Where does your dinner with Penelope and the party fit into all this?"

"Well, I mean, in the movie, he finishes everything with some time left to race his parents home from work. So I figure there will be plenty of time to have dinner and hit the party."

"I still can't believe you're going."

"You're not?"

"No."

"No?"

"That's right. I haven't had any personal battles with anybody there and I'm not going. You do and you are."

"'Battles' is a strong word. It implies that there are two fighting factions. In reality, they beat me up and I . . . got beat up. Anyway, can we drop this for the time being and focus on the task at hand?" I point at the list to draw his attention back to it.

Thibault frowns as he reads.

"You really think this is the answer?"

"It's not *the* answer. It's *an* answer, and right now, it's the only one I have. Let me ask you this. If all else failed and enlightenment eluded me despite following the plot to the letter, would it be such a bad afternoon anyway?"

"I guess not. I could do without going back to school, though."

"The school is just a jumping off point, somewhere to begin our fantastic voyage. It's far enough from home that we won't just say 'fuck it', chicken out early, and sit around diddling ourselves instead.

"We can choose how to shape this day, Thibault. We've got the script; we've got the intention. We can be Cameron and lay in bed all day feeling sorry for ourselves, or we can be Ferris and *carpe* the fucking *diem*. History only remembers the winners. When I tell my grandkids about my young dark days in the wilds of Africa, will it be a dull and depressing tale about how I liked some girl and it all went wrong, or will there be some hope and joy and lessons of will and endurance to be learned? I prefer the latter, and by god, I'm going to fight for it while I still have any time left!"

I finish my war speech with a finger pointed triumphantly in the air, but Thibault continues to stare at me skeptically.

"Dude. You're really gonna leave me hanging like that?"

"Like what?"

"I dunno. I thought that speech was really deserving of a slow clap . . ."

Thibault sarcastically performs one.

"So are you in?"

Thibault frowns again, contemplating this. I grab him by the shoulders and give him the same line The Joker gives Bob in *Batman*.

"Thibault . . . *Youuuu . . . Are my number one . . . a guyyyyyyyyy . . . .*"

"Alright, I'm in." He smiles reluctantly.

"Okay then. As we overlay our Ferris plot with our real-life plot, we're gonna have to modify things. Maybe some rewrites, a new character, something to stir up the mix."

"A happier ending would be nice."

"Hold on, let me write that down."

I take my pen from my pants pocket and quickly scrawl on top of my hand, "Happy Ending!"

"So: we start at Woodmere, and you're my sidekick, my good cop. The straight man to my comedic foil, the Garfunkel to my Simon, etc. and so on."

"If this is Ferris, does that mean you're planning on stealing one of my parents' autos?"

"Hadn't planned on it. I never learned to drive here, so it would be a tragically short remake. I would get in the car, hit the wrong gear, and drive it right out of the fucking showroom glass like at the end of the movie, decapitating myself and/or exploding in a ball of fire in the woods below."

"The film would be reviewed poorly."

"To say the least."

"Well if we need to get out there, my mom is going to Fourways anyway and could probably take us."

"Hmmm. Practical, though not particularly glamorous. Sounds less like strong-willed adventurers and more like a couple of pathetic teenagers."

"It's amazing how the truth can sound that way."

"Shocking. I guess this will have to be our MO. Our exposition is already shot. We've explained away the whole premise of the plot too early and too clumsily, so we're already off to a bad start."

"Was that guy last night a critic then?"

"Script doctor if anything. That's another problem, though. We've introduced a major conflict too soon. We haven't even built up any rapport with the main characters. We have no reason yet to care for their fate. Now that the action is already underway, how do we make up for lost backstory while still advancing the action?"

"Flashbacks?"

"A clumsy and clichéd device, to be sure, but it might be all we have."

"Maybe it doesn't exactly have to be a flashback. Like maybe you are casually explaining past action to other people throughout the movie as in the course of normal dialogue or something. Or dream sequences. Or diary entries. Or letters to other people or something."

"Again, a bit clichéd, but yah, I suppose beggars can't be choosers."

"Okay. Well I'll go let my mom know we're looking for the ride out to Woodmere."

"Don't forget to secure some auxiliary characters, too."

"Ummm... How about Sebastian?"

"The farmboy?"

"Yes. I was actually supposed to hang out with him at some point today."

I rub my chin, pensively stroking stubble I imagine will someday be there.

"Does he posses any special skills or personality quirks that will help us advance the action?"

"He likes to walk around barefoot all the time."

"That's it?"

"Yeah. Plus he lives on a farm."

"He may have to do. He doesn't have to carry the film all by himself anyway. Let's get moving. Once we've hit Woodmere and collected the farmboy in tow, we can modify the script as we go."

"Can I be more heroic and have more lines?"

"I suppose so. Not much to lose at this point."

"I shall make the necessary arrangements."

Thibault heads inside, and I wonder whether or not aping the plot of a decade-old comedy to attain enlightenment and personal triumph is a somewhat backward notion, if it is accomplishable at all.

Thibault was right—we are not men of action. We're talkers, not doers. Why *do* things when you can just think and talk about them and convince yourself not to? Why play the game when you can critique it loudly from the sidelines, just another screaming voice in a sea of thousands? I've lived my whole life this way until now and it's led me to this moment, rotting in the morning sun alongside a plate of runny eggs and burnt bacon.

Even now as I stare into the cool blue of the pool, I am thinking, only thinking. I think about being in the pool at my grandparents' condo in Boca when I was little, trying to stick my dick in one of the water heater jets when no one was paying attention.

I think about swim meets from my youth, and how at

the end, when the race was long over for any of the real competitors, I was still thrashing and gasping my way through the final lap, feeling the dead silence of the world above as everyone watched me finish last.

I think about Kim and me in my pool that day not long ago. It was one of only a handful of times in my two years here that I actually got in that water, but I got my money's worth that day. The weather was perfect. The water was warm. We glided from one end to the other, our bodies pressed together and weightless. We thought so little and did so much that day.

I think about water, and how it spends no time thinking at all. It's the most versatile substance on Earth: capable of being solid, liquid, or gas. But it spends no time contemplating what it will be and do next. It has no memory of past failures or triumphs, no consequences or benefits to consider in its daily routine, no future decisions to make. Water never thinks; it only does. I am 80% water. You figure some of this stuff would rub off on me by now.

I lay down on my stomach at the edge of the pool, my head hovering just above its surface. I imagine the water accurately reflects the current state of my face—dark and wobbly, with unsteady, vague features. I touch my fingertips to the surface once more, thinking about how tired I am of thinking, and how I would like to be more like water. I think of Mickey Rourke in *Rumblefish*—Coppola shot it in black and white with only the fish in color. He's staring at those fish saying: "*If you're going to lead people, you have to have somewhere to go.*" I'm thinking that thinking has never given me anywhere to go, only convinced me to stay where I am. And for one moment, I decide to stop thinking and dunk my head into the pool as fast as it will go. Early returns say it's the best decision I've made in a while.

The world is blurry and blue. The only audible sounds are water in my ears and the whirring and clicking of some type of pool-cleaning device moving with a mind of its own. Fallen leaves hover around me, floating through fluid patches of light. The chlorine stings my eyes but I've never minded that for some reason; I like to be reminded that I'm in the water. My breath shortened by recent pot abuse, I'll soon have to come up for air. But I'm not thinking about that.

I finally come up gasping for air, and the stink and noise of the world come back with me. My hair drips water like a garden hose. I roll onto my back to see Thibault staring at me, a mildly concerned look on his face.

"I was wondering whether I needed to pull you out, or put rocks in your pockets and push you all the way in."

"And what did you ultimately decide?"

"I dunno. Another twenty minutes and I would have figured it out for sure."

"Good to know you're looking out for me."

"Hey, I wasn't sure if you were already jumping ahead in the script to the part where Frye does his fake drowning thing, or if you were applying your 'outside the box' thinking on ways to end your misery and suffering for good."

"Another twenty minutes and you would have figured it out for sure."

"For sure."

"Don't worry, suicide is not on the menu today. Besides, that would make your mom really mad at me and I don't want that." I reach out my hand and Thibault pulls me up.

"It would certainly make our car ride more awkward."

"Exactly. Why risk it?"

We head back through the sliding glass door of Thibault's room into the dark, stale air. The room is a mess despite there being very little in it: a computer and desk in one corner, a pile of dirty clothes in another, a small TV, the blue beanbag chair I slept in—or didn't—last night, and CDs in and out of cases, strewn everywhere. A single poster, one for Nirvana's *In Utero*, hangs on his wall, looking lonely. That seems fitting. Overhead, an even lonelier ceiling fan offers its dim light to us. It gently rattles its chain underneath it as it spins, whirring around softly, making the sound of nothing, reminding us there are no prospects left here. I find my bloody, checkered shirt and hold it up to the light. Thibault and I look on in momentary silence, as if we were fellow analysts examining a Rorschach test.

"It looks like a butterfly," he finally says.

I give him a silent, dirty look, and then throw the shirt in the trashcan. Don't think, just do.

A warm breeze comes through the open sliding-glass door, and the top two corners of Thibault's Nirvana poster come off the wall in slow motion, slumping down to touch the top of his pillow.

"See that? That's Kurt's ghost fucking with you for making light of my bloodshed."

Thibault frowns at his wall, but makes no move to fix the poster.

"Time to go, I reckon."

You said it, Thibault.

3
WOODMERE

*"Everything ends badly, otherwise, it would
never end."*

- Coughlin, *Cocktail*

In Miami, my bus trip to high school was ten minutes, if that. Here, it's about an hour and fifteen. You block out certain sections of travel in your mind to believe it's closer to forty-five, though, because really—what mad people would spend an hour and fifteen minutes on a bus each way to go to some god-forsaken school out in the middle of nowhere?

You come up with checkpoints. Sandton Mall. A road sign at a certain part of the highway. Fourways Mall. A cattle farm halfway up the hill, through the twists and turns of the bush. The convenience store at the last turnoff before the last dirt road to Woodmere. And you talk to anyone about anything to pass the time.

Thibault's mother lets us both sit in the back of her car so we can talk on the way there, but we don't have much to say. He continuously rubs at the shiner around his eye, perhaps wondering if he can magically rub it out of his skin and forget it altogether. No such luck.

His mom leaves us at the bottom of the drive of Woodmere, right outside the auditorium entrance. Our story is that my mom will pick us up later. The stage is set. The afternoon is ours. We are now the bold architects of our own destiny, rising or falling of our own accord.

"Goddamn I hate the Rolling Stones! Your mom knows they have real albums and not just randomly cobbled-together collections of ballads put out by their label for cash, right?"

"That one's her favorite. She listens to it every day."

"Christ, man! That means if she's listening to that one song where Mick says 'you love' seventeen thousand times in a row, by the end of one week she'll have heard him say it—"

"One hundred and nineteen thousand times. If you're counting the weekend."

"Man, ever since that one time I placed higher than you in the math Olympiad . . ."

"I know. I can't let it go. I was off that day."

"Too bad. I retire with my crown intact. You'll never see me back here again."

"Didn't you say that yesterday?"

"Probably. Sounds like something I would say."

"Well, here we are again. How fast can we do this thing?"

"Don't say that. My mom says that every time we go grocery shopping."

"Um . . . With how much speed can we accomplish—"

"I mean don't rush me, man! Right now, you should go down by the river and try to pick from that *dagga* plant we all found last week. We'll need lots of supplies if we are to make it out of this thing alive."

"Me? What are you going to do while I do that?"

"I need a moment alone up here."

"*Jassus.* Hey, you didn't mention that interpretation of 'rescuing your love', and you should have taken care of that in my bathroom before we came here . . ."

"Not that kind of moment alone, dickhole. Just come back and get me when you've found it."

"Whatever."

Thibault hurries off down toward the river and I am alone, remembering the excitement of early mornings in this spot that once made life here just a little bit more tolerable.

Woodmere bears no resemblance to a normal school, at least to me. Aside from the commute, and it being the capital of nowhere, it's also spread out over some very wide, very green hillside. At the bottom of campus is the Jukskei river—the river Thibault has just run down to in order to pick wild marijuana. The river is one of the few things I ever enjoyed about the place.

It's a private school, but you wouldn't know it by the American definition. The students don't wear uniforms, unlike in most South African public schools, and the teachers are capable of very little discipline.

Woodmere also features a handful of cramped and modest shared houses for exchange students from other parts of Africa, along with the Mercuri residence. Kim Mercuri and her mother, Mrs. Mercuri, the school Afrikaans teacher, have lived there for many years. I've had so many good times with Kim in that house. Now that tiny, unassuming façade is suddenly menacing under the weight of the heartaches it holds.

I sit on the stone steps to the auditorium for a moment and take in the scene. The air is crisp and the sun's anger has briefly subsided. The birds are even singing. It was like this when Kim and I first started hanging out during language hour. I would wander campus under the guise of my independent Japanese study. Kim would hang out at home, a native Afrikaans speaker allowed to skirt further instruction from her mother. We discovered we were doing nothing at the same time, and started wandering around together, walking, talking, eventually making out on random occasions.

It seems so long ago now but the air hasn't changed that much. It must have been that long ago, or our love story is severely lacking something. The great star-crossed lovers— the Romeos and Juliets—they're torn apart by forces as real as a fist. This is how it's supposed to be; if love dies, it dies in a blue and purple fireball, an explosion that leaves no survivors, no questions, no doubt as to why the two can't be together. The thought that love could last forever 'if only . . .' keeps us warm in our beds at night.

In reality, outside the movie screen, love fizzles for a variety of mundane reasons. Her fingernails were too long; his breath was too stinky; he stayed out too late; she spent too much money on clothes. The audience watches the fuse burn down closer and closer to the bundle of dynamite, waiting for that epic explosion, but at the last second, a cup of water falls off a table and casually extinguishes the flame without fanfare. What sense does that make? Who watches a movie that ends that way? As the old song goes: "*Is that all there is?*"

I whisper this question to myself out loud as Thibault ambles back up toward me, looking dejected.

"Did you find the shit? As your attorney I advise that we smoke it at once."

"I forgot where it was. I looked down by the river, but couldn't even find the right general vicinity, let alone the stuff."

"Shit, man. That's cause it's off the river, underneath and back around the corner of the bridge, up past the sand bank, with the dead fallen tree on the left. I'll show you."

"Oh . . . yeah. Note to self: it is hard to remember location of newly discovered pot in wilderness when said discovery occurs while already high."

"I only remember it myself because it was one of the last times Kim and I actually spoke to each other."

"And speaking of which . . ."

"Later, I said. First we smoke, then we deal with that."

This is, of course, a terrible idea, the exact opposite sequence of events that should occur. When Kim dumped me, I took it as a cue to stay as high as possible for the remainder of my time here. To be somewhere else. Take my mind away while I run out the clock. I wanted to be oblivious and therefore impervious to any further dealings with her. In reality, constant smoking accomplished none of this. It intensified my focus on my own misery and turned me into a mute child any time I saw her since our breakup. But why break a good streak?

Thibault and I stroll through the empty campus of Woodmere like a modern Rosencrantz and Guildenstern wandering the wasteland. We did a scene from the movie version for our final project in drama class. We're still acting it out: two fools on an endless cavalcade of fool's errands, each one of us making the other dumber even as we attempt to impart wisdom. Each conversation is a garbled mess of nonsense with no beginning, middle, or end.

We start to pass the library, and I think of our English teacher, Mr. Sumner. He mentioned he'd be cleaning out his office in the days following the end of school. Mr. Sumner is the only other teacher I like besides Mr. Thomson, our art teacher.

"Hey, lemme see if Sumner is still here. I want to say goodbye. You go ahead. If he's not here, I'll catch up in a second, but if he is, meet me back here in 10. Cool?"

"Sounds like you're veering from the script."

"Yes, but I feel a moment of introspective pathos coming on."

"What's that mean?"

"I think the main character is about to learn something deep."

"Whatever."

"You know where the shit's at now?"

"If I can't find it this time, I'll throw myself in the river."

"See you in a minute."

Charles Sumner is, quite literally, an English teacher. He moved here with his wife from the U.K. just after Apartheid, hoping to live well off of a strong pound in the 'new' South Africa. She got stomach cancer only a year after they moved, though. It was quick. Except for a sister back in Macclesfield, he has no family left. Which is a shame, really; I always thought he should have been somebody's father.

Mr. Sumner's office is a thin, long room on the east side of the library, with doors at its front and back. I don't really expect him to be there when I peer in the glass of the front door, yet there he is, sitting in his desk chair, legs crossed. His back is to me and he looks out of the open back door at trees swaying in the breezy sun, smoking his trademark pipe.

It's such a perfect scene—in the movie he would be played by Anthony Hopkins or John Hurt or some well-regarded English actor like that. I can't see his face but his body says he is lost in thought. I almost feel bad disturbing him, so I knock very lightly as I open the door.

"Mr. Sumner?"

The surprised look on his face turns to a smile when he sees me.

"Well 'ello 'ello. What in bloody 'ell are you doing here?"

"I had to come back and get some stuff I forgot here. Figured I'd stop in and say goodbye if you were still around."

In lieu of responding, he motions me toward an empty chair with his eyes, his pipe still firmly between his teeth.

Mr. Sumner looks to me like a classic Englishman archetype—what David Bowie might look like in his 60s if he ever really aged. His hair is an even mixture of blond and grey, parted neatly and flatly to the left. Piercing blue eyes stick out from the rough and rocky terrain of his pale, weathered face. His teeth and fingernails are stained yellow and brown from decades of coffee and nicotine. He always wears wool slacks, dress shoes, and solid color button-down shirts, sometimes thinly striped, sometimes not. His pipe is often in his hand or in his mouth, but almost never lit.

On my first day of school, I got lost on the way to Mr. Sumner's class and showed up five minutes late. Everyone looked up at me, including a wide-eyed Mr. Sumner, clearly surprised that any student would dare to be late for the first day of his class. Before I could say anything, he snarled at me.

"WELL, WHERE THE 'ELL HAVE YOU BEEN?"

Mr. Sumner was famous for yelling shit like that at kids. The most common one was: "*'EY NOW, SHUT IT!*"

Of course, this makes everyone think Mr. Sumner is an 'angry old bastard', but after the shock of that first outburst, I never saw him that way. I liked him and Mr. Thomson for the same reason: they didn't tolerate bullshit and excuses, but had much to teach to those who were willing to learn.

Like Morgan Freeman's "Crazy Joe Clark" in *Lean on Me*. A student tries to convince him that he has good reasons for dropping out of school, but Crazy Joe just looks at him with nothing in his eyes and says, "You'll be dead in a year, son."

Mr. Sumner would never say anything like that to a student at Woodmere, but he'd give you a snarl in a heartbeat. If you care and pay attention, though, he becomes the English gentleman, fulfilling his sacred duty of imparting deep knowledge to a younger generation. Mr. Sumner should have been somebody's father, but we were the only kids he had: loud, obnoxious, spoiled, full of profanity and drugs, and with no hope of shoe-horning any sense into our heads during the few hours we were there each day.

Now Mr. Sumner lights his pipe. It's the first time I can remember seeing it lit. He puffs a few times and leans back in his chair, glancing once more towards the starched white outside through his back door. I realize just how dark it is in here; only a small shaft of light comes from the skylight. The smoke from his pipe wafts up lithely through it, the room filling with that rich, woody smell. I've always liked the smell of pipes and cigars. I couldn't say why. There's something familiar and comforting in it. Maybe it's an old movie thing; it takes a certain type of character to smoke a cigar or pipe. You don't see wimps and whiners doing it.

"And now the Far East, is it?"

"What? Oh, yes sir. Have you ever been?"

"The missus and I planned a trip to China once, never ended up taking it. But you'll be in . . . is it Japan?"

"Yep. I got accepted to the exchange program maybe a month and a half ago. I'll be leaving from the states after a brief return home."

"'ealing elixir of the African countryside not doing it for you, then?" he snidely deadpans.

I laugh unexpectedly at this, perhaps a little harder than I should.

"Ah, let's just say I'm more than ready for the next act of my life to occur, sir."

"Heh, you and me both. You'll never see me round 'ere again."

"That's funny. I said the same thing this morning. But you're going somewhere, sir?"

Indeed, much of Mr. Sumner's office is boxed up right now. I haven't given it much thought as his office always looks like a mess.

"Cape Town."

Puff.

"Cape Town? What's there?"

"A job."

Puff.

"Job? Teaching?"

Mr. Sumner slumps his shoulders in a gesture of mock disappointment.

"No, mowing a lawn. Of course teaching, you git."

"Oh, sorry. What will you be teaching?"

"English literature at the University."

"The University? Wow. That's a step up from this place. Are you sure you won't miss it here?" I joke.

He slumps again and rolls his eyes in a God-help-me look that makes me chuckle.

"Has this been decided for a while?"

"The offer came up about a month ago. I told them I would move after the year was over."

A month. And he didn't mention a thing to any of us. Good for him. Let us find out from the next poor bastard who has to deal with us.

"So who's the next poor bastard that has to try and teach English in Standard 9 now?"

"Mr. Pretorius."

Puff.

"Shit."

"Makes me look like a bit of a puppy dog, does he?"

Mr. Pretorius takes Mr. Sumner's 'angry bastard' stereotype, feeds it steroids and strips it of any intelligence or class. Serious anger management issues.

"Yeah. Good thing I'm leaving."

"Good thing."

We sit for another moment as I watch the pipe smoke dance up through the shaft of light. The breeze picks up outside, rustling the trees more, but the air in here remains thick and still. It's so perfect I don't want to move; it reminds me of being high, the way the light and shadows play off each other to frame the scene. Light always becomes very important when you're high.

"Does this mean I can call you 'Professor' now?"

"You may."

"Professor . . . Charles . . . Sumner." I space out each word, as if I'm reading it off a plaque. "It has a nice ring to it."

"Cheers."

Puff.

"So is there anything you can teach me as a professor in the five minutes before I go that you couldn't as a plain old teacher during the past two years?"

"Well, actually," he begins, dumping the remnants from his pipe. He pauses before loading more tobacco and points the end directly at me. "I've watched you these last two years. You've got a better 'ead on your shoulders than about 90% of these other gits, even despite being a yank."

"Uh, thanks sir."

"But you get weighed down so often by all this rubbish around you, human or otherwise. You'll not get anywhere if you continue to wallow in it forever. You'll just end up like the rest of them."

I open my mouth to offer some kind of defense, but nothing comes. I sit silently for a moment, contemplating the nail Mr. Sumner has just mercilessly pounded directly on its head.

"And for fuck's sake, get over that bloody Mercuri girl!"

"Mr. Sumner, you knew about that?"

"Knew about it? Are you daft? I'm surprised you don't have splinters in your lip from how much you've dragged it 'cross the floor the past few weeks! Whatever happened, it's not worth it, mate. And if she's anything like her mother, it's definitely not worth it. Move on. Go 'ome. Find yourself a nice Yankee girl with her 'ead on straight. Live to fight another day."

Puff.

My shoulders slump as I stare down at my feet. He's right about all of it, but then, it hasn't been an issue of not knowing what's right. What's the line? 'There's a difference between knowing the path and walking it.' What's it from? Some kind of kung fu movie? Fuck, I'm forgetting.

"You're right, Mr. Sumner. I dunno. She just kinda chewed me up and spit me out."

"The really interesting ones always do."

Thibault knocks on Mr. Sumner's front door and waves at us.

"Bloody 'ell, is that Thibault?"

"Yes, sir. We were hanging out today and he came with me to get my stuff."

I open the door for Thibault and he steps in, wearing a shit-eating grin.

"Morning, sir. How are we on this day?"

"Off your meds today, Simms?" Mr. Sumner deadpans.

"No sir. Administered safely under supervision this morning, sir."

"Lovely."

"I guess that's our cue to leave, Mr. Sumner," I say, standing. He stands to see me out, handing me a small scrap of paper.

"This has my contact info in Cape Town. Write and let me know how you fare in the next few years, won't you?"

"Sure thing, Mr. Sumner."

"Okay. Take care, Floyd."

His tobacco-stained fingers wrap firmly around my hand for a shake and he gives me a smile, slight but genuine, before closing his door behind us. I feel the slightest welling up in my throat but it quickly dissipates. Mr. Sumner really should have been somebody's father.

Back outside, the sun leaves me squinting again. Thibault's hand rustles nervously inside his pocket as some toilet paper sticks out.

"I'm guessing you got it this time."

"I got it. We forgot something, though. We have to dry it out before we can smoke it."

All of a sudden the devil in the details comes flooding back to me: a mass caravan rushing back to Kim's house to microwave pot we had just found in order to dry it and smoke it before lunch period was over. I was probably too busy feeling sorry for myself to remember until now.

"And the only safe and easily accessible microwave here is at . . ."

"Bingo. You can't dodge it forever."

We slowly glance up campus towards her house, contemplating the now inevitable showdown, and begin walking without another word.

"Did you learn anything from your detour?"

"I learned many things, actually. For one: apparently I am a miserable bastard and everyone can see it."

"I could have told you that."

"So why didn't you?"

"You're a miserable bastard and everyone can see it."

"Thanks."

"What are friends for, hey?"

"You know what else I learned? Mr. Sumner is going to teach English at the University in Cape Town next year."

"No shit!"

Thibault thinks about this for another second or two.

"Wait, then who's going to teach English next year?"

"Mr. Pretorius."

"Fuuuuuuuck me."

"Fuck you, indeed."

— — ———— — —

"So what are we hoping for here?" Thibault asks.

We are now back where we started, by the auditorium, less than fifty yards from Ground Zero. Thibault sits on the steps of the auditorium with his arms crossed over his knees. I'm pacing nervously, trying to come up with some semblance of a plan or, failing that, some standard of morals and dignity to fall back on if everything goes to shit.

"The way I see it, this can play out four different ways."

"*Only* four? Do tell."

"Okay. Scenario one: it's both awkward and uncomfortable. No hope for redemption or any modicum of reconciliation. We are strangers in hostile territory. Any wrong move could result in epic levels of animosity and discomfort."

"In which case . . ."

"In which case we act swiftly and decisively to minimize the damage. We emphasize the fact that we were here for other random reasons completely unrelated to being at her house."

"Funny how that story keeps changing."

"Anyway. We focus on the primary mission objectives: the drying of the weed and the retrieval of one Jimi Hendrix tape. Surely she can objectively appreciate the importance of both. Once our mission has been accomplished, we vacate the premises immediately with as much dignity as we can muster."

"But my dignity is still mostly intact, at least in this situation."

"Where's your sense of empathy?"

"I'm empathetic. What's scenario two?"

"Scenario two: surface friendliness, underlying animosity. In this scenario, you are the buffer, strong enough to keep major hostility at bay, but not enough to right all wrongs. This buys us a little time and elbow room but not much. For my part, I must act as if nothing has come between us, good or bad, now or then. Completely amicable, above the fray. The cumulative effect is that she feels killed by kindness, perhaps even shamed into some sense of regret."

"Why do I feel like I will be shamed into a sense of regret for coming here with you?"

"Shut up. Last scenario: she's friendly *and* remorseful, open to peace and reconciliation. A long shot, I know, but one has to hope."

"One has to."

"We accomplish our directives easily. Perhaps we even invite her to smoke with us for old time's sake, being that she has displayed such openness and candor in spite of all that has transpired. But in this case, I must also seize the opening for closure. I need you to fake a stomachache and go to the bathroom for a half hour, or say you have to leave early, and head down to the river where I will later meet you, after I have achieved said closure through my deft speaking skills."

"This scenario sucks. And you said there were four of them, not three."

"Well, yeah. In the fourth one, she isn't home, we microwave our shit and get the hell out."

"I like that one the best."

"Me too. Ready?"

"Wait. In the third scenario, can't I just act like I've smoked too much or that I'm having a fit of narcolepsy and fall asleep on her couch while you talk?"

"No. I'm not good with an audience."

Thibault gets up and we begin a cautious walk over to the Mercuri house. The bitter taste of adrenaline rises up in the back of my throat. The next few minutes could render the last two years of my time with Kim irrelevant if things go poorly. It would be fantastic only in how far I fell and how fast it happened.

Against my better judgment, I look up from my moving feet toward Kim's front yard. The view is pure terror: a skinny, feminine figure sitting outside, smoking and talking on a cell phone. *She got the jump on me!* A tidal wave of panic hits me; all my best-laid plans seem to only pave the road straight to hell. My confidence abandons me as fast as it can run. I'll be lucky to get out of here speaking in coherent sentences. Thibault isn't even paying attention, still staring down at his own feet.

In a surreal turn, a lithe arm waves at me, cigarette still in hand.

"Is that Floyd? And Thibault?" a male voice calls out.

A boy's voice. Not Kim. All of a sudden I remember Martin. How could I forget Martin, Kim's and my fellow student council member? Martin, who under mysterious and unknown circumstances, moved in to the Mercuri residence just a few weeks ago. Martin Erasmus: the gentleman intellectual of Woodmere.

"It's just Martin," says Thibault as we approach.

"Yeah, thanks for noticing."

"How's it, gents?" asks Martin as we approach. He leans back languidly in his chair and plays with the few long strands of hair at the front of his head. This haircut, known as a Chelsea cut, is longer at the very front and buzzed all over the rest of the head, and popular among punk-rock girls. It's the same cut Kim recently had, the one I convinced her would look good on her, the reason I initially thought Martin was actually Kim from a distance. Whether this is all irony or pure coincidence, I can't tell.

"What brings you back to this godforsaken place so soon?"

I sigh deeply, partly relieved to see a friendly face, partly not knowing where to begin.

"A movie. A Jimi Hendrix tape. Destiny. A bunch of stuff."

Martin rolls his eyes at my vague answer, ultimately not that curious, and continues to play with his hair, taking a long drag from his cigarette.

One rumor surrounding Martin moving in with the Mercuris is that his parents threw him out of the house after he came out of the closet. I never knew if this was true or not—nor did anyone else I knew—but it seemed plausible. He wouldn't confirm or deny it.

"Um . . . Are the . . . uh . . . ladies home, Martin?"

"They aren't. As soon as school ended they made for the mountains on some kind of mother-daughter bonding trip. Multiple bottles of wine and all that sort of thing. Won't be home till the end of the weekend. I have the place aaaaallll to myself."

The news hits me in different ways. The relief of knowing there will be no confrontation is tempered by something else: an unexpected sadness. This is really it—no goodbyes, no peace of mind, no answers.

I make eye contact with Thibault and I can tell he sees this all in my face.

"Well, I guess that's it, then."

"What's it?" asks Martin.

"Nothing," I try to brush it off quickly. "Let us dry out some more of this weed we found down by the river and we'll smoke you out."

"Oooohhhh! You found more, hey? Sounds fantastic! Come, we'll play some music and do it up."

Off we go into the lion's den one last time, sans lioness.

– – —— – –

For the first time in a long time, I can't stop laughing.

The Velvet Underground's *White Light White Heat* plays on record in the background, Martin's choice. I've never listened to the Velvet Underground before. I've heard talk about them through the years, but I never investigated, never bothered. But eight thousand miles away from home and on my last day here and in the home of my ex-girlfriend, now the Velvet Underground makes the enormity of their presence known to me all at once. The terrific fuzz and raucous noise; it's like I just walked into a party that's been going on for thirty years, and all I had to do was knock on the door.

We're stoned and talking about Nick Sutter, Woodmere's pathological liar, that urban legend that crosses all cultures and borders, existing in every high school in the known universe. Like the tale of the acid dealer that got caught in a sprinkler system with an entire sheet in his pocket, and now believes he's a glass of orange juice in an institution—even in high school in Sri Lanka, at least one kid will know a guy who knows a guy that happened to. And in that school, there's a Nick Sutter, too.

Nick Sutter is the kid with the girlfriend from Niagara Falls that no one has ever met. Nick Sutter is the kid who secretly trains on weekends for life as a government agent. Nick Sutter was just in Sun City, gambling thousands of rand on single hands of blackjack, a girl in one hand and a martini in the other, still managing to make it back to class in one piece Monday morning. Each tale is taller than the last, each yarn more convoluted and harder to follow than the previous one.

We are eulogizing Nick's Standard 8, which ended prematurely by suspension for fighting at school in a bizarre incident that makes less sense the more time passes. One day down by the river, Nick ended up tangling with Matthew Defoe, a bespectacled, overweight nerd—not exactly Ali vs. Frazier. No one knew why they fought; perhaps there was just an underlying instability in both of them. Whatever the cause, it was over before it really started, with both of them in tears. No one really understood what had happened. Perhaps Defoe cried the hardest and was most apologetic; Nick was labeled the aggressor and was thus banished. It was the last time most of us saw him.

Not Martin, though. He kept in contact with Nick for reasons we are only now learning in our stoned hilarity. Martin studied the behavior of the South African Nick Sutter to see if he could first predict it, then exploit it. When Nick would get going on his latest fantasy of exotic travel, romance, espionage, or whatever, Martin would pump him for more information in total deadpan. *Then what happened? What next? That must have been dangerous! But of course you had to go to the embassy; who wouldn't?*

Nick was the only student in Standard 8 old enough to have a car—evidence of perhaps being left back a grade at some point—which only thickened the plot. Sometimes Nick would run simple errands with Martin, other times he would 'lend' Martin money on a shopping trip (with neither one of them ever mentioning it again). Often, they just spent time talking on the phone, Nick outlining his latest caper and Martin egging him on. They would speak of worlds and adventures that never existed, neither one of them ever acknowledging anything close to the truth. This was the beauty of Nick Sutter as Martin explained it to us on this hot last day in South Africa.

Wrapped in clouds of smoke and laughter and John Cale guitar fuzz, Martin now offers us a front row seat to a Nick Sutter phone conversation. He sits upright in a chair, steadying himself to play the straight man. Thibault and I slump lazily and heavy-eyed on Kim's couch. Martin dials the number and holds his index finger up for silence as it rings. We hear a click through his speakerphone, and the performance has begun.

"How's it?"

"Is it Nick? Nick, it's Martin."

"Oh, how's it, Martin?"

"Not bad, hey. And yourself?"

"Eh, just came back from a business meeting in Pretoria. Same old."

We almost lose it prematurely and Martin, stifling his own laughter, reminds us with a finger to his lips to keep it together.

"Yah. Pretoria, eh? What you working on this time?"

"Well, it's actually rather delicate stuff I can't talk too much about. Some government people are involved. You understand."

"Of course, Nick. I know you've got to keep that stuff under wraps. Listen, I won't ask any more about it."

"Cheers. What's up?"

"I'm feeling a bit bored, hey? I'm thinking about getting out of here this coming weekend. Have you got anything pressing going on?"

"I've got a party or two to attend, a few ladies on the line. Something up?"

"Well listen, I know you're often very busy but maybe you could hold off on that stuff and take me to Sun City?"

We all wait dramatically to hear Nick's response, but he doesn't even give us the appropriate hang time, replying after a second of silence.

"Yeah, I might be able to shift some things around. Sounds like fun."

"Of course it will be. Can you get us a room?"

"I should be able to, yah, with my connections there."

I tap Thibault and whisper to him in between giggles, pointing in the direction of Martin's phone.

"It's Abe Froman."

"Who?"

"Abe Froman, the Sausage King of Chicago, from *Ferris*."

"Are you on about this movie again?"

"I'm just saying. Nick Sutter is gonna try and bullshit his way into Sun City like Ferris pretending to be Abe Froman."

"Whatever, I want to hear the end of this," Thibault says disinterestedly.

"Have you got someone there with you?" Nick asks as our background noise filters through.

"Oh, it's nothing. I've got the television on and it's some stupid American comedy."

I give Martin a mock offended look and he flails his free hand at Thibault and me to shut us up. Sensing he's losing his audience, Martin decides to up the ante.

"Hey Nick, listen. Something else—I'm going to need to borrow some money for gambling, hey?"

"Oh yeah, no problem," Nick answers, again without missing a beat. I can't take any more and fall onto the floor, rolling around in an effort to muffle my laughter. Thibault covers his mouth with his hand, and even Martin is hopping up and down in his chair while trying to keep his tone straight. He shakes his finger at us again to let us know he's not quite done yet.

"Yeah, I think I'm going to need maybe . . . 200-300 rand, hey? I really want to be able to play some blackjack while we're there."

"Yeah, that should be fine."

"Really, is it okay?"

"Yeah, I've got a line of credit at a few of the casinos. I can also just have some cash wired in."

"Ah, thanks man. You're a life saver."

"Yeah. When do you want to leave?"

"Agh, listen, I've got so much to do in the next few days, but I'll get back to you and we'll make a plan for it, hey?"

"Right. Sounds good. Just give me a buzz then."

"Absolutely. Ta ta, Nick."

"Cheers, Martin."

Martin ends his call, throws his phone onto the couch with an exclamation, and we all begin a new round of laughter.

"That's not real. That can't be real, can it?" I ask, gathering myself.

Martin lights a cigarette, inhaling deeply with a smile.

"We've had that convo so many times! Every time he agrees to do it, and then every time we are supposed to go, I phone him a day or two before and let him know something's come up."

"Unbelievable," says Thibault.

"Madness," I echo.

"No, you all must try it sometime. You just play along with him and he'll do anything you need. I've gotten him to pick me up from clubs after a late night. He'll say no problem and that he's just 'been right down the street at another club', but he'll really just be coming out from his home."

"Wow, that would be so close to almost making me feel slightly guilty," I say, wiping a tear of laughter from my eye.

"*Agh*, I've listened to plenty of his crap. And it's so hard not to just scream at him sometimes, 'You're full of *kaak*!' I earn it, hey. Here, you must try. Write down his number," he says, scrolling back through his calls.

"Why not?" I ask. "What have we got to lose?"

Martin reads back the number and I write it on my hand just above the 'Happy Ending!' message. Now it appears I can call Nick Sutter for a happy ending. One shudders to think.

The last few notes of "Sister Ray" trickle off from the Velvet Underground and the sound of the record's empty grooves bring us all back to Earth. I exchange a silent glance with Thibault that says it's just about time to go and he nods in agreement.

"I'm going to go to the bathroom," I say, and stand quickly. All the blood rushes to my head and for a second I see only spots. The temporary dizziness and the hunger pangs in my stomach bring me further back to reality. This high will be over soon, and then what? Is it really over? Like this? No kiss in the sunset. No apology in the rain. No tearful goodbye at the airport. Real life is what happens when the credits are done, the lights come on, you get up to leave, and you find your shoe stuck to some chewing gum on the ground. It's not glamorous or easy or fluid. Just sticky and gross.

The bathroom is right by Kim's room. I take a piss and wash my hands, throwing some water on the back of my neck to cool down. In the darkness of the mirror I look sickly and pale. Outside the bathroom, I quietly massage Kim's door open while Thibault and Martin continue talking out in the living room.

Emblems of Kim pierce my vision from every angle and I instantly forget what I'm looking for. The room is thick with her scent. The only light comes from her lone open window, its white curtains fluttering in a sad, dry breeze. Her bed supports a rainbow of pillows and sheets, mangled into massive piles. This is where we lay together during that lunch hour just a few weeks ago, during our only week of joy.

I look down on the bed now and see us in that scene: arms around each other, chests pressed together, hands running up and down each other's sides. I kiss her neck just so and she hits me with that line:

"You're lucky that door isn't closed right now or all your clothes would be on the floor."

In retrospect, I don't think I was very lucky at all. If I were, I might have lost my virginity right then anyway, despite my stupidity. Instead, I made a joke, or brushed it off, or continued kissing her, or whatever. *We've got time*, I thought. Even as my stay here comes to a close, we've got time. Now I know, for better or for worse: the only thing I should have done was close the door.

Is it really better to have loved and lost? What if Kim and I just stayed friends? I'd probably still have my Jimi Hendrix tape, that's what. Wait, that's what I'm looking for. But the tape isn't readily apparent. I'd have to go digging for it. The thought gets me panicking, and after thinking about it for a few more seconds, I decide to leave it be, closing the door. Excuses race through my mind, some legal, some personal, all flimsy in nature. Still all talk and no action.

The real reason I couldn't go through with it: I don't like this ending. I want to leave the set just as it was, the props barely moved, the lighting almost the same. We can pretend the credits rolled right then when we made out. Or maybe that day at Sandton mall after our swim, where we kissed in the square as the sun was setting on Johannesburg. We had just seen *Lady and the Tramp*. Birds flew all around us. *And scene.* I'd rather keep it alive. Somewhere in the celluloid and aether. Somehow still existing.

"I think it's time we be going, Thibault."

He hops up, scanning my face for any signal or tip-off of success. None comes.

"*Agh*! And he tells me you're going back to America tomorrow, you little shit!" Matin protests. "Not even going to say goodbye, are you?"

"Well I'm here, aren't I?"

"Something tells me I wasn't the one you came to say goodbye to."

I have no comeback for this, but then, I have no comeback for any of it. The air in the house has gone stale with finality. No words will pass between her lips and mine in this place or any other ever again. What's left but to smile, the smile of a man who knows he's been beat good?

"*Tot siens*, Martin." I hug him while he takes a drag from his cigarette over my shoulder.

"*Tot siens*, Floyd. Keep in touch, hey? And don't forget to call Nick if you get stuck!"

Thibault and I continue laughing as we plod out the door, the newly rediscovered sun bathing us in sharp whites and stark contrast. We feel the heat instantly, not with full force but as a warning of what's to come.

"Well, you at least got the tape, right?"

"Not exactly."

"WHAT? Wasn't that the whole point of coming here?"

"It was at least half the point of coming here."

"And?"

"Well, first off, it's not like it was sitting in a box with my name on it by her bedroom door. I would have had to dig through all her shit to find it. I can replace an eight-dollar tape, but could never escape the shame and failure I would feel rifling through my ex-girlfriend's possessions in her absence. That's creepy stalker territory right there."

"Right. Because there's nothing weird or creepy about this whole plan we cooked up to come here, or hanging out and getting high in your ex's house while she's not there."

"There are varying degrees of creepy and weird. Shades of grey."

"What degree of the tape would you say you retrieved, then, to justify the degree of creepy and weird you employed?"

"We already know your math skills are superior to mine. Let's leave it at that, okay? Also, what if I got caught? Eighties movies would like me to believe that even kidnapping and grand larceny are forgivable if the circumstances are just made clear. But if I did find it, later on she would notice it missing, assume I stole it back, violating her personal space and privacy, and then conclude that she was totally just in dumping me. I don't want to play the role of 'psychotic stalker ex sniffing through panty drawer'. I mean what kind of sad and twisted individual would go through the trouble when he could just as easily walk into a record store in the States tomorrow and purchase the same tape for under ten dollars?"

"It's been established that you are the kind of sad, twisted individual who would do that sort of thing."

". . . On the other hand, if I leave the tape in her possession, it will forever remind her of me, and the time, albeit brief, that we shared together, as one. Every turn of the tape will bring images of me to her mind, which will in turn make her replay the events of our fleeting romance, which *should*, in turn, with the passage of time, cause her to rethink her actions and attitudes. Thusly, the tape will become her own private torture, a prison sentence for the rest of her days. She can never again listen to "The Wind Cries Mary" without thinking of the havoc she wreaked on one young man's life. Every Mitch Mitchell drum fill will sound to her ears like the beating of my bloody heart, until the day she can take no more and is driven insane by the guilt."

"That is not only totally unlikely, but you just spent five minutes explaining to me why you couldn't do what you spent ten minutes this morning explaining to me was an absolute necessity."

"I just chickened out, okay."

"You should just say that, then."

"I just did."

"Then it's settled. At least we didn't unnecessarily devote any time to it."

"Okay, it's settled. Let's go down to the river one last time."

"*Jassus*, what fucking part of the movie is this where they trek up and down the damn school all day just waiting to get caught for no reason?"

"They say you never forget your last time, Thibault."

"Yah, last time. As in I'm not walking back up this way one more damn time and will leave via the river if I have to."

"You keep talking about jumping in the river like you wanna do it. Are you itching for a good case of bilharzia?"

"At least then I'd have an excuse to stay home and lick my wounds."

"You'd have bilharzia. You wouldn't want to be licking any open wounds. It'd be rather unsanitary."

"I'll take bilharzia over coming up here one more time. This feels like some sort of cruel psychological experiment."

"My dear fellow, that's exactly what school is. We can get up to the road by climbing the hill next to the river when we're done. I promise."

"Fine. Let's make this quick."

And with that, we head down to the Jukskei River at the foot of Woodmere for the last time. Not Thibault, actually; he'll be back here in a month. As it was in the doorway of Kim's bedroom, I see hollow projections of scenes past in my mind's eye.

We pass the auditorium on the left, and there's Kim and I hugging in the early mornings as everyone arrives for school. This is when I perfected the art of tucking my boner into the elastic of my underwear so as not to embarrass myself completely.

Thibault and I walk down the steps and into the wide-open courtyard of school, with the library just ahead and the science pod to the right. Further down the brick walkway, Mrs. Mercuri's class is on the right. Through the window I see everyone studying but me. I'm beating out the drumbeats to Joy Division songs on my desk with my hands until Mrs. Mercuri scolds me to stop. I think I am so cool, that the entire continent will bend to my will and heed my teachings like the gospels. The friends and lovers will flock to me in droves based on my novelty alone. *How's that working out for us?* I want to yell at myself. But I won't hear it; I'm not even there.

We see the foliage and hear the purr of the river below. We're getting close now, climbing down the short grassy hill to the damp sandbank below. Look, there's Karen, and Kate, and Lucille, and Britney, and Jordan, and Robby, and everyone else who smokes standing there smoking. There's even Nick shuffling around on the outskirts, dragging on a cigarette but barely inhaling, like it's his first time.

There's Kim and I talking on my first day of school. She's explaining to me where things are, how things work; the cool kids come down here to smoke during lunch. I think she's cute but don't think much more of it than that. Maybe she feels the same about me. I mean, what are the chances that some dumb American would come to Woodmere and need to be shown around, and that the person picked to do it would be the only non-exchange student resident on campus, and that they would in fact carry on a brief, confusing, and fiery affair over a full year later? Who could see that coming?

The river murmurs softly as Thibault and I stand a few feet from its muddy bank.

"Well?" Thibault puts his arms out as if waiting for some act of God to befall us.

"Not here."

I beckon for him to follow as we walk a little further up the bank to an area that is mostly untouched. The smokers don't hang out here as it's not as well covered by trees. There's also a bit more bush on the ground. I'm looking for myself one last time. After twenty yards or so, we find it—a perfect rectangular patch of flat grass on the bank of the river. It's completely open to the sunlight, like a well-lit set; trees on either side flank it with deep shade.

And there I am. There we are. Kim and I.

The sun is like it is now, the colors of the surrounding world washed out in white. Butterflies flutter around us to a chorus of cicadas and the hisses of Parktown Prawns.

I'm sitting behind Kim, massaging her neck and shoulders as we stare out at the languidly flowing river. She's taken a drug called Ecstasy, one I don't really know but will be more familiar with by the end of this language period. The rush of Ecstasy is brought on by physical touch; it's a very sensual drug. Kim asks me to give her a back massage to heighten her experience and I happily oblige, oblivious again to both immediate and long-term implications. She shutters and shakes as my fingers and the drug interact upon her skin. I have a hard-on, of course, but that is not to say much. I'm a teenage boy; any whiff of any remotely intimate activity with any girl would probably do the same. And at this moment, that's how I think of Kim, if at all: with the remote interest I have for any girl. I can't see her eyes, her face; I don't know that everything is about to change.

"I've never been to this part before. Rather nice," says Thibault, examining the surroundings.

"I know. Shhh."

I'm straining hard to hear the conversation Kim and I are about to have. My whole body tenses.

"Flo-oyd," she says in that soft, girlish voice that perks up at the end. I love it when girls say my name that way. It doesn't happen often.

"Yes?" I'm working my fingers into the points right where her neck meets her shoulders.

"Do you want to kiss me?"

My throat closes up. I stop moving my fingers for just a split second in shock, but then resume as if nothing's happened. In the heavy silence of the now screaming cicadas, I wonder, 'Why now?' I mean, I know why now specifically, but how did we get all the way here so fast? I can't believe I never actually put myself in this place mentally before now—never even considered it as a possibility. Yet here we are, at the moment of truth. A long ten seconds pass. I still can't see here eyes, but then, she can't see mine either. It occurs to me that this tension may be part of her rush. I finally decide on a clumsy open-ended response.

"That depends on what your response to my answer will be."

Smooth.

Another ten seconds pass in silence. I'm digging deep into her shoulder blades now. If I don't reign in the open air around us immediately, I'll have blown my chance completely.

"Do you want to kiss me?"

The indirect direct approach.

"Yes," the answer comes back without hesitation.

"Okay," I say, and she turns around, her smiling face moving closer to mine. For a split second I think of my pillow. Do people really practice on them? Should I have?

Her warm lips close on mine and obliterate the thought. It's sloppy. And wet. And clumsy. And terrific. And I'm good! By god, I'm good. I don't know how I know, but I can just tell. I touch her neck and gently pull her in closer to me. I caress the skin right under her ear with my thumb. Like a pro. Like I've been doing it my whole life. It seems so much easier than I ever thought it would be. What was I so nervous about? I close my eyes, because that's what people do, and enjoy the moment, feeling the sun bathe us in all kinds of goodness.

"What are we doing—" Thibault finally starts.

"Shhh!"

Just a few more moments more of Ecstasy and ecstasy before it's all over. We make out for somewhere between five minutes and two hours, occasionally looking up in the direction of a cracking branch or a noise from the river. We're doing something wrong and we know it, but we don't know exactly why, or why we should stop. We finally pull apart for the last time, slowly, her lower lip the last to detach from the grasp of mine. We smile at each other like accomplices that have just pulled off a flawless heist. Without another word, I take her hand in mine, and we get up and walk back towards school. *And scene.*

"*Jassus*, what the fuck's the matter with you?"

We're gone now. Only Thibault and I are left alone at the river. The light is surprisingly similar. It could have been today. We could still be here.

"This is where I did it for the first time, Thibault," I say, finally unclenching my whole body and relaxing into a droopy stance.

"You had sex with Kim here?"

"No, dummy! The first time I kissed a girl was right here."

"Shit, Kim was the first girl you ever kissed?" He contemplates the awesomeness of this statement briefly. "Yeah, I could see how that could fuck a guy up."

I smile weakly at him. He could see it. Everyone could see it. A blind man could see that when my inexperience met her experience, something had to give. When her sex met my lack thereof, someone would end up in tatters, and it wasn't going to be her. *The really interesting ones always chew you up and spit you out*—that was what Mr. Sumner said.

"Thanks, Thibault. I think we can go now."

"You sure you don't want to lay a wreath down, or light a candle or something?"

"You don't have a massive amount of lighter fluid on you by any chance, do you?"

"Can't say that I do, as much as I like the idea of you burning down the school a few hours before you get on a plane."

"That seems like something the American kid would do, no?"

"Brash, the Americans are."

"Indeed. Ready to get back to the script?"

"I'm sorry, at what point in the last few hours did I stray significantly from the established plan so as to derail our momentum? Was it when I spent all that time talking to Mr. Sumner? Or perhaps when I made you accompany me to my ex-girlfriend's house to confront her and get back a tape, only to have her not be there and me not bother to get said tape?"

"Thibault, did you just have a sargasm?"

"I may have. I certainly feel stickier now."

4

THE TREK

"Yes, it's true. This man has no dick."

- Dr. Peter Venkman, *Ghostbusters*

Thibault and I hike up the rocky hillside to the road and cross over the bridge, beginning our walk towards the store at the turnoff. A film of dust and sweat covers us. The sun is now very angry, as if our pot smoke got in its eyes. Waves of heat boil up from the ground and pieces of the *veld* crack dryly under billows of smoke in the distance. After walking in silence for 50 meters, our heroes engage in dialogue.

"So, are you going to tell me then?" he asks.

"Tell you what?"

"The whole story of what happened with Kim."

"Oh. Well..." I smirk and sigh lightly as if to feign disappointment in the line of questioning.

"I know you want to talk about it to anyone who will listen so why haven't you told me yet?"

"Why haven't you asked till now?"

A comvi taxi with 15 black people in it speeds by, kicking up more dust on us. It's gone from sight over the next hill in seconds.

"What do you really want to know?"

"Well, one day you're head-over-heels. I hear you even talk about her visiting you when you're back in America. The next—you're giving each other dirty looks in the hall."

"Her looks are the dirty ones. I think mine are more 'pathetic'."

"Whatever."

"Well fuck, if I knew what the problem was, I might have had a chance in hell of fixing it. The whole thing makes no sense. It's like a bizarro *When Harry Met Sally*. We're close in the beginning but hate each other by the end. Waste of a ticket if you ask me. No continuity at all in this version."

"I thought that's what most relationships were like. What was the problem?"

"We had one perfect week, Thibault. One happy, horny week of slobbering all over each other. Week two, everything changed. All of a sudden she was distant. Like she wouldn't even hold my hand. We go out to this club in Randburg to meet Abe and Cybil for a double date on a Friday night, even though I think she already made up her mind to dump me. I forget which one of us was glaring at the other more, but I couldn't stand it anymore, so I finally grew some balls and confronted her. She launched into her prepackaged breakup speech.

"'It's not you, it's me'?"

"No, it was 'I think we were better friends than lovers'."

"Were you?"

"Well, it's not like she was really looking for a seman-tic debate on the subject. But honestly, I don't think so, no. We always kinda had this unnaturally close relationship, even since the beginning. Like, sometimes people thought we were a couple just because of how we acted around each other. I'm so fucking clueless when it comes to both girls and societal norms, that I only realize the weirdness of it now. I thought you were allowed to flirt excessively yet harmlessly with someone forever, as long as you didn't cross the line. I've since realized that any guy who willingly does all that shit with a girl *without* having a sexual interest, let alone trying to do something about it—he either has no dick or prefers to use it with other guys. There's no in-between. And indeed, one day we did cross the line, then kept doing it, then we couldn't go back, then it was great for like six seconds, and now it's been terrible ever since."

"So . . ."

"So you also have to realize that we went through some shitty periods of our so-called 'friendship'. When I first got to Woodmere, Penelope and Kim and I hung out all the fucking time. Then we all drifted apart a bit. Then Kim and I drifted apart *a lot*, just didn't really run in the same circles. In Standard 8 we kinda started talking and hanging out again, especially because of the student council. Then one day we got in some stupid argument and didn't speak for like three months and I couldn't even remember why! This fiery romance shit only started up in like the past two months. So to recap: our friendship included long chunks of time when we literally didn't speak to each other or hang out at all, and when we did hang out, we crossed all sorts of platonic lines on a regular basis. But yeah, we were totally better friends than lovers."

"Thanks for bringing it back to where we started."

"Hey man, just trying to give you some context and character development."

"So back to that night . . . What did you say when she said that to you?"

"I guess I just conceded, folded my tent. What can I say? When you're beat, you're beat."

"You went home?"

"No. I should have left right then, quit while I was behind. A man with any dignity or intelligence would have. But as has been well established, I have neither."

I pause to catch my breath. Thibault and I are now sweating and stinking in the hot noon sun.

"Well?"

"Well, it's a bit of a blur, mainly because I tried to stay as high as I possibly could the whole time. Since we were all still supposedly 'friends', I guess we kept hanging out. Maybe I thought I was enlightened and could handle it or something. More likely I just couldn't let go yet and tried to disguise it as that. It didn't matter, because from that point on, it was the *Abe, Cybil, & Kim Show*. They acted like three old friends enjoying a night on the town, ignoring me while I moped in various corners. I was the third wheel, or fifth wheel, or whatever wheel it is that is totally unnecessary to the operation of the vehicle.

"Somehow we ended up all sleeping in the same bed at Abe's. Everyone was passed out after a while, but I couldn't sleep. I was lying face to face with Kim, three inches from her, but there was no connection anymore. I couldn't under-stand the distance. The next day we all hung out in Abe's parents' hot tub, and I got to stare at Kim in a bikini for a few hours, until my dick ached as much as my heart.

"Finally around 5 or 6, *finally* I realized I had nothing left to hold on to in the situation and called my mom to get me. I think they were all really getting sick of me and my moping anyway."

"Jerk."

"I know."

"But you never found out why she switched over to the dark side?"

"I did and I didn't."

"Explain."

"She never told me, but I think I learned it in hindsight anyway."

"Which is . . . ?"

I continue on in an appropriately lower voice.

"It was all a game, Thibault. Everything that happened, all the flirting—I was winning because I didn't know any better. I wasn't even trying. You can't beat the man who doesn't know he's playing; he's got nothing to lose.

But then we kissed and everything changed, at least for me. I didn't want to play a game anymore. I just wanted to be with her. Fuck, I just wanted to be *around* her. It gave me a headache, spending each day hoping to see her for only a little bit. I felt like some weird junky. And I knew the more I wanted her, the cooler and more distant I would have to act. I had something to lose and I didn't want to lose it.

"The day I finally confronted her and got her to acknowl-edge that this was something real . . . that next 24 hours was probably the happiest of my life so far. We hung out all day. We went swimming, went to a movie, made out any time we were idle anywhere for more than ten seconds at a time. We even went to see Penelope belly dance at The Khyber and she said how good we both looked together. I thought I'd beaten the game, Thibault, so I just stopped trying as hard. I thought I could retire.

"But it's like Ferris says: *'you can never go too far'*; you can never stop pushing. Once I turned into a gooey mush-like substance in her hands, she knew she had me. And when she knew she had me, knew I had no more secrets left for her to discover, no more tantalizing moves left to pull, when she saw the un-mysterious soft-and-chewy hopeless romantic me in the flesh, she lost interest. Plain and simple. Because I gave up first. That's the hard truth to swallow."

We stop again so I can talk to Thibault face-to-face.

"That's why I need you here now, Thibault. I've given up and hidden away from life too often here when things didn't go right. I knew I couldn't replace my friends back home, so I gave up and chose the lowest common denominator of people to hang out with—and we saw how that worked out. When Kim dumped me, I gave up and spent two weeks getting high in my room listening to *The Bends*. Even last night, we just gave up and sat in the corner after everything went down."

"I thought that was warranted."

"Maybe. But still. Today is my last day. I could have given up and spent it at home with my dogs and my mom, watching TV all day and night and falling asleep to some crappy cable movie I've seen seven times before. But then, what would I have learned? And what would I have proved, except that nothing breeds nothing, and I deserved everything I got these last two years? Well, we may not reinvent the wheel today, friend, but goddammit, if we keep our two feet moving in front of us all day, something is going to happen. So are you with me or not?"

"Why do you keep asking me that? I'm here, aren't I? *Jassus*. And I'm not doing a slow clap for you again."

"Yeah I know, sorry. I got flustered talking about this shit. Holy shit, I think this sun is getting to me. Maybe we should sit for a second."

"Yeah, but where?"

As if on cue, we hear voices in the near distance. We search for their origin, and notice we are directly above one of the random rundown soccer fields along the road to Woodmere. It's slightly down the hillside and is little more than two goalposts at either end of a dry grassy patch of land. A pickup game is in full swing: some Angolans, some Swazi and Xhosa kids, most of them shoeless. I tap Thibault on the chest.

"Look at that."

"It's a football game. I see."

"It's our 'sporting event'."

"Ahhh . . . but a far cry from American baseball."

"Beggars can't be choosers and I hate baseball anyway. We need a quick rest. It's in the script. Let's go be spectators."

We take a seat halfway down the hillside, digging in and stretching out, the weight of our bodies resting back on our elbows. A few of the kids stop playing to briefly watch their watchers, then continue on. A large cloud loafs its way in front of the sun and we enjoy some unexpected shade for the first time all day. We breathe and settle into something like relaxation. Thibault and I exchange a knowing look that we've made a good decision.

"'The world gets out of the way of a man with a plan', eh?"

"I'm telling you like it is, my African amigo."

"*Amigo*—now that's Spanish, right?"

"Yes, it means 'friend'. I can also ask where the library is, or where the milk is, or where the toilet is. Mainly I can ask where things are."

"Can you tell me where any things are?"

"No, and I likely wouldn't understand if you told me. What do you expect from a measly six years of Spanish in Miami public school?"

"I learned about as much Afrikaans in the same time period."

"Yes, but that language sounds like people vomiting in their own mouths and you should actively try to avoid engaging in it. There's a reason I pushed hard for that independent Japanese study."

"No real argument here. It's not the most worldly language, that's for sure. Presumably, if I go to the Netherlands someday—maybe, just maybe—someone there could decipher that I am mauling what was once their language, still without being able to know what I'm actually saying."

"Remind me not to learn Dutch either, then."

We watch the game for a bit. They don't seem to keep score or have much concern for rules and regulations; it's just a group of kids running around enjoying kicking a ball from one end to another. It's a difficult concept for Americans to understand; we need games with lots of action, scoring, and statistics to measure and quantify, played on painted and manicured fields. Meanwhile, to the rest of the world, soccer is 'the beautiful game'; they can and will play it anywhere and on any surface you can roll a ball.

As if reading my mind, Thibault begins a related conversation.

"So the whole rest of the world calls this game 'football', because there is a ball and you kick it with your feet, and can almost never use your hands. Americans call it 'soccer', which, as far as I can tell, is a word that means nothing. You call that American game where they all throw and catch and run with a ball in their hands 'football', and stubbornly refuse to acknowledge the stupidity of this. Do you understand why we sometimes hate Americans?"

"Absolutely, and it's fair. Two things: First, I can and will accept the idea that this is the definitive 'football'. Except, how does that help me? If I say that back in America, I'll get beaten up. Meanwhile, what else do you call American football? Handball? Taken, and another bad name, by the way. 'Football' may be a stupid name, but it's been around for almost a hundred years. We can't just start calling it something else because people from other countries think we're dopes. Surely, you know America doesn't work like that."

"You said there were two things?"

"Oh, that you people still can't figure out the whole fucking 'tomato sauce' thing, so we're even."

"Isn't there a song about that?"

"That song is about pronunciation, which is a different conversation altogether, but not a battle I care too much about. I'm talking about the fact that you people can't tell the difference between what you put on pasta and what you put on a fucking hamburger."

"We can tell the difference. We just can't say it."

"Maybe you should try a word that doesn't mean anything, like 'ketchup'."

"Touché."

"Now see, French is not a language I am handy with, but I know that means I'm right."

"Ah, and now you're speaking American!"

"Mmm, that's good. I see your *touché* and raise you a double-*touché*. We should get the U.N. down here. We're bringing the world together."

"One made-up word at a time. So refresh my memory . . . What happens after they go to the baseball game in *Ferris*?"

"They either go to the exchange or the art museum. The chronology is a little fuzzy for me right now. Either way, I'm not sure it's as important as the action."

"Right, but so what was accomplished by going to the baseball game?"

"Well, shit, Thibault, not much in and of itself I suppose, but we're not gonna get very far if we look at everything we're doing that way. The game is part of the grand canvas, a collage of experiences that lead to a fulfilling day. Plus, it further establishes the special nature of Ferris' character, because he and Cameron end up on TV for a second, and he manages to catch a foul ball from the game."

"Catch a foul ball? Is that what you're supposed to do here?"

"Well, I guess that would depend on my reflex—"
PING!

The bounce of a plastic ball rings through my ears and bones. Things flash white for a second, then go completely black. I was saying something important to Thibault, but I can't remember what it was now.

- - ——— - -

Fade up from black.

There's red curtains all around. A black and white checkered floor. Red velvet chairs. Wait a minute. Is this . . . *Where is this?*

"It's a fair question, given the circumstances," says Kyle Maclachlan as FBI Special Agent Dale Cooper.

IT IS!

Dale sits in the chair next to me, smiling knowingly. He looks relaxed.

Across from us sit the small 'Man From Another Place', and . . . Kim. And she's wearing Laura Palmer's dress. Oh, now that's cruel.

Off in the distance, Emmanuel from our class is dressed in denim like Killer Bob, except he's still pretty much acting like Emmanuel—standing around with his hands in his pockets, looking stoned. *What's he doing here?*

"She's filled with secrets," begins the little man.

"Well, don't I know it!" I blurt out, and hop up from my chair reflexively. I start dancing painfully and awkwardly, like The Man From Another Place usually does, and he gives me the dirty eye, as I have honed in on his action. Kim starts giggling, then whispers into his ear. His face lightens into a smile, but it's an evil smile, the kind of smile Abe and Cybil and Kim all wore the night Kim dumped me. They're both smiling like that as they watch me, and I give up and plop down into my chair, deflated.

"My head hurts."

"It's best not to try and anger them," says Dale Cooper, smiling, and he pats my hand reassuringly.

"Man, you were so good in this! What's up with *Showgirls*, though?"

Dale's face turns sour and he stands up. He buttons his jacket in a huff, then walks towards Kim, while looking back to make sure I'm watching. He leans over her and they make out grotesquely, while the Man From Another Place laughs in his wild, deranged way. Even Emmanuel is chuckling in the background.

"Really, everyone? Man, I just say the wrong thing sometimes. Hey, can I at least get something for my head?"

Everything stops instantly and everyone looks directly at me in silence. Finally, Kim speaks, pointing an accusing finger at me.

"*Ek is a seun.*"

Wait, that's Afrikaans.

"You can stop this any time you want," translates the Man From Another Place in his stilted backward garble.

"That's not what she said. I actually know that one. She said 'I am a boy'."

Everyone laughs again. This is unnerving.

"Hey, where's your responsibility?" I yell back at Kim and everyone stops silent again.

She smirks and begins again.

"*Goeimore, hoe gaan dit?*"

This is another beginners' Afrikaans phrase. It means: "Good morning, how are you?" For some reason this makes sense to me as Kim trying to communicate. I try answering back with the customary Afrikaans response: '*Dit gan goed, dankie, en met jou?*' (I'm fine, thanks, and you?) But instead of words, only gurgling and hacking come from my mouth. I look down to see that I have coughed up blood into my hand. I show the bloody hand to the crowd in an effort to shame them all. It seems to work, as the Man From Another Place hops up and does his awkward dance backward out of the room. Dale Cooper smiles at Kim and caresses her hand before turning to walk out as well.

"I thought you were good in *Roswell*, too!" I call after him.

He stops and turns back towards me, giving me a slow thumbs-up with a smile. *Awesome.* That almost makes it all worth it. Emmanuel gives me a stoned, encouraging thumbs-up, too. I feel loose now.

"So why'd you do it, K?" I blurt out pleadingly. So much for loose. But she turns into her normal unreserved self, ready to talk. I knew that Man From Another Place was a bad influence on her.

She shrugs her shoulders in a casual way, and with a smile, this time a peaceful one, says, "You know how I am."

It occurs to me that I have no answer to this. Something clicks, even if it's only a small something. What if there's no good answer or reason for any of it? Things still happen.

"So where do we go from here?"

She gets up and slithers over towards me, strobe lights flashing around us; this is the scene from *Twin Peaks* where Laura goes to kiss Dale Cooper and whisper the secret of her killer in his ear. My heart pounds, my head throbs, the strobe flashes become longer and more intense as she gets closer. White flashes blot out my vision as she leans into me. I feel her warm lips on my cheek, knowing it's the last time they'll ever be that close. She whispers into my ear.

"I'm sorry."

A pain digs into my heart as I feel the words I've been longing for. I sink deep into my chair and one final white flash envelops me fully.

"I'm sorry, too," I call out into the aether, feeling myself fading into the white.

– – —— – –

"Sorry for what?" a voice screams out at me from the white. The question sounds like it was asked at normal volume, but then put through a megaphone on full blast. It sounds like Thibault, but how'd he get in the room?

"What?"

"That's what I'm asking you: what? Are you sure you're okay?"

"I'm . . . fine . . ."

The white now fades into searing bright starched-out color, like the picture settings on a television done all wrong. I am somehow moving—putting one foot in front of the other without being able to fully see yet. It's like when Han Solo was first released from the carbonite shell, and all he could see was a white blur while he was being taken to the Pit of Sarlacc. Or maybe it's more like when Jack Burton saw David Lo Pan for the first time and Lo Pan temporarily blinded him with Chinese black magic coming from his eyes and mouth.

"Was it Lo Pan?"

"*Jassus*, what you talking about? You're starting to freak me out, hey? Don't want to have to take you to hospital on your last day. I knew we got you walking too soon. We should stop for a second."

"Okay."

We stop and things start to adjust back to normal color. Thibault and I are once again on the side of the dirt road to Woodmere. The sun is still heaving over us.

"What . . . happened?"

"What happened was that while we were talking Ferris history and right about the time you were contemplating your reflexes, they failed you completely. An errant cross from an Angolan hit you in the side of the head and knocked you out cold."

"But the room . . . I was in the room . . ."

"What room, man? You were out! They paused the game to come over and check you out—twelve Angolans and Botswanas standing over you in a circle. You looked out cold but your lips kept moving like you were trying to talk to someone."

"It was just a dream then?"

"Your getting hit in the head with a football was very real. If you had something while you were out, I guess you could call it a dream, but I dunno, is 'hallucination' more accurate?"

"Hallucinations happen while you're fully conscious."

"Well you said some things when we first started walking. That's what made me think you were well enough to go."

"What did I say?"

"You don't remember? At first it was just kinda angry mumbling. I figured you were pissed about everything and were getting it out, but then you said something else at the end."

"What was it?"

"You really don't remember? It was just now."

"No, I don't remember."

"You said: 'I'm sorry, too'."

Now the details come back. The Red Room. Dale Cooper. The Man From Another Place. And Kim. The apology. *It was really just a dream?* Man, what a cruel fucker the mind is.

"Ugh. I need a Coke."

"Probably something for your head, too."

"And some water."

"And food would be good for you as well."

"How far out are we?"

Thibault points ahead and I can make out the corner store about a hundred yards into the distance. We put our heads down and walk the last leg mostly in silence, but I can tell he wants to say something.

"What?" I finally ask.

"It's just that . . . I mean the ball is *supposed* to be hit with the head about half the time . . ."

"I guess being an American, I'm not familiar with the nuances of the game, Thibault."

The only thing weirder than having a school out in the middle of nowhere is having a convenience store out in the middle of nowhere. And yet, it never hurts for business. Perhaps it's the only game in town; the nearest actual grocery store is a fifteen-minute drive down to the bottom of the hill, and then probably another five to ten minutes in either direction from Fourways Mall. They also sell matchboxes of weed out back, and are probably the only resource in the area (good luck finding it growing wild like we did). The store sticks out like a pimple on an otherwise barren landscape.

"What's the deal with Sebastian?"

"He lives a few minutes from here. I have to call him from the payphone. Why don't you sit for a bit? I'll go make a call and grab you a few things from inside."

"Thanks."

I take a seat in some brown, dry grass a few feet from the store's entrance. The world moves by in slow motion. It was just a dream . . . In my daze, I almost don't notice the three men standing just a few feet from me, one of them waving at me. When they finally come into focus, I see the one waving is my now-former bus driver. It figures. For the past year or so, we've had this weird recurring interaction: he never talks to me while I'm riding the bus, but any time he sees me walking up to the bus, he gets this weird shit-eating grin on his face and repeats this line:

"I see you. Your friends. The corner. You *bemma* too much."

He completes this with a hand motion in front of his mouth similar to warming his hands in the cold.

Over time I have learned that "*bemma*" means to smoke weed, and his hand motion is a symbol of that act. While the act of smoking weed on a corner with friends is indeed something I have engaged in while here, I find it implausible that this man was at any point watching me, let alone on a regular basis. Still, every time he sees me, it's the same thing. He tells me he saw me *bemma* last weekend, I say I don't know what he's talking about. Over and over again. He resumes his lines now.

"*Eta*, my friend. I see you. The corner. Your friends. You *bemma*."

Maybe he is actually seeing the near future. In any case, I've no mind to argue with him now.

"Sure. Have you got the *insango*, friend?"

He points around to the back of the store as Thibault walks out with a handful of junk for me and a red apple for himself.

"The good news is: I got you a Coke, two Tylenol, a bottle of water, and some potato chips. Even got myself a good apple. The bad news is: that's the last of my money."

"Thanks. You're a good friend. I'll get this stuff." I reach into my pocket and curse myself for only now remembering that I was relieved of all my money last night.

"Oh shit. Remember that time we got mugged?"

"Oh *kaak*. I thought you had some reserves or something. Otherwise why would you be offering?"

"I know I know. Brain fart. I'm sorry. I may have blocked out the events of last night a bit prematurely."

"Well what are we going to do?"

"Uh, will Sebastian have any money?"

"He lives on a farm!"

"Good point. Well, we'll have to figure it out."

"Figure what out?" asks Sebastian, appearing from nowhere.

His skin is bronze and rough, and he's muscular yet thin—what you might expect from a native Afrikaner raised on farm work in the sun. He speaks with an almost effete tone, though, like he is the host of some English cooking show, excited by the color of the beets he's preparing.

"Crackerjack timing, Sebastian. We're broke and in a bit of a quandary. Have you got any money?"

Sebastian digs into the pockets of his tattered shorts, pulls out some lint and a five-rand note, and offers it.

"Halfway there. Let's do some finagling here."

I wave for Thibault and Sebastian to follow me around

to the back of the store. People mill around in various pock-ets. Some are woozy and stumbling, deep in Mandrax hazes. Others drink 25-cent Joburg Beer, empty cartons already at their feet. Our salesman sits on a lone rock in the center of the action, an Asian rice farmer's hat shielding him from the sun, a wooden cane in his hand. I want to laugh as he looks a bit like a wizard or an oracle, waiting to dispense wisdom only to the worthiest of subjects.

Beside him sits his bag of matchboxes stuffed full of as much shitty weed as they can hold. You'll get a fare share of seeds and stems, but for ten rand, it will do the trick. We've got to negotiate our friend down to five. I pocket Sebastian's five and tell them to follow my lead as I approach the mage.

The wizards's eyes are bloodshot, probably from a mix-ture of weed and Mandrax, and he sips a Joburg Beer as we approach. I hold up one finger to symbolize our intent. He reaches into his bag lazily, pulling out an overflowing matchbox of brownish-green weed. He holds up two hands with fingers fully extended to show the price, and my per-formance begins. I reach in my pocket and pull out the five with my best disappointed look. *How could I only have a five? What a surprise!* I motion to Thibault and Sebastian to check their pockets, and they go through a pantomime similar to mine—empty pockets and sad faces. I offer up the five with shrugged shoulders and a pleading look, but he waves it away and turns his nose upward, sipping more Joburg Beer. I clasp my hands together in mock desperation, but he simply slips the matchbox into his bag and proceeds to ignore us. Our silent movie ends in disappointment. We walk off to reassess.

"Well, that went swimmingly," says Sebastian.

"We're not cooked yet. Give me a minute to think."

I crack the Coke Thibault bought me, down my Tylenol with it, and crunch on a handful of potato chips, chasing it all by chugging the entire water bottle down.

"Follow me."

We head back around to the front of the store and I locate my bus driver. He smiles as we approach, making his universal pot-smoking hand gesture.

"My friend," I begin with a warm smile, "we need some help. We need to get a matchbox but only have this." I hold up the five-rand note for show. "Can you put in a good word for us?"

He laughs out loud. "Why you want me?"

"C'mon. You say you always see me with the *bemma*. You help us out, we *bemma* with you, too."

"Okay. Okay."

We follow him to the back again. He greets the wiseman of weed with a warm handshake and half hug, talking to him in one of South Africa's thirteen languages I do not know, pointing in our direction. The wiseman makes a face, and waves the air away in our direction, telling us to buzz off. My bus driver holds, continuing with his line of reasoning. He finally hits on something, and the wiseman begins to stroke his chin, for the first time considering an actual deal. He whispers an offer back to my bus driver, and we are waved over, but stopped with the same hand before we get too close.

"He want your watch," he says to me, referring to my digital Casio.

"For just one? It's got a calculator!"

My bus driver attempts to explain this to the wiseman, and they both laugh heartily.

"What else you got for two?" asks the bus driver.

I look around at the three of us, and fixate on Sebastian's feet, covered by unassuming grey canvas sneakers that appear awkward and unworn. I look at the wiseman's feet and see only rags wrapped around them. I smile at Sebastian.

"You don't really need those, do you?"

"Of course not," Sebastian says, quickly removing them. "My mother made me wear them because I told her we might be going towards the city."

He hands them to me. I remove my watch and hold it in the same hand with the shoes, then hold up three fingers with my other hand. This needs no translation. The wiseman eyes me, then looks at the shoes with a glimmer in his eye. He rubs his fingers together to symbolize the last piece of the deal—the five rand. I take it from my pocket, stuff it in one shoe, and stuff the watch in the other shoe. Thibault and Sebastian watch silently, nervous tension on their faces.

"Tell him we need something to smoke it with."

He relays the message. The wiseman holds for one second longer, then breaks into a slow smile and an eventual laugh. He digs three matchboxes out of his bag for me, along with some papers and a surprisingly good lighter. He says something to the bus driver as I hand him the shoes and their contents, and they both laugh again.

"He says you make good deal."

I clasp my hands together and dip my head in a slight bow of appreciation. The wiseman nods back. We head for our own corner behind the store in order to enjoy the fruits of our labor. I motion for the bus driver to follow us but he says he will stay to talk to the wiseman for a bit more and join us momentarily. Thibault and Sebastian are grinning like idiots, like they can't even believe what they've just seen.

"Gentlemen," I begin proudly, "we've just been to the commodities exchange."

"Oh yeahhhhh," Thibault says with recognition.

"Wait, what's this?" asks a confused Sebastian.

"Oh. Well, Floyd thinks his two years here in South Africa have been a morbid failure, so he is trying to reverse the trend all at once by loosely imitating the plot of *Ferris Bueller's Day Off*, not only one of his favorite movies, but also a story he believes to be one of the greatest single-day adventures in cinema history. He is likening the experience we have just had to a scene early in the movie, where Ferris and his friends visit Chicago's commodities exchange. I'm probably not explaining it very well, though . . ."

"Actually, Thibault, that was an incredibly accurate depiction of this batshit crazy plan."

"Oh. Thanks."

"Well, this sounds like fun!" Sebastian is now intrigued. "What comes next?"

"What comes next is we smoke a joint, Sebastian, because if we want to star in a movie, we've got to set the mood and get into character. What's the tallest building in Joburg?"

Thibault and Sebastian squint and look in all directions as they rack their brains, finally proclaiming "No idea" in unison. I shake my head.

"Doesn't even matter. What's any building we could go to the top of that would make us *feel* like we were in the tallest building in Joburg?"

They ponder this some more.

"It has to have an expansive view."

"The towers at Sandton Mall look out over a lot of Joburg," says Thibault. "That would be a good trek."

"I think you are getting it, Thibault."

"Oooh, this *is* exciting!" says Sebastian.

"Now, who among us can roll a joint?"

Everyone exchanges wide-eyed, almost surprised looks, and it strikes me how we can't even make doing drugs look cool. I shrug my shoulders and begin rolling the world's worst joint. Ten minutes later, we are lighting the lopsided, overflowing thing. My bus driver manages to walk over at just the right time, smiling.

"I told you. You. Your friends. The corner. You *bemma* too much."

"You were right, my friend. What can I say?" I pass the joint to him. He eyes it peculiarly but takes a gargantuan hit regardless, sighing with satisfaction as he exhales. In this moment I decide he really is clairvoyant. Or maybe more accurately, he is one of Kurt Vonnegut's Tralfamadorian aliens from the book *Slaughterhouse Five* (they made a movie of it, but it stunk). The Tralfamadorians are capable of seeing time as it truly is: as all simultaneous, not in a linear mode as humans believe it is. Everything that has ever happened is always happening. Everything that is ever going to happen has already happened and will forever continue to happen. Any notion of past, present, future, or even any single individual moment existing on its own is irrelevant. For Vonnegut, it was just an interesting plot device, but whenever I have déjà vu, I believe there is more credence to the theory than even he thought. Each time in the past year my bus driver launched into his repetitive 'you *bemma* too much' routine, perhaps he was really talking about this moment—as yet to happen, yet always happening and having already happened, forever to happen on into infinity. It all comes around. The golden circle. Like Laura Palmer's ring in *Twin Peaks*.

"Floyd!"

A drop of drool falls from my lower lip as I snap back to reality, Thibault offering me the joint. Everyone begins to laugh, including my Tralfamadorian bus driver, who laughs the hardest, shaking his head. He says he is going to go, but I stop him quick.

"Wait, what else happens? You've got to tell me."

He inhales deeply, eyes closed, unfazed by my question.

"You cry. You fall. You *bemma*. You dance. You fly." He flutters his hand like a bird floating off into the distance, then smiles and walks away.

"What was that?" asks Thibault.

"I'm pretty sure he's a clairvoyant alien."

"Yesssssss!" Sebastian exclaims out of the blue, leading to a moment of silence as we think about this in stoned limbo. I have never smoked with Sebastian before. For all I know he does it once or twice a year. We certainly all cough and heave like amateurs with each hit. Thibault I've smoked with only a few times. Still, it strikes me that here, out in the open, in the middle of nowhere, with no money in our pockets, I feel safer than I ever did in all those times I smoked with Britney, and Alo, and Jordan, and Patrick, and Robby, and all the others. Thibault and Sebastian have nothing to prove, no image to uphold, no reputation to tarnish by hanging out with me. I'm pretty sure they're not going to jump me if we get too high.

There's nothing but a mutual desire to experience an adventure together. We are trying to imitate *Ferris*, but we are really starring in *Revenge of the Nerds III: Nerds Take*

South Africa. For the second time today, I feel something like enjoyment. We are coming to the end of our joint.

"About time to shuffle off the buffalo, gents."

Thibault and Sebastian gather themselves, quickly adjusting clothes and hair like they're getting ready for a first date.

"With no money, I assume we're—"

"Hitching." I finish Thibault's sentence for him. "The wind is with us now, gentlemen. Let's go find us a tall building."

A cloud of pot-smoke follows us as we leave the store's backlot. I wave to my bus driver one last time. He is again talking with his friends. Not wanting to disappoint, he laughs and gives me his *bemma* hand gesture again.

We cross the street from the store, and put out our thumbs, hoping for anything that will take us down the hill towards civilization.

Within seconds a flatbed truck pulls off into the gravel in front of us. Two passengers in the back eye us without emotion. Thibault, Sebastian and I shrug our shoulders at each other, and run up to hop into the back. The Three Stooges. No direction home.

5

ART APPRECIATION

"Loneliness has followed me my whole life, everywhere."

- Travis Bickle, *Taxi Driver*

That's where we were this morning, boys," I say, pointing back at what I believe is the general area of Fourways Mall and Woodmere.

We are standing in one of several towers attached to Sandton Mall. They are each maybe 20 feet in diameter and allow mall patrons to get a look at all the majesty of surrounding Johannesburg.

"You're actually pointing toward Illovo right now," says Sebastian. "Woodmere is more that direction."

"Dammit."

Hot winds swirl around us. Looking very far in any direction produces that gassy, wavy image, like the earth itself is crumbling under the heat. Parts of bush in the distance continue to burn. I don't know if that's an accident or by design.

It reminds me of *Falling Down*; Michael Douglas is just stuck wallowing in this oppressive heat in traffic until he finally loses his shit and becomes the angry Samaritan. But actually, it's not like that, because I don't feel very angry right now, actually kind of peaceful, and we're mostly hidden from the heat in the shade of the tower roof. I might be close to losing my shit, though, due to my terrible working relationship with sleep.

I resist sleep's advances at every turn. I'm that guy who lies down to go to sleep and then fidgets for twenty minutes to an hour, always thinking the next adjustment will bring me peace. Naps are out of the question and once I'm up, even a little, I'm up for good.

Sleep, in turn, behaves like a spurned lover toward me, showing up only when I'm out late with friends, or in the middle of something important. *"Check out what you're missing!"* she screams, and I know it's only a few minutes before I'm fading in and out of consciousness. I've never 'pulled an all-nighter'. Never even come close. One time I was hanging out at Alo's house with him and a couple of other dudes at two in the morning and this one raver douchebag kept hitting me in the face with a pillow because I couldn't stay awake. Not even physical violence can keep me from sleep's irresistible clutches when she does finally come for me.

But right now I'm literally in no position to sleep. In broad daylight and in public, I'm forced to remain upright, even as exhaustion spreads over my body like a sickness. Burning eyes, a cold sweat on the neck, something vaguely like nausea. Now I'm Michael Douglas, transposed against the African backdrop, destroying a convenience store with a cricket bat. Joburg Beer is flying everywhere and I am screaming obscenities in Afrikaans. I shutter out of it. Wait. Was that a daydream or a sleep dream?

"Okay. Now what?" asks Thibault. We all slide down the walls of the tower observation area. Thibault and I sit with our knees propped up and Sebastian crosses his legs.

"Yes. What's next?" he seconds, with a little clap.

"Well guys. I mean, don't you wanna like *linger* for a second? We just got here. I feel like somebody needs to say something deep . . ."

"We're teenagers," Thibault says.

"Oh, that's deep," says Sebastian, pondering the thought.

"Sebastian, I think he means that teens aren't really Johnny-on-the-spot with depth."

"Oh."

"I partly meant that, but I think I also meant that as teenagers we want everything to be deep and meaningful, but maybe it isn't. Maybe we're just . . . sitting at the top of a tall building, you know?"

We look around at each other in silence.

"What does Johnny-on-the-spot mean?" asks Sebastian.

"Readily available. Thibault is saying we don't have any immediately available and dependable depth. As Mr. Sumner might say, we're 'thick'. But seriously, Thibault, I just talked to your depth and it told me to tell you that your self-awareness is really killing its buzz right now."

"Well I don't know," he protests with hands in the air. "I feel like you can't just 'get deep' on the spot; it has to come from somewhere natural."

"What about this day was supposed to be natural?" I throw my hands in the air right back at him. "I thought we were taking artificial lifestyle supplements today because we established that our natural state is cowardice, loneliness, and inertia."

"I prefer to run myself," says Sebastian.

"Okay. Sebastian's natural state is running; ours is cowardice, loneliness, and inertia. But today—as we are pretending to be pro-active, engaging individuals with active, interesting things to do in hopes that we actually become said individuals with said things to do—maybe by pretending to be deep we can actually *be* deep as well."

Sebastian raises his hand. "What actually happens at this point in the movie?"

"Uh, Ferris talks about how they are at the tallest point in Chicago and then they all lean over the railing to stare straight down."

We stand up in a line against one edge of the rounded wall, staring down below us. We are directly above an entrance to the mall, and people are strolling in and out, to and from the parking lot. It's not particularly far down, probably a hundred feet to the ground.

The sound of an irate man and whining child drifts up to us and we look for the culprits. They are just about to cross the street to enter the mall: the man dragging (what is hopefully) his child by the arm towards the mall, the child resisting and shifting his weight like a downhill skier as he pulls away. The man screams at the child and the child cries and keeps pulling futilely. Upon further examination, the man is Mr. Pretorius from Woodmere.

"*Agh*, man! I don't bloody have time to be messed around with!" he shouts at his child in a thick Afrikaans accent and voice that sounds like he's been chewing on gravel. "If you can't behave you must kiss off back to the car with your damn mother! GO!"

Mr. Pretorius lets him go, and the boy runs back to the car. His lack of hesitation makes Mr. Pretorius even angrier, and he throws up his hands in a quick fit before turning back to cross the street and enter the mall.

Without a word or a look, we all simultaneously ready our saliva charges. How do you adjust for wind? What is his rate of movement versus the length the projectile has to travel? Did Mr. Pretorius ever teach us this when subbing for a science or math class at Woodmere? In the moment, all analysis goes out the window, and all we're left with is . . . heart.

"*Hcggccggcchhh . . .*"

"*Hhhccccggggccchh . . .*"

"*Hhccggwwwyyyuucchh . . .*"

We drop three bombs on him at high velocity. Each man tweaks his approach based on his personal theory of maximum efficiency. To get one hit would be an unmitigated success. Lucky day of lucky days: we land all three—including a head shot—and slink back down behind the wall before Mr. Pretorius can get his head up and begin a profanity-laced tirade.

"WHAT THE FUCK, MAN?"

We chuckle and congratulate ourselves, sighing in momentary contentment.

"Teenagers," muses Sebastian.

Thibault nods in agreement.

"Well hell, I've got something deep to say," I begin.

"It's not necessary . . ." Thibault winces, but like a drunk at a party, I won't let him cut me off.

"No no, hear me out here." I might actually be punch-drunk from sleep deprivation. I lower my eyes and my voice.

"Well look, uh . . . I just wanna say that . . . it took me a long time to figure out what I was doing wrong here with that whole crew I hung out with—Alo, Robbie, *Patrick*—and why things kept ending so badly."

Thibault and Sebastian fall into positions of attention, realizing that I am, in fact, attempting to be 'deep'.

"But I think I did finally figure it out: I kept choosing style over substance, and making sexy choices about who to hang out with instead of smart choices. I wanted to do things that seemed cool rather than hanging out with people I get along with, who are respectful and generally want me around, which would actually be cool. But I'm not cool and I'm not sexy. And neither are you guys."

"Well thanks for that."

"No, stay with me—no wait—okay—did I say 'unsexy' yet?"

"Yeah . . ."

"Okay, yeah. The point is that I'm glad. You guys aren't sexy and I'm glad because it's good, and because I'm glad we're hanging out. I'm finally glad, fox. We're hanging is good three times right? Fox frees."

"Wait, what the fuck?"

"What?" I snap awake.

"You just started speaking some gibberish there for a second."

Silence.

"I think I might have just fallen asleep in the middle of a sentence."

"Ah, nevermind it. He's a mess!" Sebastian says. "We've got to get him up and keep him moving. What's next?"

He and Thibault hop to their feet, dragging me to mine.

"Next we appreciate art to a contemporary soundtrack," I say.

"Is there an art gallery in this mall?" asks a skeptical Thibault.

"But of course, my good friend. It's called 'the movie theater'."

"High-brow culture at its highest, huh?"

"I like movies," says Sebastian.

"Yeah, everybody likes the movies, Thibault. Now if we could just find an empty theater that Sebastian could run through while he was watching, it'd be perfect."

Sebastian considers this seriously for a second.

"Yeah, but you keep forgetting we don't have any money," says Thibault.

"I didn't forget this time. I have an alternative plan. Just leave it up to me. Speaking of which . . ." I look at my wrist but only a thin white line of pale skin looks back at me. "Fuck, I forgot. Who's got a watch?"

"It's 2:17," says Thibault.

"Good, we probably still have time. Let's head downstairs."

"Time for what?"

"To smoke and get ready."

"*Jassus*, we're still smoking?" asks Thibault.

"Yeah, I need to; it'll wake me up," I say.

"Wow, is that really true?" asks Sebastian.

"No, it isn't. But the way I said it made it sound like it, yeah?"

"I suppose so . . ."

"Also, don't you think Mr. Pretorius is the type of guy who, if he gets spit on from a tower at a mall, will be immediately after whoever did it?"

We look at each other in wide-eyed silence for only a split second before breaking into a mad dash towards the elevators. We get there to see that one is already on its way up, and opt for the stairs instead. As the metal latch of the heavy door closes behind us and we clomp quickly down the stairs, I can hear the faint "ping!" of the elevator arriving at the tower.

I'm awake again.

– – ———— – –

"I think you've gotten better at rolling these as the day has gone on," says Sebastian.

"That's good. Maybe I can go pro in a few years."

I've rolled a mostly-straight joint, without all the weed falling out from the edges.

"Do we really want to light it up here, though?" Thibault asks, looking around.

We are standing in a wide-open loading dock area behind the movie theater. Its terrain looks similar to a lot of the outdoor walkways of the mall, but it is clearly not part of them; it's just a large, deserted area filled with Dumpsters and humming air-conditioning ventilation shafts that stick out of the ground and walls. We snuck back here through a series of twists and turns and are completely alone, but Thibault looks like he is getting Vietnam-type flashbacks of last night. His anxiety is making me anxious, so I say something to calm both of us down.

"Relax, Thibault." I inhale and stifle a cough. "I've been back here dozens of times, and the only person who is going to see us is someone we want to see us."

On cue, the back door of the theater opens, and a black teenager, maybe only a year or two older than us, shuffles out slowly carrying a broom, dustpan, and a bag full of trash. He is dressed in the formal yet ill-fitting attire of a theater employee: black slacks, white buttoned-down shirt, a loud vest with a presumably interesting pattern on it, and a black bowtie. His nametag reads "Sizwe". Thibault and Sebastian freeze instinctively, as if they have just been spotted by one of those animals with poor vision that might miss them if they stand still enough. For once, I am calm as I take another hit.

"Hey Sizwe, what's up?"

Sizwe looks up at us and smiles. He gives me a low-five and then shakes Thibault's and Sebastian's hands without saying anything. Thibault and Sebastian shake back, saying nothing in return, not knowing what to make of the situation. Sizwe strolls past us and throws both his trash bag and the contents of his dustpan into the Dumpster. He pats his hands clean and walks back.

Sizwe always seems like he's moving in slow-motion, but you would never actually call him slow—maybe *deliberate*. He never wastes time or movements, or words for that matter. I forget when I first met him or how I even stumbled back here to begin with, but he offered me part of his joint and let me sneak into a movie, all without ever saying a word. I figured out early on that this is Sizwe's thing, though; he's probably said less than a dozen words to me in all the times I've snuck back here, but he always has a smile. I tell him things now and again about my life, but expect nothing in return. Some things are what they are. Some people are who they are, and trying to dissect them helps nobody. Sizwe could be a prince from a tribe in another part of Africa. Or he could just be another dumb teen like us. If he had wanted to talk, he would have done it by now.

"Here," I say and pass him the joint. He takes it, smiling and nodding as a way of saying 'thanks', and takes a seemingly endless hit. He tilts his head up and slowly exhales into the sky, watching the smoke fade into the blue around it, or perhaps just thinking and watching nothing. For all he cares, we may not even be here.

"Sizwe, I'm going back to America tomorrow."

He returns to eye level and looks at me for a bit before taking another hit. As he holds it in, he smiles and brings his hand up to my shoulder, squeezing it in affirmation. Sizwe always looks you in the eyes. I don't know why, but I feel like I'm about to start crying, and I have to change the subject immediately in order to avoid it.

"Hey, uh . . ." I begin clumsily, trying to push away the cracking in my voice, "can you maybe get me and my friends in here to see something?" I pull out the second of our three matchbooks and shake it to demonstrate its fullness, then hand it to him. He passes the joint—now nearly finished—to Sebastian, and slips the matchbook into his back pocket. He opens the theater door a crack, sticking his head in and peering around. After a few seconds, he opens it wide, waving us inside. Thibault and Sebastian frantically suck up their last hits from the dying joint and shuffle in quickly. I stop at the door to thank Sizwe for all the times he has snuck me in.

He shakes my hand and gives me the shoulder grip one more time, smiling broadly. This time, I know I can't help it, and as I turn away and the door closes behind us both, my eyes start to well up with tears. I don't mind because the theater is already dark and Thibault, Sebastian, and I are the only ones in it. Sizwe is already making his way slowly up one of the aisles. He doesn't look back. I take a seat next to Thibault, wiping away the tears as stealthily as I can. The twenty minutes of commercials that precedes all movies in South Africa is beginning. I can feel Thibault looking at me and wondering if I'm okay, but he doesn't ask any questions or say anything, which I'm thankful for. Some things just are what they are.

6

IN PICTURES

"You ever see Scent of a Woman, man? You ever see Scent of a Woman – on weed?"

- Enhancement Smoker, *Half Baked*

When you're high, life becomes more like a movie and less like . . . life.

I had to smoke a few times for it to do anything to me but the first time I actually got high, everything kept fitting together just so, like it was predestined. It was almost magical. Nothing that happened was really extraordinary, but everything was an augmented version of its own everyday reality—normalcy on steroids. Being high tightened and arranged everyday existence into a fantastical, if not cohesive story. I can only compare this state of heightened, un-real reality to a movie.

Movies are pleasantly distorted takes on reality. They have realistic elements, but aren't particularly realistic. Like if everything broke a certain way in real life, this *could* happen, but 99% of the time the most predictable, boring version of events *will* happen. When you smoke, you're in the movie, bending reality until the mundane becomes spectacular, the coincidental becomes destiny, and life winks at you through its chaos, hinting at a grander design.

Sometimes when I'm high, I feel like I'm watching the movie play out onscreen in front of me as it's happening. For a split second, I think Shakespeare was right: all the world is a stage, and everyone is acting. It's always in those moments that something totally random and unexpected occurs; some cousin from Kentucky you haven't seen since you were two shows up and all of a sudden, you're playing air hockey, you're hunting for treasure, whatever. The drama, the comedy, the tension will be at their peak in a way you only see in the movies.

I think people smoke pot for the same reason they watch and make movies—I know I do. They need to escape, if for only a few hours at a time. They need to suspend disbelief and go to a different planet for a bit, one that looks a lot like theirs but isn't quite the same. Maybe that planet has alien hunters. Maybe it features Tom Hanks and Meg Ryan, and they just can't stop falling in love. Or maybe the same boring shit you do every day seems just a little bit cooler and more tolerable there. You forget about all the things you can't do in real life and start wondering about the things you can. You try to rewrite the script of your life on the fly to make it more interesting. We're making a movie, but we don't have the budget, the cameras, the lighting. Getting completely baked is as close as we can get.

The grand irony, of course, is that being high ruins most actual movies for me. When I'm stoned, I feel like someone is producing life under bright lights and rolling cameras with props and extras galore. When I'm stoned and *watching* a movie, though, it only makes me more aware of that actual construct existing on some phony Hollywood set. Instead of making reality more fantastical, it mires down fantasy with painful reality. I suspend my suspension of disbelief.

I start to realize that someone actually wrote all those one-liners for Nicholas Cage to say in *The Rock*. And by god he hammed them up, yet with seriousness, into a camera in front of dozens of people and ultimately millions more off set. And Michael Bay put those scenes together with a bunch of other things he put on camera, and without any shame, embarrassment, hesitation, or fear of laughter and reproach, he called it a "movie" and put it out for us to watch. And when watching this while high, I ask: *Wait, is the joke on me? I mean, I'm high, but nowhere near high enough that I would believe any of this crap.*

We're currently watching the film *8 Heads in a Duffel Bag*, and it looks like the joke is on me again. It stars a lazy Joe Pesci, an uncharismatic and forgettable male lead I've never heard of, Kristy Swanson, and a host of other people who now probably wish they weren't in it. This is the movie we ended up sneaking into, thanks to Sizwe.

I can't even tell who the lead in the film is. Pesci is given top billing and placement in advertising, but the unnamed black hole of charisma appears to be the 'star'. I guess they need the bullshit romance angle with Kristy Swanson to advance the action, something Pesci can't do because Kristy Swanson isn't Marissa Tomei, it isn't 1992 anymore, and the image of the two of them together wouldn't work on any level. Pesci is phoning this one in anyway. This other guy is a drain on the whole movie. I picture the director and producer watching the dailies, thinking the same thing, sighing as they try to recall casting. *Wow, HE was really the best we could do?*

Meanwhile, is this movie really a comedy? Sure, I get it—it's a black comedy, but those are still supposed to be *funny*, right? I'd like to see the director end the movie with everyone on the same plot of land, and it breaks off into an island in the ocean that gets swallowed by a Kraken or engulfed in the scalding lava of a volcano. *That* would be an artistic choice I would respect, and a fairly unique and unpredictable plot resolution.

I just hate filmmakers with no sense of cinematic responsibility. We come here to escape the shit of our daily lives, not to have more shit added to them. When a movie is really bad, it's a turn-off, a buzzkill, a blind date with someone who is super religious and you didn't know it beforehand. It's your parents catching you masturbating, getting high in a parking lot but then getting mugged, getting dumped by a girl you're nuts over after a week and having her keep your Jimi Hendrix tape forever. It's one more lame thing real life throws at you. In the end, it just makes me depressed. And tired. So tired.

My eyes get heavier, even amongst the constant on-screen screaming and nonsense. Sleep is after me again; she knows I hate to miss a movie! But she doesn't understand—this is so bad, I won't even try to fight it. Come and get me.

– – —— – –

Fade up.

I'm back in the Woodmere library. Fuck, it's like I'll never leave this place. It's empty, and books are strewn over every table and every part of the floor. Half the books are about Japan and half are about America. All the Japanese books are sleek and reserved; some even look less like books and more like futuristic machines that have yet to be invented. The books about America are just the opposite: they use bright, garish colors. They're clunky masses of pulp that look like they have been scrawled in crayon by a clown during a child's birthday party. "USA!" screams one at my feet. At least the spelling is correct.

I now see two other people sitting at the back chess table. I tried playing a few times but everybody I played with read that book about 'how to checkmate your opponent in five moves' and if you hadn't read it yourself and weren't an avid chess player, you were getting beat in five moves. It got old quick.

I can't tell who's playing from this distance; I can only see the back of one person. He's dressed in all black, sitting very still and calm, staring up at the ceiling. It looks like he's wearing sunglasses. I decide to walk over to get a better look, but it's so much farther than it should be and it feels like I'm walking underwater. A vicious storm is raging outside. Gone is the idyllic soft light outside Mr. Sumner's office earlier today. The once softly-swaying trees now whip about hysterically and angrily, with a purple and black sky behind them. Pieces of trash and debris twirl through the air in miniature cyclones. They move too fast for me to make them out, but they look like they could be pieces of my writing journal. Boy, I hope not.

"I saw a storm like this on Coney Island once," says a lazy voice from behind me.

I turn around and I'm standing right next to the chess players. The man in black is still staring up towards the ceiling in his sunglasses, maybe in a drug daze. It's Lou Reed.

"How can you see anything in those things? Most people

wait till they're my age to develop cataracts, but it's good to see some ambition in today's youth."

This is the response from Lou's opponent. He's clearly much more focused on the chessboard in front of him, and he nervously rubs his furrowed brow above his obviously-prescription glasses. It's Woody Allen.

Lou ignores this remark and Woody continues to fret over his next move.

"Um . . . have you guys been here long?" I ask.

"We're here every Tuesday, man," Lou says. He may actually be singing, but I can't really tell because I've just learned today that Lou Reed sings in a kind of off-key talking type way.

"Really, we're here all the time, but you never notice us. You're too busy with god-knows-what," Woody seconds.

"But I love you guys! How could I not notice you here all the time?"

"People got problems. People wear shades. The sun don't come in," replies Lou from behind his own shades.

"A true poet, this one! Do you actually play the guitar on your records, or just plug it in and throw it down a flight of stairs?" counters Woody.

Lou brings his gaze back down from the ceiling to be presumably eye level with Woody.

"Hey Woody, you gonna go, man?"

Woody begins to fidget uncomfortably in his trademark manner, rubbing at his temples and tugging at his shirt collar as if it has suddenly become unbearably hot.

"Ugh, I'm going all right. I'm basically at death's door—high blood pressure, nausea. I might have a case of bilharzia. Ugh, I'm so parched! Kid, you got any water on you?"

I reach into my pocket as if I could somehow pull a glass of water out of it. Instead I pull out handfuls of paper scraps, like the ones swirling around outside. They *are* from my writing journal; I can make out touches of my own handwriting.

I reach into my other pocket, but only pull out a blue guitar pick. Without hesitation, Lou takes it from my hand and smiles, putting it in his pocket.

"Ugh, you two are terrific," snaps Woody. "A regular Laurel and Hardy."

Lou opens his mouth again to prompt Woody to action, but Woody preempts him by putting his hands up in the air.

"Alright, alright!" he says, pushing a lone pawn one square up from its starting position. Lou studies the board for about one second before moving a knight.

"Check." He adjusts his shades.

Woody throws his hands up in the air again and hops up, pacing around and continuing to rub his forehead nervously. You would think I would notice Woody Allen and Lou Reed playing chess in my school library every Tuesday.

Behind me, one of the slats of glass from the windows cracks, letting howling wind in. I look back and see the crack was caused by a horn from the African mask I made in Mr. Thomson's art class. It's lodged into the crack, its eyes glaring at me. I get the sense I don't have much time here.

"Well Lou, just got to hear some of your early stuff for the first time today and really liked it. I look forward to more."

Lou turns slowly toward me. "You'll be dead in a year, man."

"A poet and a charmer!" screams an exasperated Woody. Yes, that comment from Lou certainly seemed unnecessary.

I turn my attention towards Woody as the wind from outside howls louder.

"Hey Woody, can we talk about *Hannah and Her Sisters* for a second?"

This proposition makes him even more distraught.

"I don't want to discuss my work . . ." He sits back down to focus on the board. Another pane of glass cracks behind me but I try to ignore it.

"Okay, but can I just say one thing about the part where you were thinking of killing yourself, but you don't end up doing it?"

"No, please . . ." Woody is tugging at his collar again. "It's too hot in here. I think I'm having a heart attack . . ."

Without us noticing it, Lou has lit a joint and is now attempting to pass it to Woody.

"This will calm you down, man."

"*Knock that shit off, Lou!*" I yell, swatting his hand away. He shrugs and continues to smoke. Woody is breathing heavily. Another crack behind me; the wind is becoming louder and louder.

"Woody, please. It's just that scene . . . I watched that movie at a very depressing time in my life and that scene—"

A whole row of glass slats shatters and the wind and debris swirl in through the empty space. Woody keeps shaking his head.

"Please . . . I can't talk about my work."

I have to shout to be heard over the screaming wind.

"But Woody, this one part! You didn't kill yourself because Groucho Marx made you realize there's all this 'great stuff' in the world! That part—"

The glass from all the windows now shatters in one fell swoop and a mini-cyclone rips through the library. Books about America and Japan spin above us like psychotic pigeons. The pages from my writing journal mix in with them and whip past our heads at lightning speeds. A page of my writing slaps up against the right side of Lou's face, but he doesn't seem to care. He starts to sing off-key, but I can't make out the words. I'm now screaming in Woody's ear so he can hear me.

"WOODY! I'M TRYING TO TELL YOU THAT PART MEANT SOMETHING TO ME!"

Woody's head is in his hands now and he just keeps shaking it back and forth and saying, "No. No. My work . . ."

"DON'T YOU GET IT? I WAS DEPRESSED LIKE YOU IN THE MOVIE! BUT WATCHING YOUR MOVIE MADE ME WANT TO KEEP LIVING, TOO! JUST LIKE YOU WATCHING GROUCHO!"

"*No! My work!*" Woody screams.

Lou has stopped singing. I glance over and see that he is making out with Kim now. Well great. I had to figure she would make a cameo, keep the franchise going, you know? But I just have to tell Woody this last thing before I run out of time . . .

My African mask flies over and lands on Woody's head, turning him into some temporary artificial Minotaur. He panics and starts running through the storm in the library, flailing his arms. My voice is getting hoarse now. Not long . . .

"WOODY! I JUST WANTED TO SAY . . . THANK YOU!"

Lou and Kim stop making out and stare at me. I can't tell if Woody has heard me. It's hard to see now as pages of my own writing keep hitting me in the face. A door bursts open and Mr. Sumner runs in, wild-eyed.

"*'EY NOW! SHUT IT!*"

I awake with a start and Mr. Sumner's words echoing in my head. On screen, Joe Pesci's eight heads in a duffel bag are now singing in unison. Thibault is asleep in the chair next to me. A slapping sound is coming from somewhere in the theater, rising and falling in volume. In a few more seconds, Sebastian dashes beneath the screen at the front of the house, beginning another lap around the edges of the theater.

7

FAILURES

"The news said it's raining in New York."
    - McManus, *The Usual Suspects*

The worst part is always when the movie's over.

If the ending is bad, you've wasted your time and it wasn't much of an escape, was it? If it's a good ending, it's even worse: *Crash!* Welcome back to Earth.

Thibault, Sebastian, and I sit on a mixture of rocks and grass in an empty lot across from Sandton Mall, stoned out of our gourds, staring at cars and people heading down Sandton Way. The last of our weed is gone. All our money is gone. Our energy and ambition are gone. If it hasn't already disappeared completely, our pride and self-respect are soon to follow.

What happened to my *Ferris Bueller's Day Off* remake? In theory, you could say nothing's changed; we've completed maybe half of the plot points. We *could* continue our haphazard, backwards attempt to recreate a fictional moment in history for an end that keeps fading further and further into obscurity. But the magic is missing; we never quite caught hold of it to begin with. And now we've lost all our momentum, or maybe we just smoked it out of the bottom of that last matchbox.

We aren't speaking to each other, but then again, none of us has much to say. This is the culmination of my two years here—this lot of broken glass, Joburg Beer containers, cigarette and joint butts, used condoms, and patches of unnatural grass. Sitting stiff and staring at nothing. The lights have come on in the theater; the show is over.

This is the straight-to-video sequel: real life on tape. It would be called *Ferris II: Frye's Dilemma*. It would center on Cameron, a much less sympathetic character; you know—more *realistic*. Alan Ruck probably wouldn't even play Cameron—probably someone like Tom Hulce or some shit—and Ferris wouldn't even be in the movie except for maybe some throwaway scene where Cameron talks to his 'old buddy' on the phone and you don't even hear the other voice. In the end, as the credits rolled all the way through, the tape stopped, and the static of nothingness and white noise screamed out at you, you would wonder why you bothered to try and escape at all.

For some reason I'm thinking of that heavy religious group that visited Woodmere last year. They preached and sang family-in-a-garage-band-quality pop songs about God. Their leader—a man with thinning hair atop a hulking torso—wore a forest-green turtleneck and one of those padded-elbows beige jackets you always see on college professors in 1970s movies. He gurgled in a thick Afrikaans accent about his early days of hard drugs and fast motorcycles—about how he pummeled people with martial arts for fun—anything that would get him *high*. In the end, nothing could get him as high as God's love.

Maybe this is my rock bottom and The Lord is just around the corner. I can see myself in 20 years, recalling stories of wasted youth, of life and love gone wrong to uninterested teenagers. "*I tried everything: pot, movies, furious masturbation— nothing truly got me high until Jesus found me . . .*" Seems unlikely. It's not necessarily that I don't believe in a god, I'm just not sure whatever's out there is directing with any attention to detail. I'm sure the people who made *8 Heads in a Duffel Bag* wanted it to be good, but we saw how that turned out.

In my movie, I came to this land a stranger, surveyed what I thought to be the cultural bankruptcy of my peers, and resisted any attempt at real assimilation. In the end, my environment responded in kind: in the space of about one month, my 'friends' turned on me and attacked me, a girl broke my heart just as I was finally realizing it was hers to break, and I starred in my own anti-drug commercial—my friend and I brutalized by a lightweight criminal because smoking *dagga* made us too slow and stupid to react to an admittedly slow and stupid con. South Africa is like Donald Sutherland at the end of *Invasion of the Body Snatchers*: it's pointing at me, wide-eyed, emitting an alien howl to alert the others that I'm the outsider. So is this a drama? A bloody revenge tale? *Jassus*—an after-school special? I still can't tell.

In the dark of Thibault's bedroom, I cooked up a scheme with all that was left of my fragile mind and being—one last stab at a meaning to my time here. If it failed, at least I tried. *It can't get any worse.* But that line signals doom in any movie. It can always get lower; things can always get worse.

When they ask me how the Dark Continent treated me, how many lions and lionesses I slayed, what can I say? The only lioness I ever had a chance with swallowed me whole. The jungle ate the rest of my party, or turned them into idiot vampires. The natives stole my rations and gear. At this moment, I'm completely lost. My life here has failed to make a difference, and I have failed to make a difference in my life. It's all a bit too much to handle. I think I'm getting *the fear*.

"I want to go home."

Thibault and Sebastian stir from their own pot-induced stupors, surprised that someone in our party is trying to form a sentence. A bum wobbles into our vicinity, hoping for a smoke or a few cents towards a Joburg Beer. He sees me hunched over, rocking back and forth with my head buried in my hands, and slinks quietly away in the other direction, knowing his prospects here are doomed. Thibault and Sebastian are not so lucky.

"What?" attempts Thibault, not really wanting to know what can of worms he's opening.

"I said I want to go home!" My voice cracks in hysterics. "I don't belong here. I never have! *Why?* Why am I *here*?" I ask to no one, grabbing handfuls of rocks and dust and tossing them in the air.

"This isn't my home! This. Is. Not. My. Home. I can't live here. Fuck it! Fuck all the raves. And *dagga*. And the fucking ass-backward racism. And those assholes at school. And that fucker who mugged us!"

Sebastian's ears perk up. "You guys got mugged?"

"Long story," mutters Thibault, touching gently around the corners of his still-swollen eye.

"Last night we sure did, farmboy!" My voice is already hoarse and cracking and spittle flies from my mouth. "Out at a rave club in Randburg. The music was like: *oot-tis oot-tis oot-is oot-tis oot-chika oot-chika oot-chika oot-chika*!"

For the first time during my time in South Africa, I feel compelled to do my interpretation of rave dancing—all flailing limbs and herky-jerky hips. I've got it now: my movie's a horror flick. I tried to fight off the zombies, but they just kept coming. Eventually they ate my brain and made me one of them.

I kick pebbles around me in my frenzy, forgetting that we are facing Sandton Way, just across from the mall. Pedestrians from across the street and passengers in cars look upon me in puzzled amusement but I don't care. This is what they all want. The sad clown. I'm a different flavor of Nick Sutter.

A black taxi flies by and they all yell out and wave at me as I dance and beat-box.

"Heeeeeyyy!! *Bafana Bafana*!" I shout back.

Thibault and Sebastian are having trouble stifling their laughter, still stoned, yet remembering that they are not dealing with a being of sound mind.

"See, even you laugh at me!"

"Oh, c'mon! You're asking for it here!" Thibault fires back.

I drop back down to my seated head-in-hands rocking position.

"I just want to go home. I just want to go home."

Sebastian takes a stab at reeling me back in.

"Aren't you heading home tomorrow?"

"Noooo," I hiss back at him. "New York is my home."

Even I did not anticipate this response.

"Wait, New York? I thought he was from Florida," starts a confused Sebastian.

"He is . . ." Thibault answers, now unsure.

"New York is where I belong!" The whining demon in me takes over. "My home! It's big and it's open and it's free and it's weird and they make movies there and people don't fuck with each other because of how they look or act because everybody has better things to do with their time!"

"Well that sounds rather pleasant," says Sebastian.

"I should say so," agrees Thibault.

"So he's from Florida, but he's living here, but says his home is in New York . . ." Sebastian ponders softly with a finger to his chin.

"But he's going to Japan on exchange," Thibault interjects. "That's why he's leaving here. I mean he goes back to Florida first . . ."

"But when does he get to New York?"

"I don't know if he has considered that rationally as much as metaphorically."

"I'm going nowhere . . ." I whisper, sitting still after my theatrics, barely able to make a sound. I stare dead-eyed at the ground. A used condom has caught my eye. The waste in it could have been a different person. Instead, I'm here.

"I'm going nowhere!"

My scream rattles what's left of my head and I feel faint for a split second as I hop up involuntarily. I run across Sandton Way and a roar fills my ears. Horns blare and tires screech to my right, but I'm not looking anywhere except straight ahead. If Thibault and Sebastian are calling after me, I can't hear it. I'm breaking for the line of taxis outside the mall's main entrance. I need to go home as fast as possible.

I flail my arms like a deranged person at the first cabbie in line, until he makes eye contact with me and starts up his engine. I rip open the back door, and dive in with such enthusiasm that I end up hitting my head on the other back door.

"*Eh! Eh! Eh!*" the cabbie starts with his arms up, the universal language for 'I don't want no trouble.'

The pain comes on slow like a burn and I feel dizzy. I hold my head and wince through my fingers.

"Sorry . . . can . . . you . . . please . . . drive?" I manage in blindness.

"Where we go, boss?"

"Uh . . . Rosebank . . . 13 . . . 19 . . . Roseburg Avenue."

"*Shap shap*, boss."

He pulls away and the momentum sinks me sideways onto the back seat. I don't fight it. I'm not interested in fighting anything anymore. The argument is over. If I had a white flag, I'd wave it. There's some movie where they talk about being able to take the last breath of a dying person, but I can't remember . . . ah, who cares? We're past metaphor.

Now it's quiet and all I can see through the window are the tops of trees and sky. I turn onto my back and tears pool at the corners of my eyes. I let them fall down the sides of my face. Eventually I decide I should pay attention to this last ride home. I pull myself up and the tears on my cheek change course, gravity pulling them down until they drop one by one on the seat next to me.

The sky has changed all at once. The sun and heat have exhausted themselves, deciding to call it after a half-day's worth of work. A soft golden glow blankets everything around me. For a second, it feels like autumn instead of summer. Perhaps the sun is defying millions of years of science in one rebellious moment.

I roll the window down and a breeze gushes in like cool water, yelling softly into my ears to think of nothing, chilling the tears that settled there when I was laying down.

We round a corner and the cricket stadium appears on our left. Not long now. I never went to one match despite living so close to the stadium this whole time; funny the things you regret. Wishing for simpler things. Unsexy choices. The PG-rated stuff. On *In Utero*, there's a song called "Frances Farmer Will Have Her Revenge on Seattle" where Kurt sings "*I miss the comfort in being sad.*" I never bought that Kurt was supposed to be the voice of my generation; his lyrics were mostly unintelligible—a bad sign for us. But that one—he had that dead on.

Cab rides are still novel to me. Especially here, where everything is so spread out, and everyone either drives themselves or does some combination of hitching and black taxis. I remember when I first learned you could take a taxi to get somewhere. Even if you didn't have a parent or an older friend willing to drive you, you could pay a few bucks and have a stranger drive you wherever you wanted to go. It felt so adult.

Kim and I rode in a cab just a few weeks ago, when we were coming home from seeing Penelope dance at The Khyber. My mother dropped us off, but we adults got a cab home. Some adult I am; my old nemesis, sleep, decided to cheap-shot me on the ride home and I couldn't even stay awake to smooch my girl in the back of the cab. We held hands, but I kept dozing off. She was always the adult; I couldn't keep up.

When you fall asleep holding someone else's hand and they're not also asleep, you surrender into them and let your guard completely down. You have to trust them. I imagine

Kim in the cab next to me now, sitting the same way she was that night, staring out the window as I faded, her hand still in mind. I put my hand where it was on that cab ride, trying to feel hers there. You can do the same thing in the same place, but a different time makes the new result unrecognizable. I think of Kurt Vonnegut's Tralfamadorians, seeing and experiencing all of time simultaneously, always doing everything forever. I bet they don't get lonely.

We turn onto my street, and a sinking, burning feeling starts in my gut. I don't want to see my mom like this. She can probably tell. Wait, *what* can she tell? That I'm a total mess? That this place has defeated me? I think she's seen this movie before. There's really only a few times during my stay here that she hasn't seen it. Besides, caring about appearances is not doing a very good job of surrendering.

"Here, boss. Twelve rand fifty."

My hand still clasps the air, searching for Kim's, and it takes me a second to realize the cabbie is asking me for money. I reach into my pocket, but only a few cruel seeds of terrible pot grace my fingertips. No money. A tense heat radiates from the back of my neck and the taste of adrenaline and fear wells up in my throat. A perfect end to a perfect day.

"I . . . think . . . I think I lost my money . . ."

"What?"

"Mmmoney . . . I don't have any . . . Please . . . I can . . ."

"What the fuck, boss? No no no no . . . No boss, no."

He shakes his head and talks quickly in a language I don't know. He ruffles some papers somewhere in his front seat, and begins to fiddle with his radio, presumably to call someone about this.

"No . . . please . . . can we talk about this?"

Not like I can form coherent sentences anyway. A strong wave of nausea hits me.

"No! No bullshit, boss. You fuck me. I know you bad when you get in. You fucking crazy on *dagga*."

"Please . . . don't . . . what can I . . ."

My words become even more labored as my stomach and esophagus start to convulse. A cold sweat starts on the back of my neck. *Uh oh*. It. Can. Always. Get. Worse.

Vomiting is really one of the worst feelings in the world. It's rare that you see it coming with any real time to prepare for it. It's basically nature's imaginary hand reaching down your throat and into your guts, yanking everything out of it at once. There is no way to throw up gently or cleanly, something the cabbie and I are both rediscovering together as my floodgates open involuntarily.

"Oh, what the fuck, boss? Shit, you fucking bad, man!"

In a last-second attempt to limit the damage, I put my hand in front of my mouth. Unfortunately, this achieves the opposite of the desired effect, with my vomit spattering through my fingers onto the dividing glass, as well as into my crotch, and onto the seat below. Some small remainder drips from my hand in slow-motion. I'm wincing in pain and embarrassment, or crying again, or both. I can't tell.

"Get the fuck out, man!"

"Wait . . . I . . ."

"Get out! Go!"

I finally understand that the cabbie has tired of my standup routine and is telling me to take a hike, and I fumble with the handle to get out as fast as I can. My back foot is barely out of the cab before he screeches off. I can still hear him screaming curse words as he speeds away.

And just like that, it's quiet again. The bright purple jacaranda trees sway heavily overhead. A squirrel runs by. My right hand continues to drip vomit as I hold it away from me like a useless claw. For a moment, I watch the movie of my life as if I'm outside myself, trying to find the comedy. A few bumps in the road, a few puffs of smoke, and you can frame the picture any number of ways.

The outside gate creaks and then slams closed behind me as I step in. It seems unnecessarily loud. I haven't looked behind me the whole way home. I'm imagining that everything in South Africa is disintegrating into a vortex behind me that I'm staying only one step ahead of as I leave. Like one of those unrealistic movie scenes where the Indiana Jones-like hero is just barely outrunning a tidal wave or explosion or collapsing building. I know I can look back and everything will still be there, but why go to a movie if you're not willing to suspend disbelief?

The second inside gate slams behind me as I cross the small courtyard to the front of the house. No looking back. It's all gone. I slide the key in the front door and it makes a noise like a castle deadbolt falling open, as if there were thousand-year-old ball bearings in it that had never been heard up to this point.

What I previously thought of as quiet doesn't even come close to the silence in here. It feels like the world has been screaming at me for the last two hours and I finally just stepped into a sealed vacuum. On the flip side, the smell of my vomit is now overwhelming in closed quarters. I hear my mother stir in the TV room and get up to come see me. So much for sneaking in quietly.

"What's wrong?" she asks.

I wish I could say this is great motherly intuition, but I look and smell awful, even from a distance.

"I . . . Thibault and I were hanging out at Sandton Mall and I decided to eat some nasty street shish kebab. I started to feel sick almost right away and tried to take a cab home but threw up on myself right as I was about to get out here."

"Oh my god. Are you okay? Do you want to lie down? Or should we take you to the doctor?"

"I think I'm okay now. It wasn't pretty but I think that might have actually done it. I'm still gross and I want to get in the shower and then just lay in bed for a bit."

"You should do that. And drink some ginger ale. I'll make you some soup later if you want. Just don't leave those yucky clothes on the bathroom floor."

"Okay."

"Are you sure you're okay?"

"Yeah ma."

She crosses her arms and gives me a soft reaffirming mom smile.

"You've had a tough time recently, huh monkeynose?"

"Yeah ma."

Tears well up in me again like they did outside the movie theater and I fight like hell to keep them away. I know I said surrender, but I just can't break down in front of my mom.

"Okay. I gotta shower, ma."

"Okay. Get some rest. Don't leave the clothes on the floor."

As soon as I'm sure I'm out of her sight, I dash the rest of the way to the bathroom, stifling my crying with my hand. I close the door behind me and let it go. The tears come as hard as any time I can remember. My whole body cries; it stings in my back and neck and collarbones and guts. My vision blurs with tears and I remember Thibault's pool from this morning, how peaceful it was under the water. Maybe I need to become one of those marine biologists that swim with dolphins.

Tears burst from my eyes and roll down my cheeks and I can see again. I look at myself in the mirror: caked in fluids both wet and dry, natural and unnatural. Half-high, half-exhausted, half-sick. '*One of God's own creatures,*' I hear Hunter Thompson say in my head. '*Too weird to die.*'

I peel my rancid clothes off and place them in the bathtub, shivering as I start the shower as hot as it will go. I climb in through the scalding water and fresh steam, sniveling as the water pours over my head, and I immediately slide down the wall under the showerhead, with my knees up against my chest.

I feel like I've spent at least a whole month of my two years here under this showerhead like this—thinking, crying, thinking, masturbating, thinking some more. My move to this country has been my own personal Kennedy assassination conspiracy and this is my research facility. *How did it happen? Who was really responsible? Who had the most to gain?*

People back home who ask me always get the same response, which through repetition, I now have down to a science: "My mom's boyfriend is a lawyer for an international law firm. They opened an office in Johannesburg and asked him to come work here. He and my mom had visited the previous summer and loved it, so we all moved." That's what I tell people and it *seems* simple and straightforward, simpler than you might even expect.

Inwardly, though, no explanation satisfies me or makes it make sense to me. I've never heard of anyone picking up and moving their family from Miami, Florida to Johannes-burg, South Africa. It's too random. Certainly as a movie plot it makes no sense, unless you are making a straight nov-elty comedy based on repeated culture-shock gags. Perhaps that's what my time here has been, an unfunny black comedy set to the gimmick of a cultural divide. I'm the ninth head singing from the bottom of Joe Pesci's duffel bag.

Maybe once or twice in school you hear about some-one's family picking up and moving to some European place like . . . *Paris*. You know, a place famous for its art and beauty. Where they *read*. And paint. And make music. And food. And drink wine. A place with ridiculously attractive people. At least this is what I gather from repeated viewings of the Meg Ryan vehicle *French Kiss*.

But *Africa*? Why? Let's not even call it a bad choice, just one that pops into the script out of nowhere. Where's the context? I was just starting to learn the intricacies of American high school life. I was just past braces, past the worst of my puberty and acne, past embarrassing myself in front of the same few girls in junior high. There were a whole new slew of girls for me to embarrass myself in front of. I had cleaned up and already made some good older friends. The future was so bright, I had to wear shades.

The first time I told the 'mom's boyfriend is an interna-tional lawyer' story, I stumbled through it, my friends and I both still shell-shocked. I got better at telling the story, but never better at understanding it. A lifetime of movies has warped my sense of reality and convinced me that every story *has* to have a reasonable arc: a beginning, middle, and end based on reasonable events and reactions to those events. The characters learn and grow and lose when they refuse to do so.

But I can't make out the arc here—the cause and effect. I don't even know what part of the story I'm in. I think the only part I've gotten right is the whole 'losing while refusing to grow' thing.

Maybe it's a trilogy, *Star Wars* style. Miami was my Tatooine in *A New Hope*; I was naïve and innocent, unaware of my potential or the dark side of The Force that would oppose it. Right now, I'm stuck in shitty *Empire*, getting the shit kicked out of me by snow creatures, looking like an asshole during my training, getting my hand cut off by my own fucking dad. Depressing all around. That would make my upcoming Japanese exchange trip *Jedi*, the one where I start wearing all black and moving shit around with my mind, everything clicks, and I save the universe. I guess I'd be okay with that, except if we're in act two of the trilogy, that pretty much ensures nothing good is going to happen until I get the hell out of here and into the third act. I'm not getting my damn hand back, that's for sure.

What if it's not even my movie? Maybe it's my mom's. She's the post-menopausal woman (think Liza Minelli crossed with Sigourney Weaver) looking for spiritual enlightenment and a new lease on life in an exotic locale. Her son wants to stay in shitty Florida, living with a shitty drunk of a father (think Jack Nicholson crossed with Rodney Dangerfield), but Mom isn't about to let that happen. She's going to 'find her happiness' and save her son from having a shitty average teenage American life where he eventually might lose his virginity and have friends. Mom wins, but in the process she may be hurting the one she loves most . . . her baby boy! She researches an exchange program to a country he always wanted to visit. She helps him apply and do all the paperwork. Her son gets in to the program and Mom is the hero—still strong and happy, but not without sacrifice. *And scene.* I'm up for best actor in a supporting role.

That's a great movie for her and that's why I can't break down in front of her. This is her time to be happy, and in order for that to happen, she needs to believe that picking up and moving us eight thousand miles away wasn't completely alienating and world-shattering for me, even if that's exactly what it was. I don't have the heart to tell her that while, yes, there were a few times when I smoked some really good shit, and at least one time when I almost got laid, it hasn't really gotten better. Maybe I'm the hero after all. It doesn't change the fact that I'm sitting in my shower crying.

What scene is this: the emotionally distraught woman sitting in the shower, sobbing, perhaps mascara bleeding from her eyes as the music swells? *Fatal Attraction?* I feel like I've seen it a hundred times. Whenever I'm like this, I picture myself as the woman and it makes me laugh. I think I do this on purpose; my mind subconsciously brings up the image as a mechanism to stop feeling sorry for myself.

I chuckle at how silly I look and how silly it is to have such serious feelings about such silly things in life, which is really *everything* at my age. Especially when compared to the rest of the world's real-life problems. That's the curse of youth: we know it will all go away in time, but we still can't be anywhere but *here right now.*

I really did want Woody Allen to know how I felt about that scene in *Hannah and Her Sisters.* He was saying that when you get to your lowest, darkest point in life, the best thing you can do is laugh, even if it's at yourself. For Woody's character Mickey, it was the humor of the Marx brothers that made him believe life was worth living. For me, imagining myself as a hysterical Glenn-Close-in-*Fatal-Attraction*-type character turns my tears to laughter. In life, there really is so much to keep you laughing if you look.

The strange thing is that if I stayed in Miami all of my teenage years, the idea of an exchange program in Japan probably wouldn't have ever come up. So if being here was the price to go, was it worth it? Well, could Luke have defeated the empire without losing his hand and suffering bitter defeat first? Is equating the Japanese people to the Ewoks totally racist from the get-go? The water always starts to get cold before I ever figure anything out.

My eyes are heavy. I turn off the shower with a pang of wistfulness, not wanting to leave. I shiver outside of it, throwing a towel over my shoulders, like when I was a little boy. The only difference now is that my balls are just starting to stick out from the bottom. The lights are on as I enter my room. My mom must have turned them on for me, but I prefer to think a dark spirit has done it. It's the Ghost of Failures Present.

The Tralfamadorian in me sees Kim here constantly, the faint outlines of her exposed shoulders in the dark, the curve of her hips. I'll feel a rustle next to me in bed, or swear I feel her breath on me. All madness; mirages in the night. I've seen them so much recently that it's difficult to sleep here. I'll stand at the doorway of my room, replaying it all like a Tralfamadorian peeping tom: us making out and body-locked on my bed, then two weeks later when she wouldn't even hold my hand, everything in between, before and after. I often decide to sleep on the couch with the TV on instead.

I put on a pair of boxers and a t-shirt, turn off the light and get into bed, praying my current exhaustion is a good counter for my overactive imagination. The room is dark, even though night is only just starting to fall outside. Thick wooden shutters outside my patio door and windows are almost always closed. When they are, the only natural light I get is from a sliver at the top of my windows where the wood does not reach. Through it now I see the sky slowly bleeding pink and purple, and my eyes get heavier.

I flip through CDs in bed, squinting to see names in the dark. I settle on Joy Division—*Closer*. It's the first name I can make out in the dark. I instantly know it's the right choice. Something about the production of this album—it's cold and far away, like all the air is very still and stiff around it. This is what my room feels like now, cold and still. I search for the perfect falling-asleep volume, and then pull the covers up over me. Everything becomes heavy; the bed and my pillow push back up around me. "Heart and Soul" is my favorite song. It begins after I've been laying here for a bit and I sink into its trance-like rhythm. Short synthesizer swells pulse in and out like my consciousness. Ian Curtis sings, "*Heart and Soul – one will burn. Heart and Soul – one will burn . . .*" His voice fades into a wash of guitar that seems to go on forever. I fade into it.

– – ——— – –

Fade up.

It feels like I've been stuck here for a while.

In this line. In what looks like the lobby of some tall building. I wish someone would tell me where we are. Seems popular enough. The line begins to move rapidly and I'm face to face with an old female security guard in one of those cheap blue and gray slacks and sport jacket combinations. A red velvet rope separates us. She reaches for my lapels, and I feel like we're in a bar fight in some old Western and I'm in serious trouble; it turns out she's actually putting some kind of pin there. I swallow my own neck and create a few extra chins scrunching down to try and look at the pin, but I still can't make it out. She shakes her head at me sadly as she opens the rope.

"Okay," she says, "but I'm telling you: *you can't get there from here.*"

The floor opens up and I'm walking towards three elevators. I can't locate anyone who was in line in front of me. In fact, it looks like I'm the only one to make it past the initial rope. The rest of the lobby is starting to look familiar, though; maybe I've been here before. I see one of the elevators ahead of me closing and I run to jump in and catch it. I'm not sure how, but I make it. It feels like I just squeezed my body through a space much thinner than it could possibly fit, all in one chaotic, spinning moment.

As I regain my composure, I notice my fellow occupants in the elevator. Sizwe from the movie theater is here. He looks stoic as always, staring straight ahead, lazy-eyed, seemingly focused on something, but revealing nothing. He's dressed in a different uniform now. It's a full-length red one with black buttons and trim that looks much older and classier. He looks like an elevator operator from an old movie, which makes sense, I guess, because he's operating this elevator.

Next to Sizwe is Matthew Defoe of the aforementioned Defoe-Sutter heavyweight bout that got Nick Sutter expelled from Woodmere. I don't know why he and Sizwe are here together. Defoe is in the process of lighting a massive joint. It's totally out of character for him, but then, his whole demeanor and dress seem out of character, too. He's wearing a suit—a tuxedo actually—and sunglasses, and he's moving and talking in a fluid, relaxed way I've never seen him possess or thought he was capable of before. I wonder if he's just playing a character. Or if he was just a character before, in school—the "nerd" comic relief from some movie.

"Are . . . you . . . *the character?*" I ask slowly.

"No, I'm fuckin' Joan of Arc, baby!" he says like a weird South African Rodney Dangerfield, yukking and nudging Sizwe in the ribs as he gesticulates.

"All the world's a stage, right, baby?" he cackles into Sizwe's ear as he passes off the joint. Sizwe only smiles and shakes his head before taking a hit. The elevator fills with smoke, and Sizwe holds out the joint for me to take.

"Oh I dunno, fellas. That's not going very well for me right now."

I look at it for a second longer and silently wave it off. Sizwe shrugs and hands the joint back to Defoe.

"Hey, everyone's a critic, hah?" Defoe begins to laugh again before taking a large hit of his own.

Are we all characters? Different clichés and archetypes to advance the action in one direction or another? Maybe this is what Defoe is trying to tell me with his drastic changeup: we're always playing to the audience and what we think they're looking for, even when we're not sure there's an audience there. True depth only comes when we play against type.

"So we're all just starring in the wrong pictures, Defoe?" I ask.

"Get a load of this guy," Defoe starts, mugging to Sizwe and continuing to nudge him mercilessly in the ribs. Sizwe stares straight ahead, acknowledging nothing until it's his turn to take the joint.

Defoe now has the joint and he gets serious momentarily, studying it as if it were a rare butterfly specimen. He flicks its ashes off distinctly while examining it.

"You can choose the ending," he says, inhaling, "or you can let the ending choose you."

Sizwe glances sideways at Defoe, as if this is the first thing any of us have said that is of any value. Meanwhile, the smoke is overwhelming.

"Sorry, guys, but can we stop for a minute? This is getting to me."

"Like I said, everyone's a critic," Defoe responds. He signals Sizwe to stop the elevator. Sizwe shrugs and pulls the lever down.

The doors open and smoke pours out. Down a dark hall, I can hear people stirring. It's a group of four or five, and it only takes a second for them to go from roused attention to an angry, screaming stampede of zombies. They run towards the elevator, foaming like wild dogs. I can now make out the faces of my former "friends": Jordan. Patrick. Alo. Mr. Pretorius leads the mob.

"No," I whisper without moving, paralyzed with fear.

Sizwe hits the elevator lever smoothly and without panic.

The doors close with still a few feet left between us and the snarling mob, Sizwe staring straight ahead as before, unfazed. The shrill screams and banging of metal are briefly heard as we begin climbing again.

Defoe is equally unconcerned with the display we've just seen. He whistles slowly as he pulls another joint from his pocket and lights it.

"They can smell you coming from outside. So why do you even want to get in with them?"

I know what he means. Why do I want to be friends with snarling animals? I stare at my shoes in lieu of a response. We must be quite high up. I can feel an altitude change.

"How far are we going?"

"All the way to the top, baby," Defoe starts. "If you can keep your head on until we get there."

The floors go by faster and faster. The speed becomes temporarily nauseating and dizzying and my guts sink lower in my body until finally, abruptly, we stop.

The doors open and it looks like we're on some kind of roof observation deck. Spotlights adorn its edges, pointing somewhere higher above it. A thin fog covers the whole area.

Defoe offers the path from the elevator like Vanna White showing a vowel, grinning as he does so.

"Remember," he begins while removing his sunglasses and replacing them with his standard corrective lenses, "you can always change your face."

As Defoe puts them on, his face morphs into one of helpless fear and awkwardness, maybe the same face he wore in the heat of battle with Nick Sutter. This is the type of face I think of when it comes to Defoe, the one I might have expected when I first noticed him in this elevator. But just as quickly as he changed it, the face rights itself back into the new, confident Defoe and the sunglasses come back. He's smiling and elbowing Sizwe in the ribs once more, as if to say 'look what I just pulled.'

I step out of the elevator onto the foggy observation deck and the air is charged with energy and longing. I've been here once before on a class trip in junior high: it's the top of the Empire State Building. Defoe calls after me.

"You can't wait forever! They'll be coming soooooooooooon!" he yells through the last crack of the closing elevator doors.

A man and woman in trench coats stand side-by-side with their backs to me. They're the only people I can see on the observation deck. The view is surreal; we are so far above the tops of any other buildings that I wonder if they're real or toy models. In the fog, each building's bottom disappears. Or perhaps there aren't any bottoms and the tops just float in space, circling the Empire State Building.

I walk to the edge of the deck where the man and woman stand. They turn to greet me before I make a sound. It's my friends from back home, Jason and Gina. They have big smiles on their faces. Jason offers me a firm handshake, an odd gesture in the context of our friendship. I'm not one to argue, though, and I accept heartily. He even continues the act with an accompanying arm grab. The wind picks up.

"Good to see you made it back to the mainland."

"Almost," I say, wanting to be cautious. "I still have to cross the border and it could prove difficult."

"How much time?"

"Can't say." He could be asking how long before I'm back

or how long before the angry mob catches up. The answer is the same for both.

"Well, you know we'll always be here." Gina chuckles, pushing strands of windswept hair away from her eyes. She's wearing what looks like a tiara and a lot of makeup, and she has a happy glow. She looks like she just won a beauty contest.

"You've gotta keep moving if you wanna make it, though," Jason cautions.

"I know, I know," I mutter as I glance back towards the elevator. The lighted numbers up top seem to be moving from low to high.

"Wanna smoke?" Gina offers.

"Boy, I really do, guys. But we're so far, and time . . ."

"We'll be here," Gina says again, and lights her pipe.

"We'll definitely be here," Jason echoes, laying a reassuring hand on my shoulder. They smile at me.

"Just don't let yourself get caught," he says, but the moment is shattered by the elevator door opening and a haunting, guttural scream coming from my old friend Jordan's mouth. The mob has grown in size, and they claw out of the elevator doors and onto the deck. In a panic I turn back to Jason and Gina, but they've disappeared like they were never there.

I back towards the edge as the mob closes in on me. They are too numerous to count now. I can still make out the faces of Mr. Pretorius, Jordan, Patrick, and Robby, but they get blurrier and less distinguishable as they get closer. They become one with a mass of blackness, dirt, and hands reaching out in anger. I see flashes of fangs and red eyes. They're going to smother me. My throat closes in anticipation.

Instead, the hands lift me off my feet and into the air like I'm weightless, up the wall and above its protective enclosure. I have no ability to resist. The hands push me backward off the final ledge, and I fall forward, my fingertips making one last desperate attempt to cling to something. The earth screams towards me as I plummet through fog and lights. It still seems beautiful.

The last thing I hear is the distorted voice of a man screaming Chinese in my ear. Or maybe it's Japanese.

8
FRIENDS

"All right, then. I don't care. I've had enough.
To tell you the truth, I'm relieved."

> - Rosencrantz, *Rosencrantz and*
> *Guildenstern Are Dead*

My heart is pounding before I'm even awake. I open my eyes and gasp for air, heaving and covered in sweat. My room is still dark, but now the darkness is strange and suffocating. I'm scared, confused. How long have I been trapped here?

Sleep, the spurned mistress, has taken her anger out on me again.

I fumble on the light and kick the covers from my body and onto the floor. The room remains defiantly still. *Hey man, I've been like this the whole time; you're the one who just decided to freak out right now.*

Eventually, I'll be fine. I'll remember what the world actually looks and feels like and why I (think I) am in it. I'll remember the order of things, both bad and good. Right now there's only aggressive confusion eating away at my brain.

I don't know why a nap does this to me. They are supposed to be refreshing and enjoyable, but instead I wake up afraid and disoriented. The world has moved on without me and I feel lost. I feel dirty, almost ashamed. It's like I'm the politician at Fredo's nightclub in *The Godfather II*: I wake up covered in the blood of a dead stripper and can't remember how I got there.

I turn on all the lights in the room, confirming its state. It feels particularly still and quiet right now. There's something that came out of that dream, though, an ominous feeling I can't shake. It sits in the back of my throat, sour and burning, like bile. A sense of foreboding. There will definitely be an ending tonight. I can feel that now. Maybe it's not *Ferris*, but I'll have my full movie. Something is going to happen. Something *big*.

I have to leave here as soon as possible. It's 6:30 now. I'm supposed to meet Penelope for dinner at 7:15. In theory, that should be plenty of time for me to walk down to the video store, return my last rentals, and then walk across the street to meet her. In practice, I already know I'm going to be late. Post-nap distraction and confusion will win again. I throw on some clothes as quickly as I can, grab the last of my allowance stash, and bust out of my bedroom door as if a burning building were collapsing behind me. In real life, the hero can't outrun everything.

— — —— — —

"I gotta go, ma," I say, grabbing the videos off the top of the TV.

"I was wondering if you were going to take those back or leave me to do it and pay late fees." She's lying on the couch, watching some schlocky TV show.

"How could I ever do such a thing like that?" I ask facetiously. "Besides, I'm meeting Penelope right across the street at the shawarma place for dinner."

"And then?"

"There's this party I might go to so I can say goodbye to some folks."

She gives me a look that is part disappointment, part sadness, and part passive-aggressive anger. Actors could work years to perfect that face. Mothers are born with it.

"What?"

"Am I going to get to see my son at all before he leaves or am I just a chauffer for the airport?"

"I've seen you almost every day for the past sixteen years—"

"Don't be a smartass," she interrupts, but I can see she's genuinely upset. Her eyes become watery and she wipes at their corners as she continues.

"All you ever talk about is how you don't get along with kids here, how they're not as good as your friends back home, but you're going to spend your last night at a party with them instead of here with your mom?"

I look down and shuffle my feet momentarily. She doesn't even know about me getting beat up.

"I think if you thought about that question some more, you would see it's rhetorical."

She huffs in annoyance. I walk over to the couch and kneel down beside it.

"Mama . . . you have to let me make peace with this place."

This is not what I expected to come out of my mouth, yet we both now realize it's what I needed to say. She considers this and wipes away more tears. I decide to roll with the momentum.

"*Some* of these people I hope I never see again. A few others, I'll genuinely miss. I just want to say some proper goodbyes."

"Do you think you'll ever want to come back here?"

I stare down at the floor again, considering the accumulated dog hair on the carpet. It's a better answer than screaming '*God, no! Why would I want to do that?*' My silence says everything, though.

"All I wanted was for you, me, Arthur, and the pooches to have a happy life in a beautiful country. I'm sorry you don't think it worked out for you."

"That's not true, mama," I lie. It's not the first, nor the last time I'll lie to my mother, but it never feels good. I try to make it true.

"I learned a lot from the experience. I wrote a lot. I made a lot of music. And I'm going to Japan."

"And you never could have done that if you were still in Florida."

"And I never could have done that if I was still in Florida," I echo. She smiles and I lean in and kiss her on the forehead.

"What time will you be home?"

"Late. I'm at the mercy of Romuald and his sister and when they want to head home." This isn't true either, but I can't just say to her 'I don't know how I'm getting home or when.' She becomes serious in an instant.

"Be careful. Don't get into a car—"

"I know—don't get into a car with anyone who's been drinking."

"Even if you have to call me to come get you."

"Even if I have to call you to come get me. I know ma. I'll be careful." This is also probably a lie, but I can't tell yet. How can you explain a phantom future evil you're counting on?

"Okay. Be safe. Love you."

"Love you too, ma."

And with that, I leave the safety of my mother's den once more—telling lies in order to do so—to venture out into a cold, unforgiving world, one capable of killing me quickly and without mercy. There are plenty of natural wildlife and jungle metaphors I could make given my surroundings, but I'm pretty sure I've made them all already. Any way you slice it, I'm going out into a dangerous place filled with animals. And they all come out at night.

This time I don't feel like I have a choice, though. There's something inevitable, something *final* about it all. Like Rosencrantz and Guildenstern, the nooses around their necks, waiting for the end. I'm just trying to think like the audience. I need something with hard edges and stark contrasts one way or another—no gray areas. If doors close, I wanted them slammed shut forever. Don't leave us guessing. This isn't an art film left open to interpretation. It's a populist flick about tried and true subject matter: the teenager coming of age amidst uncertainty. Lessons have to be learned. And they will be learned in blunt terms during dramatic crescendos. That's what's coming. The movie is nearing its end.

I round the corner into the parking lot of the video store. It's the last safe place for me in this country—my sanctuary, my museum. The place where I judge without being judged. The air is stale and musty—comfortable, a static atmosphere that remains unchanged even as the years pass. It feels like an old English study to me, even though it's just grey carpet and drywall. It looks more like the filing library of a doctor's office: videos in innocuous grey, black, and brown cases, stacked in symmetrical rows from one corner of the store to the other, their only demarcations being the title written in Sharpie marker on the side and front of the case. Sections are divided by pieces of cardboard with handwritten classifications, frayed and dog-eared from the years, some of them almost entirely faded. There are no garish signs pointing out deals, specials, or late fees.

The store is small, with never more than a few people in it at any one time; it could probably fit a maximum of 10. The blinds on the front window are always drawn. With no outside light seeping in, it feels like an actual theater to me. A clock ticks patiently on the wall, unmoved by anything around it.

The video store's faithful steward is Jeffrey, a slightly pudgy gay Jew in his late 20s. I guess he's my friend, even though we never talk outside the video store, and our talks are really 80% movies and 20% personal. Jeffrey and I have spent long hours digging into our favorites, debating the merits of one gangster flick over another, or a particular scene that always gets us. He's stayed to talk to me in the store long after closing many times, and just as often, I've gone in simply to return a movie, and only come out after I've heard the repeated honking of my mom's car horn telling me I've been in here too long.

I don't know what he gets out of it exactly, why he is willing to give up even a second more of his evening than he has to just to shoot the cinema shit with a teenager, but I have my guesses. For one, I think he's kind of lonely. Jeffrey lives with his grandmother, a hard old Afrikaner bitch who doesn't know he's gay and wouldn't have anything nice to say about it if she did. Taking care of her probably monopolizes most of his non-working time. I'm sure he appreciates any sort of companionship he can get outside of that.

I think he also likes feeling important and appreciated for his movie knowledge, like an old librarian. Jeffrey is a keeper of adventures and mysteries for the young and enthusiastic with a passion for other worlds: sad sacks like me. He'll help them explore, guide them in their quest for knowledge and *The Great Escape*, either as a concept or the actual Steve McQueen movie. He also has a wealth of tasteless jokes and off-the-cuff commentary for you, or a cup of coffee to pass the time. I don't drink coffee so Jeffrey keeps some Cokes in the office fridge for when I come by.

Our conversations often take place outside the store, him smoking a cigarette and me thoughtfully sipping a Coke.

I stroll up to see him smoking outside for the last time.

"Oh my god, man, is this it?"

"Afraid so. I'm leaving tomorrow and I don't think I could afford infinite late fees."

"*Agh*, you could have kept the bloody things! At least I would know they were in good hands and not stuffed under someone's fucking couch forever. What did you have out anyway?"

I show him his own handwriting scrawled across one grey case and one brown. *Blade Runner* and *Barton Fink*. His eyes widen.

"Oh yeah, hey, two goodies. Come in. Let's talk."

He stubs out his cigarette early and unlocks the store, heading straight to the back to grab me a Coke. I hear him setting up the microwave, probably heating up some popcorn.

I lay the videos on the counter as he pops the top of the Coke for me. He taps the *Barton Fink* case.

"This one. *Fucking. Brilliant.*"

"Yeah, I loved it, but we'll get to that. *Blade Runner?*" I shrug. "I dunno, pretty good? Me thinks it was hyped too much, though. Instead of watching this organically and coming up with my own opinion, I came into it thinking '*Blade Runner* is required viewing. I MUST rent it so I can understand *why.*' In the end, I couldn't get past the hype. I certainly liked it. The story is good, love the visuals, too, but Christ, I didn't shit my pants over it."

"Listen: Ridley Scott couldn't get his cock sucked more as a director than if he went to the men's room of The Hungry Horse on a Saturday night. People fawn over him as if he invented cinema, but if you dig deep, what's he really done? *Alien*—okay, very good. Classic even. But what else? *Thelma and Louise?* Please, man, c'mon."

"Some weird casting in this one, too," I pile on. "Harrison Ford's awesome. But I dunno about Edward James Olmos as the futuristic FBI agent. I mean, what, they can't fix pockmarks in the future? And Daryl Hannah as one of the droids—I dunno if that's a good choice or bad given her acting chops."

"You can really see who was hot at the time in that one." Jeffrey taps the box. "Sean Young: she bursts onto the scene here. Cold sex appeal. You figure she's set up for a long time. But she completely crashed to earth."

"It was that Catwoman thing!" I jump in.

"What's that?"

"She thought the best way to convince Tim Burton to cast her as Catwoman in *Batman Returns* was to dress up in a homemade costume and go on Oprah or something, hamming it up and looking half drunk."

"*Yes*! That was it. Oh god! And now you see what her last two films were: that terrible fucking *Basic Instinct* spoof, and *Ace Ventura* where she turns out to be a bloody man!"

"Note to self: do not lobby for part in next Batman movie by making own costume and going on morning show on SABC 2."

"I wonder if she still has the costume."

"She probably sold it for more painkillers."

"*Agh*. Depressing. So now, talk to me about *Barton Fink*."

"It's definitely sick and twisted."

Jeffrey chuckles.

"What's that line? *You're a sick fuck, Fink*," he does in his best gruff American accent. Like all South Africans trying to impersonate American accents, he sounds like an overwrought version of Jeff Spicoli from *Fast Times at Ridgemont High*.

"*We were men, we wrestled!*"

We both laugh at the lines.

"Man, the Coen brothers—I think they're my favorite. They just nailed so many different ones in a row. *Hudsucker Proxy*—it's in my all-time Top 5. *Raising Arizona*, now *Barton Fink*. *Miller's Crossing* was a little harder to get into, but still quality stuff."

"But what does the second brother really do?" Jeffrey asks in an over-dramatized fashion with his finger on his chin.

"The one directs all of them, the other produces all of them. Must be nice to have a good working relationship with your brother."

"Maybe they're not brothers after all. More like gay lovers."

"You think everyone is gay."

"Everyone is . . . at least somewhat. You'll find out when you go to University in America."

"Please. Don't mention school to me right now. I haven't even been through with Standard 8 for a full day and I already went back this morning."

"Why the hell would you go back to school after it just got out? And did you at least participate in any random acts of vandalism or juvenile delinquency as a farewell?"

"I got high in my ex-girlfriend's house on campus with pot that was grown on campus. Does that qualify?"

"Yes, I should say it does. Explain."

"I dunno, it's complicated. Or maybe it's not and it's just dumb. Anyway, my ex lives on campus with her mother, who's a teacher there. I went back with a friend of mine to try and say goodbye to her and to get my Jimi Hendrix tape back, but she wasn't home. We ended up picking some of this stuff we found growing wild down by the river last week, smoking with her roommate and listening to music."

"Wait, back up. This is *the* Jimi Hendrix tape? The one you told me about before? So *this* is the girl who borrowed the tape," Jeffrey says in long, eager tones. "And that's why you went back. But she wasn't home?"

"Negative. And that's what was funny. I had so many mixed emotions on my way to see her and all these weird scenarios playing out in my head. After everything, I just wanted to say goodbye and wipe the slate clean. What would any of it mean if we couldn't even do that? But she wasn't there, not even close; she was on vacation with her mom. So it's like, certainly don't have anything to be nervous about anymore! That was it. Not even a chance. I'll probably never see her again."

"Well you can't beat yourself up about it, then. You have a clean slate no matter what happens. Just don't be such a sentimental bastard. This part of your life is ending; another one is beginning. In the new part of your life, you may meet another girl who puts this one to shame. Or at least that's what straight people always believe is just about to happen, right?"

"Right. We do things like 'meet the one', 'go steady', and 'settle down'."

"*Agh*," Jeffrey sneers in disgust. "Get over it. Go forward with your life! Don't look back."

"Are you singing the chorus to DEVO's 'Whip It' right now?"

"No. I'm telling you to end the pity-party early. Send everyone home. No one is having a good time, least of all you."

"You're probably right. I've looked at this thing from every angle, but the more layers I peel away, the less sense it makes. You know what gets me the most? I just can't take how everything fizzled out. Stories are supposed to climax and end, right? Tension and release? It's the basis of every movie on these walls—"

"Sorry, what about tension and release?"

"Just let me finish, you. So what if there are no fireworks? What if instead of defeating Darth Vader and killing the Emperor, Luke just spent the last half hour of *Return of the Jedi* eating space Cheetos and watching TV on his couch? Or what if instead of turning out to be a homicidal maniac that burns down the entire hotel, John Goodman's character in *Barton Fink* stays just a regular guy, and he and

John Turturro just exchange pleasantries through the wall the entire movie? I wouldn't pay two rand to watch stuff as crappy and underdeveloped as that. Neither would you. But we're supposed to accept it when it's actually happening to us? As LIFE? How am I supposed to believe there is a skilled auteur working the light at the end of the tunnel when he clearly has such contempt for his audience? That's the rub right there: I spend all my time in here, chasing after perfect endings, but life just keeps handing me anticlimaxes."

"Eh, real life is mostly boring." Jeffrey rolls his eyes nonchalantly. "But that's why places like this exist. These bits of flavor and fantasy make it worth living. Think: if your life were only bullets constantly whizzing past your head and femme fatales looking to fuck you and then kill you with an ice pick, you'd get sick of that, too."

"Maybe. At least I'd be alive."

"Think so? You've got to consider the law of diminishing returns. Really spectacular things in life are rare. That's what makes them spectacular. If everything were spectacular all the time, then nothing would be spectacular, because you would have no baseline of crappyness to compare it to. So accept that most of life is boring, but that a select few moments are so extraordinary they make it worth living. Put those moments in a special place when you have them—maybe in one of these."

He gestures to the walls of celluloid around him.

"Wow. That pep-talk was equal parts optimistic and hopeless. The net result may actually have been neutral."

"Well thanks. Wasn't that the same speech your president gave in that movie just before he asked them all to *win it for the Gipper*?" Jeffrey employs his American Spicoli voice again on the last line.

"Our president? Man, you're out of touch. That guy hasn't had his finger on the button in years."

"*Agh*, man! You think it's my job to follow American politics? Of course I'm just going to know the one who was a movie star! We even have a section for him over there."

Jeffrey points to a sliver of about three videos with their own divider in a lower left-hand corner of a shelf. I walk over to read the section title: "*Popular World Leaders in Dramatic Roles*". Ronald Reagan is the only world leader featured in them. I chuckle out loud.

"You're the only one who gets that joke."

"But of course. I'm going to miss you, Jeffrey."

"*Agh*, I know. Who the bloody hell am I going to talk to in this shithole now?"

"C'mon, I bet you'll have plenty of great future conversations with customers about the finer points of *Patch Adams* and the big screen version of *The Mod Squad*."

"The best is when they come in and try to explain what they're looking for by describing the plot. They don't know actors, directors, or names, just 'it's that guy from all the other action movies, and he's a spy this time, and there's a woman . . .'"

"I bet you figure those out more than half the time, though."

"Well shit, yes, I feel I must make a game of it to stay sharp! Sometimes they are so damn vague, though . . ."

"Let me try one. A real one you've gotten before."

"'The one where the guy from *Star Wars* is the American president.'"

"Come on, are you serious? *Air Force One*. I said gimme a real one."

"Okay, that was just the warm-up to make sure you fully understood the parameters. How about 'the one where the comedian dresses up as a woman nanny to see his kids'?"

"*Mrs. Doubtfire.*"

"'This one's got the really young heartthrob guy and the old black oke that everyone likes, and they're detectives, and it's quite dark . . .'"

"*Seven.*"

"'The really ridiculous funny guy has a stupid bowl haircut, and he's with this other blonde guy who isn't as funny, but they're both gits.'"

"*Dumb & Dumber.*"

"Okay. These are too easy for you. Let's up the degree of difficulty. These you might need more than one guess for, points for how few it takes you."

"Do your worst."

"'The one with the Italian gangsters who are all like '*hey ho ah ah ahhh*!!!'"

Jeffrey puffs out his chest, shaking his shoulders and arms in his best worst Brooklyn mobster impersonation.

"*The Godfather*?"

"'With the little guy and the 'you talking to me?' guy.'"

"Oh. *Goodfellas.*"

"'The one with the people in space.'"

"That's it?"

"You are permitted to ask a follow-up as I did."

"Does it begin with the monkeys and the music?"

"Yes!"

"*2001: A Space Odyssey.*"

"'The two guys who are in everything together.'"

"Abbot & Costello?"

"Newer."

"Chris Farley and David Spade?"

"Older. And they don't know who those people are."

"Hmm . . . Redford and Newman?"

Jeffrey continues as if he's the customer, placing his index finger on his chin and wondering aloud: "Maybe . . . are they the rugged handsome guys?"

"Are they cowboys?"

"'No. Not a western. More 'old-timey'. They're trying to trick somebody or something . . .'"

"*The Sting.*"

"Very nice. 'The one with the retard—'"

"*Rainman. What's Eating Gilbert Grape. Sling Blade.*"

"'—who's famous for doing a bunch of different stuff.'"

"Oh. *Forrest Gump.*"

"Should have let me finish."

"Should have let you finish."

"I've got one to stump you though, actually. And you've got to get it in five guesses or less."

"Five? Have I proven nothing yet?"

"Just you wait . . . 'It's a movie where they switch bodies.'"

I stare at him in silence for a second, waiting for the rest to come.

"And?"

"And nothing. None of my follow-up questions helped. The customer didn't have any information more useful than that to offer. He said he'd probably know it if he saw it, but couldn't recall anything else about it on his own."

"And did you actually end up finding it for him?"

"Yes. We fast-forwarded through the first five minutes of every body-switch movie I know of here in the store until he finally recognized something. It took half an hour. It was actually kind of amusing to see him squint at everything trying to figure it out. He was the only one in here. Five guesses."

"Five guesses. No sweat. Here we go. Judge Reinhold and Fred Savage in *Vice Versa*."

"That's one."

"Jimmy Smits and Ellen Barkin in *The Switch*."

"Two."

"That old movie *Freaky Friday*?"

"Is that a guess or a question?" Jeffrey asks on his toes.

"*Freaky Friday*."

"Two left."

"Shit. George Burns in *18 Again*."

"Last one. Better make it count."

"You really went through all of these?"

"Yes."

My eyes dig into the carpet under a furrowed brow, searching for a clear answer but none comes. Damn body-switch movies.

"Eh . . . *Like Father Like Son*?"

"Thanks for playing. The correct answer was *All of Me*, starring Lily Tomlin and Steve Martin."

"Fuck. I also would've guessed *Dream a Little Dream* with Corey Feldman before that one. At first I thought if I were in your shoes, I'd lose it with the guy, but then I realized it'd be the opposite. After a while I'd be so dying to know if I could actually get him the right one, I'd take as long as I had to."

"What else have I got to do, really?"

We laugh and I remember I haven't checked the time in a bit. I look at my wrist and a pale strip of white skin looks back at me again.

"Hey Jeffrey, what time is it?"

"7:25," he says, consulting the wall clock behind him.

"Damn. I'm late to meet my friend for dinner."

"Boy or girl?"

"Girl."

"But not the one who kept your Jimi Hendrix tape?"

"Not the one who kept my Jimi Hendrix tape."

"Would this girl ever do a thing like that?"

"Never. She's as sweet and straight an arrow as they come."

"Marry her. It's what you—"

"I know, I know. It's 'what us straight people do'."

"Exactly." He points and winks with satisfaction. His pointing hand changes into an open palm and I hear his Spicoli impersonation for the last time.

"Put 'er there, pardner."

Maybe it's John Wayne.

"Jeffrey, you're a gentleman and a scholar."

We shake warmly.

"Remember, you can always change the ending."

"Wait. What?"

His words. The dream. The elevator. Defoe.

"If your movie's not going well, change the ending. Reshoot. Rewrite. Fire the actors, the people you work and play with. If they don't make the film work, get rid of 'em. Keep working on it. If it's a flop, no one will pan it as much as you do, and if it's a hit, no one will be as proud either."

His words pass through me. I'm still thinking about the dream, staring glassy-eyed at the carpet.

"Hey. Where'd you go?" Jeffrey asks. "Aren't you late?"

"Wha? Oh, sorry. Yeah, you're right about all that. Just the way you said it reminded me of something else in a weird way."

"Like a line from a movie?"

"Something like that. Gotta go. I'll keep in touch with you."

"Get out of here. Or my Bogart from the end of *Casablanca* is next."

"Can't risk that. It'll sound like a cat dying."

"Identical to Afrikaans actually."

"Take care, Jeffrey."

"Fly safe."

We wave as the door jangles closed behind me. I imagine Jeffrey feels the type of loneliness I've felt most of the time here. The feeling of too much space between you and the walls. The feeling of too much quiet in your ears. The feeling of being too familiar with the sights of hands on ticking clocks and telephones that don't ring. Why not watch something else instead?

I can't believe it was *All of Me.*

– – ——— – –

Penelope sits alone at a small table at the back of the restaurant, lit dimly by a lone candle. Her cheek rests bitterly in her hand. Her eyes shoot laser beams at the door. I am seventeen minutes late to meet her. If the shawarma place weren't right across the street from the video store, it would have been worse.

I walk in the door and her eyes turn nuclear. I wither inside. I'm going to miss that look. I can tell she thinks I'm on drugs. I would think I am, too. Despite sleeping off the worst of my *dagga*pocalypse, the sleep itself has made me look I look like I've been up for three days smoking crack. This is going to be equally difficult for both of us for completely different reasons.

I rush up to her table and end up hovering awkwardly an inch off of her, unsure of what to do for some reason. She eyes me for a second, her head still in her hand, her hair cascading over it down on to the table. She finally gets up to hug me, but it feels weird and strained, like we're suddenly forgetting the hundreds of times we've done this before. Now I can only believe that when men and women hug, ultimately bad things happen. It's all marred by genitals coming within any reasonable distance of each other. Fuck, Kim has ruined the way I think of everything.

"*Agh*, man! Have you been smoking *dagga*?"

"What?" Penelope has caught me staring intently at nothing. "Um. Not in the past few hours, no."

"*Agh*." She doesn't believe me and turns away briefly in disgust. I don't blame her.

"I've actually just woken up from a nap. I'm a little disoriented."

"I thought you never take naps."

"Well now you see why."

Silence for a bit.

"Well, have you had a fun last day?"

How do I answer? I never lie to Penelope about anything, but I just can't tell her all the events of the last 24 hours; the culmination of my failure would make easy fodder for her condemnation of the people, places, and things I've fallen into as my time here has progressed.

In the beginning, Penelope, Kim, and I were actually like the 3 Musketeers. We'd sit in the center of Fourways Mall, them making fun of anyone and everyone passing by for their amusement, me watching them do it for mine. And I was the only one in all of South Africa who never thought it weird that I spent all this time hanging out with two gorgeous girls without ever even breathing heavily in either of their directions. I was just happy to know anyone.

Penelope always lived out in the middle of nowhere, though, on farmland, and it took a lot of doing to see her outside of school. So I started hanging out with a bunch of gigantic assholes that weren't as nice and positive as her, but lived closer and had good weed. She would occasionally call and we would talk about getting together and seeing a movie or whatever, but without cars or good public transportation, it was always difficult. And somehow it was just sexier to hang out with Jordan, and Patrick, and Robby, and Britney, and Alo, smoking bushels of pot and watching boring skateboarding videos—going nowhere, but at least doing it quickly.

And now all I have is a last 20-minute dinner in a shitty shawarma place to see her. This whole two years we could have been harmlessly sipping herbal tea together, making fun of people in malls, and seeing movies I actually wanted to see (Penelope would always let me pick). Instead, I've kept busy by destroying my mind piece by piece, dragging myself to turds like *You've Got Mail* with Britney and the rest of her stone-stupid girlfriends, and getting beaten up and embarrassed repeatedly, all so I could end up staring at condoms in an empty lot.

"It was alright," I lie about the day.

"It doesn't look like it," she says. I now realize that I've been grimacing like a bad Edward G Robinson impression.

"Well, I ended up back at Woodmere with Thibault."

"*Jassus*! What for, man?"

"I realized I never got a proper South African wedgie the whole time I've been here, so I tried to find Mr. Pretorius to see if he could give me one."

Penelope laughs out loud and it breaks the unseen tension in the air. It's so nice seeing her smile. I'll for sure miss that. She covers her mouth and gathers herself, eyes staring out knowingly from beneath a few strands of wild hair as she is about to ask a serious question.

"But you really went to see Kim?" She asks it in that slightly bitchy authoritative tone that all girls know and mothers just love to hang on you.

"I saw Martin Erasmus at Kim's house. Thibault was with me and we all got high and made stoned phone calls to Nick Sutter. No Kim to be seen, though."

"Smoking with Thibault and Martin? *Jassus*, you've gotten into that stuff a lot, hey? No wonder you're brain is for *kaak*!"

Penelope's never even touched a drop of caffeine; she's one of those people who tells you they are on a permanent "natural high". I almost believe her, too, because she is just so damn bubbly and upright. They tell you that real life is "full of magic" and that drugs are just for escaping reality (probably true). I usually hate people like that, but I could never with Penelope; she's just too earnest about it.

"Recent times have been tough, Pineapple."

"Oh crap, man!" She's getting genuinely angry now, but I'm not sure why. It's something other than just talking about my drug use.

"You don't need that stuff to have a good time and I know it's not making you feel any better . . ."

She trails off when she notices me staring at my shoes like a scolded child. She crosses her arms nervously and bites at a thumbnail. I may not understand most female behavioral tendencies, but I somehow know this look means *'crap, I forgot this is his last night here and I'm supposed to be his friend and I may never see him in person again, so I should probably stop lecturing him now.'*

"Well, nevermind. Did you at least get your Jimi Hendrix tape?"

"No. I think I'm resigned to it being a casualty of war. I probably could have gone in her room to get it, but I just couldn't make myself do it."

"For fuck's sake, why not?"

"Well to start, there's a legal implication in me being there and going through her stuff, plus—"

"Crap," she interrupts. "Everyone goes to her house when she isn't there. You were already smoking *dagga* in her house without her there. And she had your property."

"Well yeah, but then I also had to go looking for it—"

"*Kaak*, man!" she interrupts again. "She probably keeps all her tapes in one place. You probably already know where that place is. And if not, so what? You see one or two pairs of her panties while you're digging through a drawer. It's nothing you haven't seen already, right?"

"I . . . well, I . . ."

"Nevermind," she pulls back. "I'm sorry. That's none of my business. Continue on, please."

"Well, I . . . you see, it's putting those two elements together that seems totally stalker-ish, and, I don't know, what if she came back? I just couldn't do it."

"There's a part of you that wants her to keep that tape. You want her to keep it in a special secret place away from her other tapes. You want her heart to break every time she looks at it or listens to it. You don't want to give up your place in her mind. You want to secure it so you can move on first."

"Well . . . Yeah . . . When you put it that way, of course."

"But you want that even more than actually getting your tape back. You know you could have gotten it pretty easily. It was probably actually the perfect situation for it. Why did you leave it? Because you can replace your tape, but the memories it makes her have—you hope they never get replaced."

My shoulders slump to their lowest point. I've gotten a lot of good looks at my sneakers today.

"Man, why do you have to know me so well? Okay, fine! Even though I dreaded the idea of a final conversation with her, I wanted it more than anything in the world. But fate played a trick on me by having her not even be in town when I got there. So the fall was complete. I was about to slip away into the night without a trace. There was only one piece of evidence I could leave that could prove we actually happened. All I had to do was not look very hard."

"I know you because I'm your friend. I know you because I care about you. Maybe someday you'll stop chasing after the people who don't care and stop bending over backwards for them."

"I know. I know. I mean *now* I know. It took me this long to figure it out. Probably too little too late . . ."

We are both looking down at the table in silence now. By default, our eyes go toward the flickering candle at its center. As if on cue, a stiff breeze extinguishes it.

"You're never coming back here, are you?" Penelope asks without looking up.

"Not if I can help it," I say, answering the question truthfully this time. I pause at the end of the sentence, thinking I have more to say, but nothing comes. That was another goal of today's adventure: to search for a last beacon of light and hope on the African horizon, anything—any sign that would ever make me consider coming back here by choice. If that candle could blow out again right now, I'm sure it would.

I stare into the center of the dark and damp wick. Above it, at the top of my vision it looks like Penelope is silently wiping her eyes. I almost miss it.

"Wait, what's that?"

"What?"

"What did you just do with your eyes?"

"Oh, shut up." She wipes underneath one again, this time openly, but still not calling attention to it. I was not prepared for this. I never am when a female cries in front of me.

"Hey . . . I . . ."

"*Agh*, I said *shut up!*"

Half the restaurant turns to look at us. I give my best 'nothing to see here' sheepish smile.

"I'm sorry," she composes herself. "I shouldn't have said that. I have to go in a few minutes."

"I . . . It's okay. Work, right? You can't get out of it?"

"No, I can't. Tonight we're doing a private dance event for some foreign dignitaries. It's been planned for a while. I told you about it. That's why we're supposedly eating dinner right now."

I realize we have no food in front of us.

"Oh, sorry. Did you wanna get something?"

"Not hungry. Gotta go."

"Right . . ."

She snatches up her bag, standing in a huff as her disgust reaches a boiling point.

"I'll follow you out," I blurt in a desperate attempt to reshape our last goodbye. She glares at me and heads for the door. Our candle is still the only one on any table that's been blown out. I slip around her and turn around, trying to block her quickening progress.

"Wait wait wait wait wait," I begin, "please don't be mad at me. I feel like I have too many people mad at me right now. I can't take another one."

Her eyes widen and her nostrils flare and she's ready to begin another tirade, but I cut her off in unexpectedly calm tones that catch her by surprise.

"I get it. This was our last time to hang out together and I blew it. I'm sorry. It was a long night and not in any good way. I'm not at the top of my game."

She rolls her eyes, but I preemptively cut off any heckling again.

"I've blown it in more ways than one. You were right. It took me too long to figure out who the good people in my life were, and that I should be spending my time with them. It should be easy but I make it harder for myself on purpose. All I can say is better late than never. You and Thibault are the only people I really trust or care about enough to want to try and keep in touch. And you're the only one who's been a true friend to me from day one till now."

The anger subsides from her face and she hangs on my words.

"I'm sorry we drifted apart. I know we live far away, but that's not really a good excuse. We had a good thing going there for a little bit, Pineapple, and I should have tried harder to keep it up. Now it's too late. I have to live with that. But I want you to know that I want to keep you in my life however I can, because you're not just one of the good ones; you're like the best one."

She sniggers and shakes her head lightly.

"What is all this?" she asks.

"All what?"

"These lines? Where is this coming from?"

"These are actually the opposite of lines. I panicked at the notion of our last ever interaction ending in such a shitty way. I thought we deserved better, so I just opened my mouth to let what was in me out. My brain eventually caught up to form the rest of the words around it. That was all true."

"You should try that more often. That 'truth' stuff."

"Okay, howbout this: Some people will say I didn't give a fair shake to my time here. That I should have tried harder or relaxed more or done as the Romans do: just shut the fuck up and go with it. If they want to make that case, you should be their first, best, and only piece of prosecuting evidence. You're a once-in-a-lifetime person and a once-in-a-lifetime friend, Pineapple, and I never would have met you if I never moved here. That's got to count for something."

She smiles into my eyes, looking deep into me. She's thinking about something but I can't get at it. Her gaze not only blocks me but tells me she's digging through my skull for answers of her own. I feel vulnerable and begin fidgeting.

She takes my hands in hers and studies them, tracing the cracks and contours with her fingers. I realize for the first time her hands are so much smaller than mine.

"Well, you're not the worst friend in the world . . . You could use some work, though. And of course, meeting you has made my life better, too."

"I'll write you electronic mails."

"I live on farmland. Do you think I even have a computer, let alone some 'electron mail' crap?"

"Okay, so I'll write you letters. You're worth it. Maybe I'll send you each one twice for when the first one inevitably gets lost."

"The post has gotten better here over time."

"From what?"

She continues to examine my hands.

"So then what are you going to do with the rest of your last night here?"

"Go to Richard Koening's party."

I am focusing on Penelope's mouth as it falls open, probably why I don't see the pale hand rocketing towards my face, stinging me hard and fast. A flash of hot rage wells up in me instantly, to go with the stinging pain and disorientation.

"What the fuck?"

"What the fuck yourself! Here you've been feeding me this bullshit about how you finally learned who is important and who isn't; you say all this shit with a straight face, but you're going to turn around and go to that party on your last night here?"

"That's something different—"

"Bullshit. You're going to go get high with the same stupid

bunch of arseholes you always do, the ones who turn their back on you in a heartbeat when anything goes wrong."

"Will you just listen to me? Okay, you're a spiritual person, right? You believe there are things and forces in this world that you can't see in front of your face, but that are still real, right?"

"It sounds like you're working up to mocking me, but okay, yes. So?"

"So I'm telling you something is *making* me go to this party. There's an energy and pull from the universe telling me I need to be there for the final act of my story here. Now could I physically refuse to go? Probably. But all that would accomplish would be me closing the door on any number of endings I'm meant to have, and I'd just be running out the clock until my flight tomorrow morning. A safer strategy, maybe, but I tell you I'm not going to learn anything from it."

"What are you going to learn by going, though? Let's say you're right—you feel something undeniable pulling you towards this party tonight so you can learn some final lesson. What if that final lesson is more of the same things you already feel? That the people here are bad, this place is shit, and you never want to come back here again? What if it's even worse than that?"

"That doesn't sound like you. That sounds like you trying to think and sound like me."

"Yes, I was really trying there . . . You're right, I guess I would have to do it, too."

She squeezes my hands in hers.

"Just please be careful. If you're letting an energy guide you, please listen closely to it. Don't fight it. Don't try to cheat it. You'll only make it worse."

"See? Now you're getting me."

"Maybe. Or it's more bullshit, and you're just telling me this so your 'new age hippie chick' friend won't hassle you for the last time about going to smoke *dagga*." She says the words 'new age hippie chick' in her version of the Jeff Spicoli American accent.

"No, I'm telling you straight. I don't even think I want to smoke tonight. The good times with that seem to have expired. By the way, some day I have to come back to teach all of you how to properly do an American accent. You all sound like you're about to grab a surfboard in Southern California in 1983."

"I'm from America, man." She makes herself as graceless as possible, shrugging and slumping her shoulders while sticking her hands out from her sides in mock confusion. I can't tell if she's doing her Spicoli or trying to imitate me. That looks like my posture.

"See, that's what I'm talking about. That's terrible."

She pushes me in the chest in some combination of real anger and play.

"I have to go now. Give me a good hug, you."

We wrap our arms around each other like we've done so many times before, but she's squeezing a little tighter and longer now. Not knowing when I'll ever see her again, I return the favor. Her hair smells like millions of fruity shampoos and conditioners I'm sure she would never use because they are full of chemicals and tested on animals. Does Penelope even wash her hair? She must; how can it smell so good? Knowing her, she probably uses cow dung and it still smells that good.

We're hogging up a good chunk of sidewalk, locked in a game of hug chicken that neither one of us wants to win.

Penelope can hug for hours. I finally waive the white flag and pull my head back first. Our faces are only inches apart, and we stare into each other's eyes, still hugging, a weird kind of heat and energy there I've never felt before. My throat closes up. There's something different in her eyes now; they cut through me, and the energy spreads down into the rest of me, to my stomach, my pants. It's pulling on my insides, pulling me towards her. She's never looked at me this way before. Or . . . maybe she has, I've just never noticed it before.

She plays with an old spot on my shirt while distracted. I have maybe five seconds before I am completely embarrassed by the movement in my pants. She looks me in the eye again before leaning in and kissing me slowly on the check. I don't know what this means right now. I don't know what anything means right now. As usual, I'm missing something and don't know what it is.

"Wait . . ."

"Be careful," she repeats, and steps back out of my arms, still looking into my eyes. The energy screams out in silence as we separate, and I feel a phantom pull back towards her. Freed from the constraints of the tight space it was only so recently smothered by, my erection now decides to stretch and rise in honor of the body that so recently awoke it from its slumber. Thanks, puberty.

I move with the grace of a street pickpocket, adjusting myself with a sleight of hand that would make a magician jealous. The naked eye cannot possibly keep up.

Penelope flags down a passing taxi. It goes from 30 mph to stopping right next to us in about two seconds. She looks back at me, smiling again. God, I'm really going to miss that.

"I'll see you again. I know it."

What's funny is that I know it, too. She's telling the truth; we'll see each other again someday. We have to.

My fingers tingle with longing as she backs away. My mouth is open for something to say. Anything meaningful. Poignant. Real. Anything I've learned from the thousands of hours of happy and sad movie endings alike I've witnessed. I must have an 11th-hour hero speech for this from somewhere. But it's still too early. I don't even know what's happening, let alone how to talk about it. Instead, my mouth just sags and bobs open, like I'm the singing Little Mermaid who just lost her voice. Yes, I can't think of anything meaningful to say, but a *Little Mermaid* reference comes to mind.

She gets in the cab and rolls down the window, still looking me in the eyes and smiling.

"You should take care of that before you go out in public. You don't want to embarrass yourself."

Fuck. The cab screeches off while I'm distracted with readjusting my pants. I look back up in just enough time to see Penelope's waving hand fading into the gray of the cab as it speeds off. I'm left on a street corner with a raging hard-on and my arms out in slow-motion confusion. People stare at me as they walk by, probably wondering what fool let me out of the hospital so soon. It occurs to me that I find myself acting out a scenario similar to this one far too often.

I trudge back toward the shawarma restaurant, trying to piece things together. My stomach growls and churns with hunger, so I finally order a shawarma, stuffing most of it into my face before I head back outside.

For what feels like the thousandth time, something big has just occurred right under my nose and I barely even sniffed it. I think I would make a good detective and a horrible beat cop. Good at chasing leads and analyzing evidence after the crime occurs, powerless to stop it while it's happening. A frog in slowly boiling water. The light bulb doesn't come on till they've already got my 40 rand in their hand.

That last gear always clicks into place for me years later, on some crowded street corner, long after I can do anything about it. I'll mutter and curse violently to myself, people staring at me as I walk by. '*Don't mind me, I only just figured out that Stacy Forbes named her rabbit after me in elementary school because she had a crush on me.*'

Let's try and expedite the investigation this time: I met both Penelope and Kim on my first day ever at Woodmere. They both showed me around school. I remember thinking how ridiculous it was that I met two such good-looking girls on my first day of school, and that they were both basically required to talk to me! I became friends with both of them, and for a brief moment we were all inseparable. I even flirted with both of them, although Penelope's flirting has always been much more harmless than Kim's. Of course, I've since learned that no flirting is really harmless.

I never wondered about my connection to Kim before the first time the flirting went too far. I never knew I wanted her until the day she kissed me. Could it be happening again with Penelope? How many times can the same frog be slowly boiled alive?

Two beautiful roads diverged in the bush and I took the one . . . more traveled? Kim had the darker features: darker hair, darker skin, darker personality, darker eyes containing darker secrets. The proposition was like hopping on the back of a motorcycle with a drunk. You could crash and burn, or have the time of your life. Part of the thrill is not knowing.

Penelope is all sunshine and moonbeams. Golden flowers and tie-dye. When she smiles, her teeth and cheeks look like they could explode with sunlight. There's no dark mystery there. No bullshit or game-playing either. Just a good friend who continually treats you well and cares about you—that old boring nonsense. The Library instead of The Party. I fell for the dark and dangerous stranger while the kindhearted townsfolk were right in front of me. *Gosh self, cliché much?*

Penelope. There was that strange conversation we had weeks ago when I was telling her how everything had just gone completely wrong with Kim. It was like she knew the whole story already. She said she knew Kim had been attracted to me from the first day. She could tell. How can she tell everything?

"You're smart and funny. Very charming . . . when you want to be. What girl wouldn't like you?"

What girl wouldn't like you?

Penelope. She got unusually mad at dinner. There were tears. Tears! *'Don't fight it... I'll see you again.'* Has it really been there all along? They used to call me Duckie after Jon Cryer's hopelessly longing character in *Pretty in Pink*, because they thought I looked and acted like him. But . . . was I really Molly Ringwald?

"WOT ARE YOU LOOKING AT, YOU STUPID GIT?"

A car screeches to a stop right in front of where I'm sitting on the curb. It's Patrick's car—Lucille's Patrick—and Lucille is sticking her head out of the passenger window, giggling at me like a maniac. The sky has turned completely dark as I've sat finishing my shawarma on this corner. I'm still moving in slow-mo.

"Pull yer head out of yer arse and get in. The light's about to change."

I have a split-second decision to make: see the final act, or walk away? *Don't fight it*, Penelope says in my head. I pull myself together, open the back door and get in. Patrick peels off almost before I close it. Whose energy is it, though? And where does it lead?

I can't remember how Lucille and Patrick met me here, if I called them earlier today or we made plans a while back. Maybe we never even talked about it but they still knew. The universe knew and told them. Doesn't matter. Don't fight it.

9

A HELL OF A PARTY

*"There's something out there, and it ain't no
man. We're all gonna die."*

- Billy, *Predator*

So who all is going to be at this party?" I ask, already
knowing the answer. Who knows; maybe someone got
hit by a bus on the way there.

"Well, there'll be Britney, Camilla, Robby, Alo, Jordan,
Patrick . . ." Lucille's list becomes labored as she mentions the
inflammatory names, and she trails off, leaving a stale silence
in the air. I can tell she's thinking of something positive to
say while I process the names.

"You know, Floyd, you mustn't let those fucking gits
ruin everything for you. Britney and Alo are decent people,
but Jordan and Patrick and them aren't worth fuck all and
they can all go to hell."

Lucille is one of those South Africans who want to pretend they're of British descent because they're ashamed of

the backwardness of their countrymen. I weigh the relative truth of her statement before responding.

"I don't know, Lucille. None of them have tried to make any real amends with me or say it shouldn't have happened. The whole thing even started with harmless old Alo thinking he was going to punch me because I was 'getting too weird' or whatever, before Patrick just took the initiative and did it for real. They all still hang out together and nothing's changed, except somehow I turned out to be the bad guy who had it coming. Maybe Britney and Alo aren't as bad as the rest of them, but they're not exactly breaking up the band, either."

"*Agh*! I've told Brit so many times what arseholes they all are and how she should just fuck off from them. All they do is sit and watch those stupid skateboarding videos! And Alo you know is just completely fucking thick."

At a stoplight, Patrick calmly lights a cigarette before offering his own reasoned, more mature take. He is older and already in University and avoids that crew when Lucille is hanging out with them. He barely knows them, and doesn't much care to.

"Fuck 'em," he begins with a long puff. "You can't treat people like that and just blow it off. This is your last night, so you must enjoy it and just ignore those fuckers. And if anyone wants to fuck with you tonight, they can talk to me first."

"Thanks, Patrick."

"Yes!" Lucille jumps in. "It is *your* night and you are going to have fun and that is that, and everyone else must fuck off!" She declares it as if she were Mary Poppins telling the children they must eat their vegetables during dinner or not get desert.

"I hope you guys are right."

Is it my night? It still feels like nothing good can come of this. And yet I am doing it anyway. It's the story of my life, or at least it has been for the past two years, a Top 40 hit that plays endlessly in my mind.

> *"Nothing good can come of this yeah yeah yeah*
> *but let's do it anyway oh baby baby . . ."*

I suppose I could murder Lucille and Patrick right now in order to get out of it; just strangle Patrick or club him in the head with my shoe while he's driving. We've already established that I've bought my ticket tonight and am taking the ride, though; a murder-suicide would be an unequivocal copout.

For the sake of argument, let's just say I *did* spend tonight back on the couch, watching *Only You* or *French Kiss* for the umpteenth time, or renting a last movie from Jeffery at the video store. Of course I checked the TV schedule, knowing it could very well come to that. I made mental notes on how I could potentially spend the evening:

7:45 PM- *Dune* – I fell asleep one night while watching this and never saw the end of it (man I hate that). An interesting artful choice, sure, but entirely humorless. I never got that into it and would only be watching it to get that ending. I hate not having endings.

9:20 PM- *Bulletproof* – Adam Sandler and Damon Wayans. Sheesh. Dumb comedies are great when you need them (like now), but this would be a trap-viewing. How do I know? Because just weeks ago, coming home after Kim dumped me, I needed a dumb comedy to take my mind off things and this is what I rented from Jeffrey. It failed miserably, partly because it wasn't really funny to begin with, partly because nothing would have been funny to me at that time. In all honesty, I can barely remember it.

10:30 PM- *Monty Python* – A rare tasteful offering from SABC 2. I still don't get these guys, but man would I ever try. At this point, I'm so desperate for a laugh I'll even give that sitcom *Chef* another try.

11:25 PM- *Delta of Venus* – I mean, we're really getting in to the straight jacking-off hours of the night here. My mom has rented this before; it's one of those "erotic exploration" movies that adults watch just before they take a bath together. The horny teens suffer through them just to get to the one or two decent smooth-jazz sex parts. Like *Red Shoe Diaries* or something. In fact, Zalman King is the guy who did both of those. Fuck, why do I know that?

1:45 AM- *The Dark Backwards* or *Back to the Future* – Of course I've seen both of these movies before and neither one all that long ago. *The Dark Backwards* was actually a weird little movie that was surprisingly likable. Judd Nelson plays an unfunny comic who becomes popular after mysteriously growing a third arm out of his back. Bill Paxton is in it, playing the same kind of sleazy weirdo he played in every movie until he inexplicably became a leading man dodging tornadoes with Helen Hunt. The movie ends with Judd Nelson losing his third arm, but actually becoming somewhat funny. It's twisted, sad, and lonely—right up my alley—but a terrible choice for my last night here. *Back to the Future* is the clear winner, and it's not even close. By the time Marty McFly sings Johnny B Goode at the Enchantment Under the Sea Dance (the worst suspension of disbelief for movie lip-synching in history, by the way), I'll almost be able to taste the cold South African Airways jet air in my mouth, thinking about my flight home.

3:30- *Dazed and Confused* – I hated this movie when I first saw it. I just didn't get it. Everyone just rides around, getting high and drinking; the story goes nowhere, nobody learns anything. When I finally got high myself and watched it with friends for the first time, it all made sense. It's an 'adventure in a day' movie. Except it's less about the adventure and more about that moment, a snapshot of wayward youth. It's about that last moment of being young and stupid with your friends before you turn around and it's gone forever. I'd enjoy that movie, but it's one you should really watch with friends.

All of a sudden I remember Thibault and Sebastian, and how I ditched them unceremoniously in a moment of insane panic. I feel rotten inside and remind myself I have to somehow get in touch with them from the party and apologize. I ran away from the good people again. Nothing good can come of this, and yet I'm doing it anyway.

Patrick throttles his tiny hatchback to the red to make the next light. We speed over hills and past a blur of random Joburg life. Bums stand on dimly lit corners, lost in a haze of mandrax, eyes bloodshot, double-fisting cartons of Joburg Beer. Robert Miles' "Children"—an instrumental techno song with a cheesy piano lead—comes on the radio and Lucille blasts it to start the night in earnest.

Why does South Africa have such a predominant rave culture? Is it that life—and with it rhythm—began in Africa, that rave music is the bastard descendant of the first tribal drumbeats? No, that's too wholesome an explanation. I've always found it sinister—the continuous thumping—like 'The Telltale Heart' on speed. It's certainly been the soundtrack to every bad time I've had here.

Through these two years, I've tried my damndest to avoid meeting rave culture face-to-face. Once or twice Britney or somebody dragged me to some club somewhere, and I sat in the corner exclusively. Last night was only one of a handful of times I willingly journeyed towards the belly of the beast. I realize it's come full circle now; I've got my own rave song mapped out already:

> *"Nothing good can come of this"*
> *(oo-chka oo-chka oo-chka oo-chka)*
>
> *"But let's do it anyway yeah yeah"*
> *(oo-tis oo-tis oo-tis oo-tis)*

I can hear the lead singer of Faithless reciting the lines now in his smooth British monotone. Just repeat that for 20 minutes while on Ecstasy.

Patrick opens the windows wide, and Lucille cranks the radio louder still. The wind roars like a jet engine, but I can still hear that evil pulsing heartbeat underneath. I am on a collision course with the ugly side of destiny.

I'm thinking of a movie I never even saw except for a preview on an American TV show; it was an indie in limited release and it never even came out in South Africa. Johnny Depp plays a guy about to be murdered in a snuff film so his family can pocket the cash from it. In the preview, he's talking about knowing you're walking into death and doing it anyway. In my melodramatic teenage mind I equate my scene with that one. The weird calm. The sense of inevitability. But who would benefit from my death? Or learn anything? I'm telling you—my movie is poorly written and constructed. The main character is too much of a drama queen: whiny, self-obsessed, and unsympathetic, even in dire circumstances.

Ten hours ago, I was imagining myself as the star of a live-action remake of *Ferris Bueller's Day Off.* Now I'm Johnny Depp marching to my inevitable death. In the moving picture business, they call this role a "departure" from the last one. Thump thump goes the 140-bpm beat of the telltale heart.

— — ———— — —

Richard Koening's house lies down the same type of dirt roads as Woodmere, surrounded by the same type of misshapen and unforgiving bush. Another out-of-place palace among the weeds where nothing grows. His parents are of course gone for the weekend. That he is hosting is in and of itself unusual; everyone knows Richard as the longhaired ginger with glasses who always reads Tolkien novels on the bus. He wears the same combination of black jeans and black t-shirt every day. He's been witnessed engaging in Dungeons and Dragons-related activities as recently as a year ago.

So why is everyone here? To me, the simplest explanation is of course that Richard has created a Kelly LeBrock-type supermodel with his computer ala *Weird Science*, and his mere proximity to this mythical beauty has increased his popularity tenfold. Really, any time someone can throw a party with wide open spaces, free booze, and no parents within miles, there's bound to be a good deal of interest.

I'm not altogether off from the truth, though. Richard didn't invent Kayla Vermeer—one of the most attractive, popular girls in school—but he may have pulled the greatest Jedi mind trick in the history of Woodmere by somehow convincing her to not only go on one date with him, but multiple dates in full-on-boyfriend-girlfriend-yes-this-is-really-happening capacity. That's the real reason we're all here. We're curious as hell.

Even as we arrive, I hear faint whispers of 'how'd he do it?' and 'I don't get it' from others. Once upon time there was no opinion of Richard; his Q score simply didn't rate. Now he is looked at with equal parts respect, amazement, and confusion. I myself expressed all three when one day I cornered him, needing to know how he had achieved the feat of successful dating. The answer was simple and came without revelation, except there was a coolness to his explanation that hinted at how he'd done it.

He smiled and said he had liked her for a while, and had just decided to ask her out. No smoke. No mirrors. Just a question posed to a girl he had barely talked to over the course of two years of high school. It was maddening. Real life can't even get *good* romance right.

And now here they are, greeting guests together as they arrive, like some bizarro power couple. Richard gives me hope in a world where few other things do.

"How's it going, Richard?"

I make a point to shake his hand and say hi. After more thought, Richard is more like Skolnick in *Revenge of the Nerds II*: the alpha nerd leading his troops from a desert island and back to civilization. He seems relaxed.

I say hello to Kayla and recognize an all-too-familiar look on her face—the distraction, the disinterest—it's that same look Kim wore out just a few weeks earlier pre-, mid-, and post-dumping me. My heart sinks; so much for escaping off the island. Maybe I'm contagious. Patrick and Lucille hightail it towards the booze, and I slink after them as quickly as possible to try and avoid the blast radius of another exploding heart if and when it happens.

There's maybe 100 yards of open dry bush between Richard's house and a covered barbecue and picnic area like you might see in a state park. Out in the wide-open space, pockets of people mill about or rest on blankets, discussing a rave later on at a warehouse somewhere in Illovo, passing around a spliff of Durban Poison. It reminds me of the water tower party in *Dazed and Confused*. Everyone has that look in their eyes like we just narrowly escaped another year of hell. People are already cooking up burgers and various other animals on the barbecue. On one of the picnic tables sits an impressive assortment of beers and hard alcohol, curacaos and crèmes, all ripe for teenagers with poor judgment. I get the feeling someone here tonight will end up pregnant.

The only light comes from the house in the distance and a few lights in the picnic area. I thank the bright stars above that they are not bright enough to make the Britney-Jordan-Robby-Patrick contingent easily visible to me or vice versa. They probably wouldn't even be here this early. I sneak further away from the glow of the lights to improve my odds of remaining incognito.

Around the back of the picnic area, in almost total darkness, I find Richard's friends Damian and Henrik, the ones he would be talking Tolkien with if he hadn't recently become a rock star with his dating coup.

Damian, Henrik, and Richard have that weird nerd power trio body-type distribution. Damian is the small skinny nerd. Henrik is the large, wide nerd. Richard is somewhere in between, neither too big nor too small. They travel as a pack, asymmetrical but still balanced. Of course, they all wear glasses.

The boys are having difficulties adjusting to 'the other woman' in their friend's life. Sure, they get to go to more parties now, but Richard's hard-fought gains in the social strata haven't quite carried over to them. The only real difference for them is that now they are alone *at* the party instead of miles from it. That, and their best friend spends less time, energy, and attention hanging out with them than ever before. He's especially impossible to talk to at a party like this. It's no wonder we found each other on the dark edges of town.

Damian and Henrik have with them a bottle of something dark, something too strong for them. They hold cups filled with way too much of it, sloshing and spilling them left and right. They have clearly drunk too much already. I give them each about half an hour before they are vomiting or passed out or one followed by the other.

"Alec Guinness!" proclaims Damian with drunken gusto and agitation.

"*Jassus*, You. Are. Mad. It's James Earl Jones," Henrik counters without emotion.

Their body types work with the alcohol to show biology in its purest form: Damian's drunkenness burns him up like an angry little firecracker; he pulses and gesticulates with fury. Henrik becomes even more slow-handed and mono-toned than usual. His eyelids shrink to slits as he clings to the comfort of his internal drunk.

"Me? I'M MAD?" Damian says, exasperated. "Did you watch the bloody movie? You're telling me when they pull off the mask and he's dying—that's a black oke I'm looking at right there?"

"Makeup, man. Makeup," Henrik slobbers.

"MAKEUP! You know that's not makeup! The voice doesn't even sound the same. It's a different guy. A white guy: Alec Guinness!"

"No, you are off it, man." Henrik waves him off with closed eyes. "Alec Guinness is somebody else completely."

"Alec Guinness played Obi-Wan," I chime in.

They turn to look at me, equal parts dazed and confused.

"You're wrong and he's only half-wrong. James Earl Jones *was* the voice of Darth Vader when he had the helmet on, but when it came off at the end of *Return of the Jedi* it was a totally different guy: Sebastian Shaw."

"Eh, who the fack is Sebastian Shaw?" Damian snarls at me.

I shrug my shoulders.

"I dunno. The guy who played the unmasked Darth Vader at the end of *Return of the Jedi*?"

"But *Jassus*," interjects Henrik with hurt in his voice. "Why must you say I'm 'half-wrong'? I got the voice part right. Can't I be 'half-right'?"

"Well yeah, I suppose that's true. Some people call me a pessimist . . ."

"Yeah!" Damian jabs a finger at me but it wobbles in the air without conviction. His face changes back from anger to confusion.

"Hey . . . Aren't you the guy with the Jimi Hendrix ta—"

Before he can finish, his face slams into the table, emitting a snore before it hits. His arm knocks the rest of his drink onto the concrete below. Henrik grimaces and sucks his teeth, wincing.

"*Jassus* . . ."

"Shit. Is he gonna be okay?"

"He's getting better at this. Usually this happens an hour earlier and he throws up first."

Henrik gently lifts up Damian's face, removes his friend's glasses, and tucks them into Damian's shirt pocket. Damian doesn't stir; his eyes are rolled back up in his head. Henrik lifts him up again and puts a hand next to his mouth to check for breathing before dropping him solidly back on the table. I shudder with the crash.

"He's fine," Henrik says matter-of-factly, taking another gulp of booze. He grimaces and groans immediately afterward. His movements become even more labored; he's running a marathon inside his body just to stay conscious.

"You got friends?" he asks, staring down into his lap. He's

barely audible except for his heavy breathing. I wonder for a second if he's really talking to me.

"Hard to say," I hedge as I take a seat next to the comatose Damian.

Henrik sneers with a half-chuckle.

"They remember you when cooler people come along?"

"More like I forgot them when cooler people came along. Now I wish I hadn't."

We sit in silence for a bit, Henrik's breath the only sound. Thibault and Sebastian and Penelope smile silently at me in my head.

"The good news is: you'll have your old friend back soon." I pat Henrik on the shoulder lightly as I stand.

"Like—without *her*? How do you know?" He looks up at me with all the energy he can muster.

"The Force, man. When Darth Vader is defeated—when the helmet comes off and he goes from James Earl Jones back to his old self of Sebastian Shaw and he is at death's door— he feels a peace. A remembrance of the man he once was. When he at long last forsakes power and the pursuit of it, he frees himself of the chains of those who use it to control him. He loses his life but regains his soul. He remembers family. He remembers love. The Force. You could call it an 'energy', really—"

I'm interrupted by Henrik's snoring. His eyes are closed, while he still sits upright.

"Thanks for the talk. That helped. See you around."

I leave the quiet of a passed-out Damian and Henrik, determined to find a phone to call Thibault. I'm Bill Murray in *Scrooged*, kicking my burning feet at the bottom of my own coffin until I realize I've been given a second chance at life. I want to change my evil ways. On cue, Thibault and Sebastian waltz in front of me.

"Wow, you guys came. And you're here fashionably early."

Thibault and Sebastian look around uncomfortably without acknowledging me.

"Okay. You got me. That was my whole make-a-bad-joke-to-gloss-over-the-paranoid-drug-freakout-I-had-earlier-today approach. You're telling me it didn't work."

"Not particularly, no," says Thibault.

"Not sure I even caught the joke," seconds Sebastian.

"Guys, I'm sorry. I really am. If I had a logical reason for doing it or a sensible way I could have avoided it, it wouldn't have been a freakout. I guess I cracked open like an egg. I apologize for any feelings of discomfort, distaste, and disdain I may have inspired in you."

"I was outraged," Thibault says casually.

"I never . . ." says Sebastian.

"Wait, are you guys serious?"

"Not in the least bit," Thibault says. "We weren't that mad."

"I was actually a bit amused," adds Sebastian.

"We came to your initial thesis on our own: while your freakout and abandonment on its own may constitute the behavior of a 'dick', the behavior itself suggested that we were looking at a man who's mental faculties—once proud and at least mildly functional—had temporarily turned to mush."

"Total poop," echoes Sebastian.

"Thusly, we could not judge harshly lest we be judged ourselves if the tables were turned," says Thibault, adding after a pause, "One could only counter that I was a victim of the same attacker as you last night, subject to many of the same indignities, and that my haircut does not look as good today as it initially did yesterday."

"Oh, c'mon, I think it still looks—"

"That said, you *were* a dick, which is to say you deserved the guilt that lead you to make this awkward yet heartfelt apology, and we deserved to have the apology, and you deserved to have it considered with a certain weight and dignity, which it was, and accepted accordingly."

"Wow, what's gotten into him?" I ask Sebastian.

"After you . . . *departed* . . . we went back to his house for a bit. He slept for about twenty minutes but it only made him more tired; we almost lost him for good. He kept saying we needed to stay up for this party because you'd be here, and it would be our last chance to see you, so he started drinking a bunch of soda."

"So he drank too much soda just so he could stay up and come here? Damn, Thibault . . . Thanks . . ."

Thibault nods his head quickly up and down while slowly turning it side to side.

"Well yeah, but that's not why he's like this. The soda wasn't working so we stole some of his mom's caffeine pills and that seems to be doing the trick."

"I see."

Thibault makes a clicking sound with his tongue.

"Thibault . . . I just wanna say—"

"Well, what's he on about?" interjects Lucille, appearing from nowhere. "And who cut his hair?"

"Kate cut it," Thibault clicks out robot-like. "It was Kate's cut. Cut by Kate. A cut that was a creation of the cutting Kate," says Thibault.

"Wot the fuck have you been smoking?" Lucille looks at him wide-eyed.

"He drank lots of soda," answers Sebastian.

"He took some caffeine pills to stay up but he's half-delirious from not sleeping anyway," I answer.

"But the soda probably was bad, too," Sebastian says.

"Nonsense!" Lucille proclaims in her Mary Poppins accent again. She produces an open can of Coke for me from behind her back and places it delicately in my hands. "Soda is for *good* boys and girls."

"I still think he drank too much," mutters Sebastian.

"Wow, thanks, Lucille. My favorite!" I hold up the logo and mug for an imaginary camera as if I'm in a shiny print ad.

"Eat this, too," Patrick adds, also appearing out of nowhere. He places a cooked burger in my hand and walks off.

Thibault and Sebastian wave to him to order two more.

"Yeah yeah, coming right up."

I take huge lusty bites of flesh and slosh them around and down with Coke before I'm even done chewing, like some Viking warrior celebrating victory. In a bit, Patrick returns with a burger apiece for Sebastian and Thibault and we all chew in dumb smiling silence for a minute. Lucille seems the most excited of all, displaying her Mary Poppins perkiness the whole time, grinning like a loon. She occasionally bugs her eyes and shakes her head dumbly at me, making me laugh.

Is *this* the moment I feared? Or is it just the magic of the mundane I was supposed to learn about? That a burger and a cold soda can make you just as happy as any drug or movie escape. We could actually fade out right now and it'd be perfect: the last of my friends and I munching burgers in idyllic silence happily ever after. *The end*. The fingernails of the message are on my skin but they don't dig in. Some context is missing. Something just isn't all the way there.

For one thing, Lucille's face is getting to me. At first it was funny, but she's been staring wide-eyed at me this whole time I've been eating and drinking my soda. She looks like she's dying to tell me something.

"Lucille," Thibault begins in a fake British Cockney accent, for some reason, "I do declare I am flummoxed by dis distribution of food and drink." He spaces his words out in between mouse-like nibbles on his burger.

"While your companion provided us all wit' delectable morsels of satisfaction, it appears only our esteemed colleague should be privy to da liquid form of said things. And since dis offering came from you, must we also curry favor wit' you for da same?"

"Speak English, you bloody fool!" snaps Lucille.

"Can you give us a Coke like Floyd's?"

"NOOOO!" Lucille blurts in her theatrical Mary Poppins style.

"Yes, I don't think he needs any more soda . . ." seconds Sebastian.

"NOOOO!" Lucille repeats in identical fashion. She quiets down to a whisper now. "You may be able to have one, but *not* one like his."

"Why not?"

"His"—she points at me—"is *special*."

All eyes turn toward my can of Coke. I sip down the last of it quickly, in case someone tries to attack. I get a weird feeling though, like I want to know what Lucille means by 'special'.

"Lucille, what do you mean by 'special'?"

Lucille begins to rub her hands together and fidget, then sort of shuffles and dances while avoiding a straight answer.

"Well . . . it's speeeecial because . . . um . . . it's like a good old regular Coke that yankee boys and girls love . . . but with like an"—she searches for the words—"extra kick!"

She punches her fist in the air like she's selling the stuff in a commercial. My stomach feels weird.

"What is the 'extra kick', Lucille?"

Patrick walks up with a cigarette and a beer just as Lucille is puckering up like a fish out of water, about to explode.

"I put a tab of acid in your drink."

Her lips quiver for a moment before she lets out a hysterical guffaw. Thibault, Sebastian, and I look at each other, wide-eyed and clueless again. Lucille brings her laughter to an abrupt halt when she sees she's alone.

"You're not laughing," she says nervously.

I am now the puckering fish out of water.

"Jesus Christ, Lou," says Patrick, exhaling his cigarette smoke and giving her a disbelieving sideways glance. "You put one of *our* tabs in there?"

"Yes," Lucille answers. Everything sounds like a question now as she's instantly rethinking and regretting her decision. Patrick shakes his head and walks away.

"Pat, no, wait!" Lucille calls after him, and starts to go. I grab her arm first, perhaps with a bit too much adrenaline. It startles her.

"Ahh!"

"Hehe, uh sorry about that. Um, could you maybe just hold up on the pursuit of Patrick for juuuust a second and maybe back up to my Coke and me? I feel like you may have glossed over an important tidbit and I just want to make sure I got all of this clear."

Cold sweat forms on my back and neck. I feel like I could choke on adrenaline. I'm getting familiar with this feeling now. This full-body fear.

"Floyd . . . I . . ."

I put my hands firmly on her shoulders.

"Lucille. What did you put in my drink and what will it do to me?"

She's mumbling now.

"A tab. Of acid. In your drink . . . You're going to trip balls."

My hands drop to my sides.

"Or maybe not!" she proclaims. "Maybe you'll be fine and nothing will happen!"

"Fuck, Lucille!" I shriek, beginning to pace.

"I told you you didn't need more soda," Sebastian whispers in Thibault's ear as they both look on, fascinated.

"I'm sorry, Floyd!" Lucille is pleading now. "We said it was going to be your night, remember? An adventure! All that sort of thing? I wanted you to try something you've never tried before! It might make you laugh like hell. And we'll be here. Oh wait, hey, I'll be right back. Pat! Wait up . . ."

Her last few words fade into one long one as she chases after Patrick.

I'm muttering to myself with increasing intensity as a scene starts to play out in my head.

"Stupid . . . just so . . . stupid . . . what was she . . ."

Two smartly-dressed executives sit down at a table across from each other.

Executive 1: Okay. Pitch me.

Executive 2: Okay. It's a kid, a teenager. Latchkey kid growing up. Bit of a loner, but not the cool, dangerous sexy type. Bit awkward but still salvageable. Has a thing for movies. Grew up on 'em his whole life. He's got a reference and a line for every situation.

Executive 1: Loving it. Who doesn't like the movies?

"WHY? What made her think . . . so misguided . . ."

Executive 2: Okay. You love it? Good. Kid moves to a different country. Stranger in a strange land—

Executive 1: (Interrupts) Love it. We talking some cultural slapstick here?

Executive 2: Eh, not exactly . . . Maybe think of it as some . . . black humor.

Executive 1: Okay. Hearing some red flag words right there. I'm hearing "low-budget", "indie"; not a real moneymaker. But I'll let you keep the floor for another thirty secs.

"Not like this . . . this isn't . . . no . . . not this . . ."

Executive 2: Okay, well . . . he falls into drugs—

Executive 1: Ooohh. You just killed family audiences right there.

Executive 2: Just pot! It makes him feel like he's in the movies, see?

Executive 1 (sucking teeth): Still a bridge too far.

Executive 2: There's a romance angle.

Executive 1: Loving it again. Star-crossed lovers. Stickin' it to their parents. Stickin' it to The Man. Breaking down barriers. Showing once again that LOVE. CONQUERS. ALL.

Executive 2: Not exactly. She dumps him and he spends most of his time complaining about it.

Executive 1: You've got fifteen seconds left.

"But this it! It's right here. This is what I'm here for, no?" I'm looking at my hands, which feel hot now for some reason. I'm pacing wider and I'm starting to yell. Thibault and Sebastian continue to watch, afraid to do anything but whisper to each other.

"You think he's gonna do it again?"

"Could be . . ."

We're nearing the end of the scene.

Executive 1 (exasperated): So where's the hook here? I mean what are we selling?

Executive 2: Okay, he loves the movies, right? But he thinks his real life makes for poor story, so he tries to copy a movie to fix it. Just when he feels like he's finally got something figured out . . . (dramatic pause)"

Executive 1: Ahhhh??

Executive 2: He goes to a party on his last night in the different country, a friend puts drugs in his drink as a practical joke, and he goes crazy and dies. Surprise tragic ending. Think Easy Rider.

Executive 1 (slumps over): What are we, a foreign studio here? I would never greenlight a depressing piece of shit like that.

Executive 2: I know. It was some straight-to-video shit I saw in the video store the other day on my way to the back to get a porno!

Executive 1: Ahahahahaha! (slaps his knee)

Executive 2: Right? Hahahahahahaha!

Executive 1: Hahahahahahahahahahaha!

"YEAH HERE I AM!!!" I'm screaming to no one in particular, "IN THE AIR TONIGHT!!! COME ON!!!! COME ONNNN!!!!"

My whole body itches. I kick off my shoes and start hopping around like a cartoon character revving up to run. My head feels like it's expanding, taking in air in order to eventually pop. *This* is the moment everything has led to, that Phil Collins told me was in the air tonight. *You see the hook is that he loves movies and hates reality, and can't stop talking about how he would rather have one than the other. Then his reality disintegrates into pure nonsense just before things were about to get better organically.* Maybe 'black comedy' isn't the right term for it either . . .

"I'M COMIIIIIINNNNNGGGGGG!!!!" I scream and—fully revved—take off into the night, barefoot, the trailing sound from my lungs my last thread of connection to conscious humanity. People laid out in the field prop themselves up and stare. Any faces I see, I turn and run in the opposite direction. I'm sure I'm screaming the entire time, but I can't really tell. The air is roaring around me. The Tralfamadorian me is always screaming, always running.

I run until I can't see anyone around for a million miles and then I finally fall to the ground. I realize I've been trying to imitate the sound of a jet engine with my voice, pushing out a continuous drone.

I feel the pricks of scorpions' tails all around me and I swat at my sides. Maybe it's just grass. Whatever Lucille gave me has come on fast, and will be fully kicking in soon enough.

Now my skin feels like it's crawling with insects. Maggots. Or maybe ants? They chew my flesh to pieces as I writhe on the ground. Maybe they are land piranha. Maybe they don't even exist. Maybe there's a reason I never touch psychedelics. Maybe I'll be the first person to commit suicide using only their own mind, another poster-child of the menace of illicit drugs.

Hours into the future and miles away, a plane will take off for America with one extra empty seat on it. I'll watch it fly overhead from my living grave, unable to understand what it is, my once-working brain now a bowl of soft maggot food. I'll drown in the summer sun, my flesh rotting off my bones like melting candle wax. I'm Johnny Depp nearing the end in the last movie playing in my head, the one I never even saw. I'm going to die out here.

10

LOVE OR CONFUSION?

"There's shadows in life, babe."

\- Jack Horner, *Boogie Nights*

I'm floating alone in this world.

The rest of the party could be a thousand miles away or ten feet; I wouldn't be able to tell the difference. My body vibrates with tension. Do I want to stand? Do I want to run and jump and fly off into the night, exploding into a million pieces? No. Better to just lay here and not risk making the universe any angrier with me.

The stars throb out of the sky as I lay on my back. They leap toward me in a rush, then recede just before they're about to pummel me, like bullies trying to make me flinch. I keep flinching. Eventually I try to scream, but no sound comes from my mouth. I think of Patrick, strangling me in the bushes outside of Alo's house. I can feel his hands around my neck and I gurgle for air. Everyone said I was too loud. Even Alo was getting pissed at me. But I was just scream-whispering; almost no sound was coming out. The more I tried to demonstrate it, the madder they got. Attack and strangulation. Conflict resolved. I just couldn't *hang*. I couldn't modulate. I can't control. I have lost control.

The back of my throat cracks and a low moan leaks out. I think it's the life slipping out of me, my dying breath. How do I hold it in? In a panic, I grab handfuls of air to horde into my mouth. Then I remember the shower scene. Me crying in all those movies, the mascara running. Wait, was it *me* in all those movies? No, it wasn't me; that was make-believe. It's funny when things are make-believe and less funny when they are real.

A song bubbles up from the earth, a prehistoric rumble from a million years ago. I can only hear the undertones right now. The ground moves in waves in response to the soft edges of melody. It's "May This Be Love" by Jimi Hendrix. *Really? That song?* Is it really playing or just in my head? And who would play it now? The bass line morphs into a human voice, someone else's low moan even. At first, it's barely audible, a second later it feels deafening, as if it's being pumped through a megaphone. Whatever it is, it's clearly worse off than me right now. Things can always get worse.

If I can find the location of the voice and help, maybe I can keep from flying off the earth. I sit up and the stars spin like loaded dice. I swear I catch a glimpse of a hyena trotting by a few feet from me. They say hyenas can chew through bone.

The moaning is coming from behind some bushes. Or are the bushes themselves groaning? They expand with each grown, then contract as it dies down. Am I Moses in the beginning of *The Bible Part II: Electric Boogaloo*?

I stand and make my way towards the bush, and a groan

inadvertently stumbles out of my own mouth. I am trying to groan in harmony with the other voice. Misery loves company, after all.

Perhaps on the other side of the bush, the sinister hyena awaits. It mimics a human groan in order to lure its prey. It smiles the same evil smile of the Patricks, the Jordans, the Robbies and Alos, the Mr. Pretoriuses, the Abes, Cybils, and Kims. I finally got too close to the animals. They'll smile at me that way before they crush my bones to powder.

I tiptoe towards the bush, but in my present state, my movements are more cartoon-ish than practical. It's an exaggerated up-and-down prancing motion, my tiny T. Rex-like arms tucked close to my side, like I'm Vincent Price set to scare you in a 1957 movie. I will surprise the groaning hyena in its natural habitat, grab it by its tail, and swing it over my head till it makes a great whirring sound that signals I have conquered this land of Africa. Kind of like the sound of the Aborigine communication device used in *Crocodile Dundee*.

Hey, whatever happened to Paul Hogan by the way? Was he typecast after playing a character that was just *too* good, too iconic? He made like three movies later in his career, and they were all watered-down takes on an affable, fish-out-of-water, Dundee-esque character. A tough thing that must be, having your career ruined by one epic portrayal that people just can't get past any time they look at you. Wait, did I just call Paul Hogan's portrayal of *Crocodile Dundee* 'epic'?

Another groan emanates from the bush, and I freeze in my cartoon tiptoe stance. I start giggling at myself uncontrollably. I am not a zoologist, but I believe the element of surprise would be key in attempting to capture a hyena. Maybe I would still succeed by a different definition of "surprise", the hyena seeing a laughing buffoon tip-toeing toward him, and being like "I don't get it."

I picture us having a conversation behind the bush—the hyena and I. I would obviously try to make it laugh, because humor is my defense mechanism in uncomfortable situations. If I were successful, we would become friends and we could run back to the party together, where I would encourage him to crush the bones of those who had wronged me. I've talked myself into this plausibly happening now and casually stroll over to the other side of the bush, fully ready to entertain the hyena. But it's not a hyena at all. In fact, it's Richard Koening, sprawled out on the ground, looking lifeless, his face covered in bloody scratches, his shirt sopping with dark, glowing, green ooze. Did the hyena get to him? Is he dying?

"Richard, are you okay? What happened, man?"

"Uuuugghhh. I drank too much."

The dark ooze on his shirt is the green Sambuca I noticed earlier. Or I guess it could be Predator blood. Or Richard could be an alien himself, bleeding to death. Just trying to cover all the bases here.

"Sambuca is traditionally served in a snifter, Richard, not on your shirt."

"Uuuuugggghhhhh. My face hurts. What happened?"

"You tell me. It looks like you're all scratched up. Well, actually it looks like your face is melting but I'm hoping it's still mostly intact and that's just me. Did the talking hyena get you? Or did you fight a Predator?"

"Whaaaaa? I fell . . ."

My powers of deductive reasoning briefly return.

"Did you fall into the bushes here, Richard?"

"Yes," he continues with his eyes closed. "I think so . . ."

I reach out to touch the bushes, and my hand comes back screaming; they're thorn bushes. In a rage, I decide to kick the thorn bush in retaliation. It rattles in place as a few leaves drop to the ground but otherwise remains unmoved, embarrassed for me as I shriek, spin, and dance in pain. The spectacle is enough to make Richard at least open his eyes.

"What's . . . going . . . on?"

"Nothing. I just had to make sure there were no wild animals in the bush. I think we should get you back and cleaned up, Richard."

"Uuuuuunnnnhhhh. Okay."

I reach down and clasp his wrist, pulling him up to his feet. He waivers and threatens to topple back over for a second before I can put his arm around my neck and get my full weight under him. He's bigger than me, so this should be fun. His face looks like that skinless dude in *Hellraiser*. Or maybe it's more like the Nazis at the end of *Raiders of the Lost Ark*. I've just got to take it on faith that he won't be a talking skull in minutes.

"Okay, Richard. We need to walk now. Can you walk with me?"

He groans in confirmation. Head tilted towards the sky, eyes slits, my body acting as his, we take one step forward and nearly topple over again. I catch him, and my whole body buckles to keep him off the ground. He dangles, mostly lifeless, just above it. Stars flash in front of my eyes and I'm sweating through my clothes under the strain of holding him up. I swear I hear a hyena sniggering at me.

"Shut up, you."

"What?" Richard looks up bleakly.

"Not you. Let's try this again."

Richard repositions his arm around my neck and we begin a slow slog back to humanity.

"How far?" he mumbles.

I look ahead to the faint lights of the picnic area in the distance, but have no depth perception. We appear to be walking in pitch-black outer space toward our destination.

"Looks like maybe 100 miles or so. Wait, you're on the metric system, right? 350 kilometers."

"Unnnnhhh," he groans, and we continue to stumble through the dark towards salvation. I can't see anything around or in front of us. I picture us walking through the insect tunnel in *Indiana Jones and the Temple of Doom*: centipedes, millipedes, and maggots all around us. I guess being on acid really makes you think of Indiana Jones movies. We walk in silence for what seems like forever. Maybe the universe has stopped around us. Richard's head remains down the whole time. Finally, he tries to talk.

"What's wrong with me?"

"You're drunk and you ate a face full of thorn bushes. What else?"

"No . . . I mean what's wrong with *me* . . . She's . . . She's not really . . . paying attention to me anymore . . ."

"Who?"

"Kayla . . . She's ignoring me . . . I think she's . . . dumping me." He seems almost on the verge of tears.

I must be on South African Candid Camera or something. The look I saw on Kayla's face when I arrived—it *was* that same look Kim had. That utter indifference. That look that says "I'm already light-years past this." I know that face, I know the cracks and nuances in it; I could pick it out of a lineup on anybody. It's been burned into my mind for all time.

Turns out Richard didn't make it off the island after all. He probably made the same mistake I did: he played the game up until it needed playing the most, then stopped. We spent all our time and thought constructing a durable, efficient boat to get off the island, paddled as hard as we could till we were only just out of sight, then sat back lazily, counting the clouds in the sky, not realizing the tide would carry us right back to its shore.

Well, he may have to suffer the same fate as me, but he doesn't need to suffer the same indignity. There's still time for me to try and prepare him.

"Hey, Richard, listen—"

"HHHLLLLLRLRRLRLGGGGGHHHHH!!!!!!"

Richard turns in towards me at the precise moment he starts projectile-vomiting, splashing my shirt with a warm stream of forest green-tinted puke. In a moment of instinctual panic, I almost throw him off me, but then catch him before he hits the ground. Falling back into my arms, he squishes into his own fresh puke. We squish together in the night air. I steady him back in our original position but he is mostly comatose now. The world is red and hot as I use all of my strength to lug him forward. It's not often you end up covered in vomit twice in one day. On the plus side, it's a good distraction from an otherwise completely splintered reality.

"Richard. Thank you—for—the—gift—but—I need you—to help by—walking with me. RICHARD!"

He temporarily snaps awake, droopy-eyed and pale.

"We're almost there, Richard. Move your legs a little."

Richard somehow puts one foot in front of the other. Lucille is one of the first to notice us stumbling back to the picnic area.

"Jassus and for fuck's sake! What the bloody hell?" she screams, running over to us. The image of me running off in screaming, paranoid hysterics at the beginning of an acid trip, then returning back however much later with a bloody Richard in tow, I'm sure leaves some questions wanting to be answered.

"Richard fell into some thorn bushes, then vomited on my shirt."

Actually, that seems like it about covered it.

"Hot Christ, let me go get Kayla. And are you okay?"

"I'm pretty sure a hyena is tailing us. If it asks about us, just make up a story."

"Nevermind," says Lucille as she scampers off. Patrick helps me bring Richard over to a bench and sit him down so he's mostly upright. He slumps in place, his hair wet with blood and chunks of his own vomit. I have yet to address my current state of hygiene.

Kayla comes back with Lucille and her face sinks at the sight of Richard.

"Well I guess we better get him inside then," she says, a sigh of resignation in her voice.

Richard floats off in the arms of Patrick and another guy I don't know. They carry him nimbly between them so as to keep his various fluids to himself. Kayla follows close behind, checking her phone along the way. I follow along behind her. Because a head full of acid makes me feel like I need to tell her something. And because I'm still covered in Richard's vomit and I need new clothes.

Inside Richard's mansion of a house, we make a beeline for the bathroom. I waddle at an angle of ninety-three or ninety-four degrees to the ground, to avoid dripping vomit on his parents' carpet.

Kayla knocks on the bathroom door and quickly tries to open it. She pushes on it lightly and motions everyone in but the door sticks at halfway open. She smacks it back and forth a few times and the obstruction stirs and groans. It's a live being: my one-time friend, Canadian Robby.

His legs block the door. His face is buried in that stupid backward baseball cap he always wears. In one of his hands is an empty bottle of something. An upturned toilet seat watches over him while something gruesome sits in the bowl.

"For fuck's sake! Can *anyone* keep it together here?" Kayla screams to no one as she shuts the door again.

We march upstairs and deposit Richard in his parents' shower. No one wants to go through the task of undressing him and cleaning him off, so any valuables are removed from his pocket, and he's given a shower while fully-clothed and seated. Patrick and the other guy quickly check themselves for collateral damage, rinse their hands, and head out.

"Richard owes me a pair of clothes," I tell Kayla, showcasing the abstract artwork her soon-to-be ex has painted on me. She sighs heavily.

"Follow me."

We walk down a long hallway to Richard's room. She opens the door and points me toward his dresser.

"Will you help me with him?"

It's less a question than an expectation.

"In a sense."

"What?"

"I said 'yes'. Go make sure he's not drowning."

I close the door behind her. Richard's room sparkles and shines, his favorite possessions glowing under now-wavering lights that make them look like museum pieces. On the walls, under track lighting, are framed Boris Vallejo fantasy posters—dragons, demons, women, and creatures that may be some combination of dragon, demon, and woman. The images rock gently from side to side in their frames as I focus in. This is a constant side effect of the acid; everything vibrates or sways slightly at all times, pulsing in place. If I stare long enough I notice I start swaying in time with them, a lanky vomit-covered palm tree in the breeze.

On Richard's desk, under lamplight, are his painted figurines: men bulging out of full battle regalia with swords bigger than their bodies; women busting out of strategically-placed brazier armor; hundreds of dollars' worth of high-end plastic and molded clay, standing guard in silence.

In between and around Richard's Comic-Con souvenirs, the rest of his room is immaculate. The floor is empty except for multiple pairs of combat boots lined up at the foot of the bed. A wall of bookcases houses what looks like at least a thousand books, many of them boasting that fantasy-sized thickness and frayed edges. His white walls contrast with the black furniture and display pieces and for a second I feel like I'm in Superman's Fortress of Solitude.

I chuckle a bit—or a lot, as any time I start laughing now I can't easily stop—at the thought of Kayla entering here for the first time. What was it like the first time she saw toy models and paints! Did they make out here, under the watchful eyes of barbarians, man-beasts and Amazonian princesses? They must have. What music did he put on?

Richard and I probably ran the same playbook with our respective romances. We played dominoes, figuring the first one was so immovable that if we somehow managed to tip it over, all the rest would tumble under the momentum. If a girl said yes to you the first time (which was the hardest to get), it didn't matter how many "Woman Slays Dragon" Vallejo prints you had mounted on your wall. You were golden. But girls play chess. You can take every small piece off the board and it won't matter; they can get your most important piece at any time.

Staring longingly into the quivering bosom of Richard's latest woman-warrior model, I momentarily forget I'm covered in his vomit. The smell returns to my nose, and I almost lose it myself. I take off my pants and underwear and put them into his trash can. The shirt comes last; I remove it as delicately as possible to try and tame any more stray vomit. I hold the shirt out in front of me as I carry it toward the trash.

The vomit on the shirt morphs into a face. Some detail is lost, but it looks like a young Matthew Broderick.

"Finish the work!" he exclaims with a bullshit exuberance typical of a faking Ferris.

"Shut up, you. I don't want to hear any more out of you."

Pieces of Richard's lunch dance around and form another face. It's Woody Allen.

"The work!" he says with exasperation.

"The work? Don't talk to me about work! Where were you when I wanted to talk about work? Jerk!"

The vomit dances tightly towards the center for one last face. It's my Tralfamadorian bus driver. His universal smoking hand gesture hides his puffy cheeks and smile.

"I see you. Your friends. The corner. You *bemma*."

"Aw, fuck off already!"

"What's going on in here—*Ahhh!*"

Kayla peeks her head in to see me totally naked, screaming at a shirt covered in vomit. I recoil and shriek myself, channeling some previously unknown female instinct, bringing the shirt quickly in front of my chest and not my exposed bottom half. It slops into my naked chest.

"Fuck!"

"What the fuck are you doing in there?" Kayla screams from behind the cracked door.

"Ugh . . . Sorry! Sorry you had to . . . see that! I got . . . uh . . . this shit on me . . . aaaaaand . . . I need to clean it off!"

"Can you hurry up???"

"Gimme a fucking second!"

She pounds the door in disgust and walks down the hall. I throw the shirt in the trash with the rest of my clothes, and do a quick rinse and towel off in Richard's bathroom.

His wardrobe is no optical illusion; it really is all just varying shades of black. In his underwear drawer, I find a small box in one corner. Curiosity gets the better of me and I open it. It's a necklace, an egg-shaped cubic zirconium enveloped in a metal eagle's talon and attached to a chain—a renaissance fair special. There's a card with it:

"Dear Pearl Ear,
Thanks for a wonderful month.
Love,
Rich Bitch"

Putting the box back, I notice something shiny underneath it. It's a condom. The writing on its wrapper frowns at me in slow motion. I nod back in solemn agreement. Poor bastard.

I choose some black boxers, a ratty, faded black t-shirt,

and a pair of black jeans from his closet. I avoid any socks or pairs of the combat boots. I hate boots, plus I'm telling myself I must have had some sound super-intuition that initially led me to ditch my shoes and that I shouldn't go against it now.

In Richard's mirror, his clothes are slightly big on me, just enough that it's noticeable. Defoe's words come back to me. *You can always change your face.* In the mirror, my face stretches to look more like Richard's while my hair lightens in color and grows to match his. He has an extra pair of glasses on his dresser and I put them on to complete the image. Through the blur of his prescription, I'm Richard. Jeffrey said I could change the ending, too. But if I change my face to Richard's, am I already changing the ending just by being him, or does me changing into him allow me to change both our endings because doing things as him will make them both different for him and me? Wait, how long have I been standing here as Richard?

I thrust his glasses roughly back on to his dresser as if ridding myself of some possessed artifact. I'm me again; I rub my eyes, forehead, and hair to make sure. All our endings need changing. Body-switch movies are such a cliché, but at least I know them. I think I just winked at myself.

– – —— – –

"I don't look too good, do I?"

My words startle Kayla as she's looking out a slightly open window, smoking a cigarette. Richard still lies in the running shower, out cold. At least the blood and vomit have been washed from him. Fresh pink cuts line his face and arms. Kayla eyes me up and down in Richard's clothes.

"What are you talking about? You look fine. He's the one that's a mess."

"No doubt about it. I mean look at me," I say, gesturing towards Richard pathetically. "I've never looked worse."

"Look, I don't know what the fuck they teach you in America, but it sounds like only *kaak* comes out of your mouth. I asked you to help but now it seems like you were the wrong person."

"Oh, I'm the only person, Kayla. But I should back up so things make a little more sense. It's me, Richard. That's Floyd in the shower. We switched bodies earlier in the night as part of the sacred Ritual of Zarathustra—"

"Okay." Kayla throws her hands up in the air. "Now I know all Americans are fucking psycho."

Her eyes narrow as she points her finger at me.

"And I don't know why Jordan and them kicked your arse, but I can tell you probably deserved it and they should probably come up here and do it again."

"Now Pearl Ear, why do you want to talk to me like that?" I ask in a singsong voice.

Direct hit # 1. She pauses dead in her tracks.

"Wait . . . what did you call me?"

"Your nickname. Pearl Ear. The one I came up with for you. You remember where it comes from, right? Your family name: Vermeer. The painter. *The Girl with the Pearl Earring*? Remember we talked about it?"

More silence. That gamble, otherwise known as direct hit # 2, comes courtesy of our Standard 7 art teacher, Mr. Thomson! See, good teachers are worth something.

"Okay, okay, okay." Kayla shakes her hand at me as if she's

trying to push thoughts from her mind. "Listen, just listen . . . Just . . . please . . . you musn't . . ."

"Please don't what, Pearl Ear? You can tell your Rich Bitch."

Her hand goes to her open mouth in slow-motion, her eyes widening.

Direct hit # 3. I may not know how to checkmate someone in five moves, but I think I just sunk her battleship.

"What's. Going. On," she whispers between her fingers.

"I already told you it was the ritual of Jumanji that made us switch bodies. I sent away for a kit out of the back of one of my books; there was a monkey skull and everything, but we don't have time to go into all of that. I knew you would want me to prove I'm me right off the bat so I tried to get it out of the way quickly, but I'll go you one better and tell you something else about you that only I know, something about you that only I can see."

"What what what . . ." she stutters out.

"I see the look in your eyes. I know you're done with me but you don't say it."

"Wait . . . you?"

"I know it, Pearl Ear. I got to know you real well real fast. I thought we had a good thing going but I guess I was wrong."

Kayla rubs the back of her neck with one hand and begins to chew the thumbnail of the other.

"I was gonna tell you, but—wait!" She flails around desperately and hysterically. "I still don't know what the fuck is going on! This can't be actually happening, hey? This is some American voodoo or whatever. I saw the movie!"

"Oh, which one?" I can't help but break character for a second. "*Angelheart* is the darker flick for sure, but I guess

I'm a just a Martin Sheen fan because I thought *The Believers* was pretty good, too—"

"What—what the fuck?" Kayla shrieks.

"Look, we're stalling here. The Curse of Marrakesh is incredibly dangerous and complicated. The accursed that switch bodies attain a higher consciousness and insight towards themselves while out of body, but the curse demands they forget it all when they return to their own flesh. Floyd fell victim to the rare reverse double-curse, the demon goat scarring him and showering him with green vomit."

I shake my head sadly at Richard slumped at the bottom of the shower.

"Again, time is running out, though. The curse will expire"—I look at my wrist; still no watch—"any minute now! I'll awake in that shower, not remembering anything. Floyd won't remember anything either. And even if he did, he's going back to America for good in mere hours! He'll never come back here! Nothing you say will leave this room."

"I just don't know if I can . . . I just . . ." Kayla wrings her hands under the weight of the supernatural burden I have just unleashed on her. I grab her hands slowly, as a lover might.

"Pearl Ear. Just talk to me. Where did I go wrong?"

She is still, looking into my eyes.

"It wasn't you . . . You . . . You know who you are already. You have your friends and your favorite things figured out now and forever. The same ways of doing things. But I'm always changing. I get new friends and things to follow all the time. You should be you, but I have to keep changing. We just do everything differently."

"But you liked my differences enough to get together with me in the first place."

"I did. I mean, I do. It's just that . . . well, you didn't think we were going to get married, do you?"

"Kayla . . . We're in high school . . . I didn't—"

I think she just turned the tables on me . . . er, Richard.

"I didn't either," she continues. "We'll be going to different universities . . . I can't believe I'm telling you all of this now—I guess you won't remember. We're going to be different people next year in different places. We were pretty much different people in different places when you asked me out. They say opposites attract, but then, you know, that wears off, and you just have someone different from you. I had some fun with you, Richard. But we weren't going to last either way. That made it easier to see the differences."

Now I'm speechless. Kayla Vermeer *has* turned the tables on me. And all of a sudden I get it. *I can't have it both ways.* I can't lament that real life pales in comparison to movie life, but then put the first girl I ever kiss up on a pedestal like she's Juliet and I'm Romeo.

"So let me go, Pearl Ear."

"You know I never liked that fucking nickname."

"Yeah, I wondered about it."

"You came up with it."

"Oh yeah, right."

"Sorry. What were you saying?"

"Let me go easy. When I wake up, when I'm conscious and we're alone, tell me all these things again. I won't remember them anyway and you've had a little practice now. Remember our brief good times together and be civil; don't ignore me or give me that dead-eyed disgusted look and let me drag on in this confusion."

"Okay. I don't want to do that."

"And to appease the cursed monkey skull of Shasta, you must tell other attractive friends of yours that you wanted it to work out with me, but I just had too many deep, dark layers you couldn't get inside. I was too much for you to handle."

"What? Why do I need to do that?"

"Ah, nevermind. This should cover most of the appeasement."

Kayla now grabs my hands gently as I just did hers.

"Richard. I'm sorry."

The words freeze me. They're the only ones that could have—the ones I've needed to hear. Not every two people who get together will love and cherish each other forever. That's real life. Most people deserve to be treated better than they are, though, and deserve to learn life's tough lessons easier than they end up having to.

"Thanks, K."

"See, I like that nickname better. I've told you that."

I smile at her.

"I know you do."

The real Richard stirs and groans in the shower. I groan with him, clutching my head in a dramatic fashion.

"Uuuunnnngggghhhh!! What happened? How did I get up here? Kayla? Richard? What's going on?"

Kayla quietly composes herself, eyeing me cautiously, finally accepting that she's the only one who knows what just happened.

"Richard got sick drunk, but you helped him up here. I think maybe you hit your head or something and passed out for a bit."

I feel around my head frantically for an imaginary bump I know isn't there.

"Oh, weird! Well, I gotta go. Early flight to catch home in the morning."

I start backing my way out.

"Guess I probably won't be seeing you all again for the rest of our lives. Kayla, good luck to you in University, life, love, and all that shit. Richard, hang loose, buddy. I took a few souvenirs to remember you by."

I show him I'm wearing his clothes but nothing registers. Just more groans.

"Okay. Great talk, everyone. *Tot siens!*"

I close the bathroom door behind me. The last image I see before it shuts is Kayla once more nervously biting her thumbnail, trying to process what just happened to her, or what she thinks just happened to her.

Maybe there's some universal desire expressed in body-switch movies that keeps people coming back. What would you say and do differently if you weren't you and the people you were talking to weren't them—if you could somehow be more yourself by being someone else? I see the appeal now. Kayla thought she was talking to Richard. I thought I was talking to Kim.

11

ANOTHER LONG TRIP

"A man's got to know his limitations."

- Harry Callahan, *Magnum Force*

Do you remember when we both first got here, and we first met, and it was like some silly movie shit because—hey look—we were the only two kids in school from North America and had *this* in common and *that* in common and of course we were going to be 'best buds'?"

"..."

"It seemed destined to me at first, too, or at least it made basic sense. I mean we dug hanging out with each other. But I think we figured out real soon it wasn't going to go that way—it was that one Friday you came to hang at my place. We played tennis down on my tennis courts, which was probably the first mistake, because neither of us knows or cares how to play fucking tennis, so why were we even trying, right? Mom suggestion—whatever, I know. I'll take a mulligan on that one."

"..."

"So yeah. So you were all like 'what are we gonna do?' and I was all like 'I like to make soup and watch movies. How do you feel about making soup?' and you kinda, like, *sniggered* for a split second, then realized I was serious and walked it back a little, trying to politely say you weren't *that* into the idea."

". . ."

"And it's like—*I get it*. Making soup isn't cool. No, it's not fucking *coooooooool*. It's *delicious* is what it is. Some people like to eat it and some people even like to make it. And I asked—you know—if maybe *you* were one of *those* people. And—you know—maybe you're not, and that's fine, but you got all *whatever* about it, and I was like '*Fuck you, man!*' *FUUUUUUCK YOU.*"

"Ungh."

I hop off the bathroom counter and peer over the top of Robby to see if his eyes are open. They aren't. This is the first sound or movement he's made in the past fifteen minutes. I've been talking to him for as long.

I stand there for a period of time between a minute and four thousand years long to see if he'll stir again, but he doesn't. I hop back up on to the bathroom counter and sit with my back again to the main mirror, looking back into another mirror. Fifty thousand Mes look back at me. They all move at a slightly slower rate than the real me. After a while, their trails become jumbled and I have to look somewhere else.

This may be the longest conversation Robby and I have ever had. I find him surprisingly easy to talk to in this state—both his and mine.

"I lost my place. Where was I?"

"..."

"Right, so we weren't really gonna be 'best buds'. No big. We may have spent more actual time together when Jordan and Patrick and Alo and everybody were around, but it was clear we just didn't connect like the rest of you guys did, and we never really hung out one-on-one after that first time."

"..."

"What's funny is that I still don't have much of a strong opinion about you either way."

"..."

"Okay, well you got me. I mean, I do think you're a dick, but you're no criminal mastermind, or even a competent henchman. You were always just kinda there. I never really wanted you to burn like the others. But then again, you aren't funny and hapless like Alo to where I would forget you being a dick either. You're somehow smarter and dumber than him at the same time."

Someone knocks on the door.

"Use the one upstairs, please. We're busy here."

From beneath the door comes the flickering of shadows and the sound of someone shuffling off quickly.

"I hope you don't mind me sending them off like that, Robby. I'm just really into our conversation."

"Ungh."

I hop off the counter and stand over him again, looking for moving eyes. He opens and closes his mouth and swallows once before lying still again. I only wait a few more seconds this time before hopping back on the counter.

"Of course, the one thing I've always despised about you is your tendency to be a joke-jumper."

"..."

"Oh come on! You may not have heard that term before because I just coined it, but I'm sure you can figure out what it means. And I know you know you did it and when."

". . ."

"You did! You did. Just about every time we were on the bus together. I would make a joke on the fly, and you know, you're right, I'll give you that I have some problems annunciating and projecting—that's on me—but you just take that joke, turn right around and say it louder as if it were coming directly from you. Because you're mildly smart, you were able to do it a lot of the time before I even finished the joke. Like you would mirror me very closely and then yell the punch line so people couldn't even tell you were repeating what I just said."

". . ."

"And shit, everyone thinks Robby is *soooo* fucking funny. But you're not that funny. And those were all my jokes. Nobody likes a joke-jumper, Robby. It's like the shooting the messenger thing in reverse: don't go sucking his dick for delivering someone else's good news."

". . ."

"But backing up, I just want to reiterate that I've never really had too much of a problem with you. You're a bit of a goon, that's for sure. I'll say that's the Canada in you. You're also a bit of a dick and a spoiled rich kid, but hell, you could probably say that about me too, and you probably would if you had the chance, am I right?"

". . ."

"Haha! Totally. So I can't be mad atcha. I can't even remember where you were when Patrick was strangling me. Cowering in the bushes for all I knew. Just there. Just around."

". . ."

I stand up from the counter and fold my arms in introspection. One of Robby's ankles rests between my bare feet.

"Maybe we were two sides of the same coin. That's why it seemed like we were gonna be great friends. America and Canada might as well be the same when comparing either of them to South Africa. But it didn't materialize. We had the same internal machinery but used it in totally different ways. The same things that hit your sweet spots just hit me over the head, and you love it here, or at least say you do, which I don't get, but whatever. Jordan and Patrick became your best friends. I only thought they became mine, and—shock and surprise—turns out there is a big difference."

". . ."

"But hey, I'll say it again—not mad atcha. I guess I hope you have a good life? Or at least pull your head out of your ass and that stupid baseball cap."

". . ."

"Listen. This has been great. Really heartfelt. But I think I should go. I want you to stay loose, though, okay?"

". . ."

I stroke my chin, thinking. I can't just leave him like this. It doesn't seem right. Maybe he needs something from the movie back catalog. I've already used body switch, we kind of did heart-to-heart, and rousing speech followed by slow clap just isn't applicable. Hmmm.

". . ."

"My friend, I think you need Summer Camp Movie pranks to remember tonight by. As a prankster yourself, I'm sure you can appreciate them."

I remove the empty bottle from his hand (I have learned it was once Vodka), urinate in it and place it back where it was. I fill a soap dish with warm water from the sink and place his other hand in it. His 'tagging' pen—the one he uses for his asinine attempts at graffiti—is in its usual place in his back pocket. In my most ambitious move, I pull down his pants, boxers and all, and use his pen to draw eyes on both butt cheeks. I stand over him, admiring my handiwork. His ass cheeks stare back at me blankly, looking for guidance. One last thing is missing. I deftly remove his hat from under his face, drop it down the back of my pants, give it some familiarity back there, and then return it gently to its original position.

"So long, Robby."

I leave the door ajar behind me as I squeeze out.

"Bathroom's open!" I yell to anyone who wants to know.

— — —— — —

"Meet me at the back patio in 0200 minutes."

"You're alive!" exclaims Thibault. "And *what?*"

"I'm better than alive. I'm *back*. Meet me at the back patio in two minutes I said."

"I don't get it, though. Didn't Lucille spike your drink with that acid? Aren't you way out?"

The combination of caffeine pills and sleep deprivation has made Thibault punch drunk.

"Oh, god yes! I'm out of my mind completely! But I'm also back *in* things. Meet me out back in a minute and thirty seconds and I'll explain."

"But how could you be back *in* anything if you're currently so far *out?* And what things could they be that would allow you to be back in them even while you were so out?"

"That's why I need you to meet me out back in a minute and ten seconds so I can tell you about them."

"Tell us about what?" Sebastian walks up, munching on another burger. "Some kind of universal truth? I've never had a conversation with someone on acid, but I hear that's what happens; they discover universal truths."

"I don't know what you'd call it, Sebastian. Maybe a 'local truth'. If you just meet me out back in fifty five seconds, I can probably explain it to you."

"Fifty five?"

"Okay. Fifty."

"So you've managed to grasp something powerful in your way-out altered state," Thibault reasons, "something you could only achieve in said state, and yet you actually believe it has a practical local application in the real world, despite the fact that it was pulled from the aether of a different dimension."

"Well you're kind of running with it, but yeah, if you could just meet me in thirty seconds—"

"Maybe it's that Floyd's mind is constructed differently than ours," Sebastian interjects. "A drug like that would make a lot of people crazy in the head, but maybe instead it soothed him and allowed him some cool, crisp thought and vision, one in which problems can be easily solved and truths easily attained."

"I dunno," says Thibault skeptically. "I'd have to hear about it."

"Did you guys smoke while I was gone?"

"Oh, most definitely."

"We were gonna hold off after earlier today, but when we saw your drink get spiked we thought all's fair."

"Indeed. The blind leading the blind. Speaking of which, do you guys wanna follow me out to the back patio and hear some things?"

"Sure, I'd like to," Thibault says.

"That sounds wonderful," Sebastian concludes.

"Follow me."

We head back to my original lurking area when I arrived at the party, close to where I left Henrik and Damian.

Thibault and Sebastian stand a few feet away and I begin pacing like an army general once more. How will I shape this argument? How can I put together the concrete plan of attack for what I can only vaguely see in my admittedly derailed brain? Will I be able to form coherent sentences? I got into a little bit of a comfortable roll inside and now I'm having trouble readjusting to being back out here.

"Um . . . you guys still down to hang out and do stuff with me tonight?"

Thibault and Sebastian look at each other, shrug, and nod in unison.

"Yeah."

"Yeah."

"But like—even if it's more weird stuff like this morning that doesn't make a whole lot of sense?"

"More *Ferris* stuff?" Sebastian asks excitedly.

"Eh, I dunno, Sebastian. We're still making a movie, I just don't know what it's called now. But we're gonna finish it this time. I'm back. I'm ready. Look in my eyes."

Thibault and Sebastian both squint to try and get a good look into my eyes in the darkness.

"No. Not seeing it just yet."

"Here. Come in the light more, then try and look maybe right into them . . . maybe head on."

Thibault and Sebastian reposition themselves and squint harder as I jut out my face for them.

"Oh! There, I see it," says Thibault.

"Yes, I got it, too!" agrees Sebastian.

They repeat their looking, shrugging, and nodding ritual.

"Okay."

"We're in."

"Okay. Well I'm glad we got that discussion over with. Follow me back into the light and I'll show you the plan."

We kneel down on the concrete under one of the patio lights. I pull out a piece of paper and Robby's pen, drawing an 'X' on the paper.

"This is a map of Java and its surrounding areas," says Sebastian, reading the bottom of it. "It looks like you ripped it out of an atlas from Richard's parents' library."

"Yes. I brushed up on my basic knowledge of hyenas there as well, but we're already getting off track."

"You put us somewhere in the Java Sea."

"Well Christ, Sebastian, the map isn't exactly to scale. Can I finish?"

"Sorry."

I draw another 'X' on the edge of Borneo.

"There's my Jimi Hendrix tape."

"THE TAPE!" Thibault and Sebastian both scream.

"That's right, the tape. I blew it the first time, got caught up in my own bullshit and panicked. But this is now bigger than me, bigger than Kim, bigger than a Jimi Hendrix tape. It's about finishing what we started, riding the wave."

I put my hand out and conjure up the universal wave symbol as I wobble it up and down. Unfortunately, I become too engrossed watching it throb and change shape in front of me, and Thibault has to remind me to continue.

"Sorry."

I put a third 'X' on the map in the middle of Sumatra.

"If you were ripping maps from an atlas, maybe it would have made more sense to rip out one of Joburg or just South Africa in general instead of—"

"Shut up, Sebastian. This third X is The Khyber. This is our final mission destination."

"The restaurant?" Thibault asks.

"The restaurant."

"What's there?"

"Penelope."

"Penelope Vermaak?" asks Sebastian.

"Penelope Vermaak."

"Why are we going to see Penelope?" Thibault asks, losing clarity.

"It's a long story . . . You ever make the wrong choice? I mean, everyone does, but I mean, you ever look down the wrong path so hard for so long, that you miss the right one right in front of you? It's easy to see if you would just try but you've been so conditioned to look in one direction that it never even occurs to you. It's a matter of perception, not effort."

"So we're going to see Penelope because . . ."

"Because I think I like her a lot, Thibault. Because we said goodbye earlier tonight and something happened between us. I don't know if I can explain it properly, but there was an air, a feeling that came up that I hadn't felt with her before. Or maybe it was always there, I just wasn't paying attention. I have to know what's there before I get on that plane tomorrow."

"What happened? Did you kiss?" Sebastian puts his cheek in his hand, fascinated.

"She kissed me on the cheek. But it wasn't just the kiss. It was that charged air that really got me thinking. I met her right at the beginning of my time here, same time as Kim. But unlike Kim, Penelope wasn't up, down, and all around with how and when she would interact with me. She never ignored me for long periods, then flirted with me ferociously, then ignored me again. She never broke my heart, never mistreated me. I don't think Penelope is capable of mistreating anyone. She's always been a great friend."

"So but maybe she's just that: a great friend. Why this now?"

"Excellent counter, Thibault. All I can say is that when we said goodbye, I had a Keyser Soze/*Usual Suspects* moment."

"Great flick," says Thibault.

"Isn't it, though? The scene at the end with the coffee cup crashing down and breaking. 'Kobayashi'. I had that moment."

"Great ending," says Thibault.

"I never saw it," Sebastian laments.

"That's okay, you won't need to now that we've ruined the ending for you."

"Definitely, Sebastian. Don't even worry about it. All you need to know is that a cop is talking to a bad guy for hours without ever realizing he's actually the bad guy. The cop keeps trying to pin the crime on a different, more likely bad guy. After the guy leaves, though, the cop finally notices one small detail that makes him rethink all the other small details he's been told, and he finally realizes he just let the real bad guy walk away."

"Sounds like a bad cop. I probably don't want to see it," says Sebastian, now feeling justified.

"You're right. It's a piece of shit and you probably shouldn't bother."

"So?"

"So I'm the cop. I'm the cop and I've been so busy trying to pin the crime on the suspect that I'm sure has to have done it, that I completely ignore the other one right in front of me who may be the real criminal, but who doesn't have the same M.O. or give off the same signals."

"So Penelope is a criminal? I'm confused . . ."

"Well, it's a metaphor, Sebastian. But she might be, yes. She may have stolen my heart out from under me while I was distracted by Kim. I might have gotten on that plane without ever even realizing it.

"But when we said goodbye today, I had the Keyser Soze moment. A small, seemingly insignificant detail occurred, and forced me to go back through every small seemingly insignificant detail from our past history and reexamine it. Every hug to start or end the school day. Every casual conversation we've had. Every hello and goodbye. Every comment she made in passing about me, Kim, or other girls, or herself. Every seemingly harmless flirtation. Every piece of evidence now points back to a larger picture, one I couldn't see till now—the coffee cup crashing on to the floor.

"Now look, Kim was in all the Standard 7 and 8 classes with you guys and me, and she and I had that free language period to hang out together all the time, AND we were on the student council together, AND she was more mobile, making it easier to do things with her, AND she flirted at a level which of course I only now realize is unusual, AND despite all that, she still had to literally ask me to kiss her before I even considered the possibility that I might like her."

"So . . ."

"So Penelope, on the other hand, was always a standard above us, lives in the middle of nowhere and can't get anywhere, and although she does flirt, it's not nearly so shameless and aggressive. Who knows where my story would be if her and Kim's circumstances were switched."

You can always change your face, Defoe says in my head.

You can always change the ending, Jeffrey says in my head.

"Let's say it *is* there, then," says Thibault. "Why hasn't she made more of an effort toward you?"

"Well, Thibault, a couple thoughts on that. First off, you could be totally right—she's just a friend, and I'm seeing this wrong and leading us on a fool's errand."

"For a change."

"Yes. Nothing new. If that turned out to be the case, though, it would at least answer your question in a roundabout way."

"How thrilled I'll be."

"But let me trust in myself and my instincts for once and say I don't think that's the case. Aside from that, it's simple and complex at the same time. The simple part is Penelope's personality. She's not shy, but she's not overly aggressive either. It's all that hippie-universal-flowing-energy stuff. She never gets too upset, too excited, too anything. She never oversteps her reach; she always lets things come to her in time. And it works for her. If we never got together, she would believe it was the will and order of the universe and that there was a good reason for it, and she'd probably be right, too.

"The complex part is the stuff with me and Kim, the logistical issues with seeing Penelope at all that I just mentioned, and whatever else has gone on in my own head to ruin things up to this point. It's quite possible that she *has* dropped the right hints and messages, the right suggestions to encourage me time and time again, done everything short of mount me in public, and I've missed it all. I am entirely capable of that."

"I've seen you do it many times," Thibault enthusiastically seconds.

"Thanks, Thibault."

We all stare down at the Java/South Africa map for a second in silence. Sebastian runs his finger over the final X.

"Okay. So when we get there, what do you say? What do you do?"

"That's the part I haven't figured out yet, Sebastian. Going with a specific goal in mind doesn't seem to be the point. In time, I don't know what any one thing that happens tonight is going to mean. But I want to feel that energy again, the one I felt today when we hugged and she kissed me on the cheek. It was crazy, a pull that was half physical and half emotional; it felt like we almost couldn't get out of it. I need to feel that energy again, just to know if it's real. If we get all the way there and that feeling is there . . . it'll all be worth it."

A slow clap comes from behind Sebastian and Thibault. We all turn to look and see Damian and Henrik are the perpetrators, sitting in just about the same spot as they were before.

"Go for it," says Henrik slowly. "That Penelope Vermaak is hot."

"Yeah, I'd fuck her," seconds Damian.

"You'd fuck your hand," counters Henrik.

"I'd fuck your mom's hand!" Damian snarls back.

We go back to looking at our map.

Thibault traces all three Xs with his fingers.

"This map . . ." he begins. ". . . this map bears no topographical resemblance to anything existing in our current reality. I'm not even sure you've put the locations in their correct relative directions. From what I know, we're going to have to go from one end of the bush to the other to get this tape, then go back into the city after all that to get to Penelope. And we have no ride. It'll take hours . . . if we're lucky.

"Plus, we've trailed after you a lot today, following your plans and schemes. Are you gonna ditch us again if they go wrong?"

This is the first real indignation I've seen from Thibault during this caper.

"I know, Thibault. You've been a better friend to me than I have been to you. I keep making the same mistakes and I can't fix them all in one fell swoop. But I'm not letting you down any more tonight. And what we're about to do will stay with you long after I leave this godforsaken place. That's my promise to you both right now."

I look at each of them nervously. They look to me like different species of bird right now, but I'm not sure telling them that would help our situation in any way.

"Fuck it, it's your last night here," Thibault finally says. "Let's do it."

"Yesss!" Sebastian pumps his fist in the air.

"Alright. I've got good news, too. We won't be completely stranded thanks to *this*."

I thrust my hand out over the map so we can all look at it. The faint outlines of the words "happy ending" can be seen. The phone number that was below it is gone, washed off in the shower.

"Gahhh!!!" I scream.

"I'm not sure how getting jerked off will help us here," questions Thibault.

"Is *that* what that means?" Sebastian asks innocently.

"Yeah. I have an uncle who takes a lot of business trips to Japan . . ."

"Shit. That was Nick Sutter's number . . ."

I bring my hand closer to my face, as if I just wasn't looking hard enough for the number before. A million pores dance and laugh back at me.

"Nick? Yeah, from what I heard today, he could have been a big help if we told him we were on a government mission. Stop looking at your hand."

"Sorry. We'll just have to get going another way, and hook up with him later on. Something tells me we're going to need him."

"For what, though? And how are we going to get in touch with him later if we can't now?"

"Thibault, it's going to work out. You looked into my eyes, remember?"

"That's true, we did," Sebastian offers.

"*Jassus*, okay! Where do we start then?"

"We need a ride to Woodmere, but since that isn't going to happen, we just need a ride out of here to somewhere else where we might better acquire a ride to Woodmere."

We all think for a minute. Thibault snaps his fingers.

"We got a ride here from Romuald and Agnieska Paw-lowski. They said they weren't going to stay too late because they had to pick up their granny early in the morning. Maybe we can ride back with them to their place if they're ready to go."

"Where do they live in relation to Woodmere?"

"No idea."

"That sounds much closer than where we are now. Let's do it. Find them, and meet me back here as soon as they're ready."

"Got it."

"Okay, break."

Thibault and Sebastian scurry off towards the field to find two needles in a dark haystack. As they leave, Brit-ney passes them in the opposite direction, making a beeline toward me, bleary-eyed.

"Oh shit . . ." I mutter to myself, trying to turn away.

"Floyd-o!" She drunkenly grabs me by the hand and begins pulling me after her before any further explanation.

"Uh, what's up, Britney?"

"What's up? *What's up?* It's my buddy's last night here and I gotta make sure he has an awesome time before going home! Plus, you know, some other people wanna talk to you, too, you know . . ."

Oh god, no. I try to drag my feet behind us, but Britney is at a forty-five degree angle to the ground, using her whole body weight to pull me after her.

"Hey Britney, I'm already having a really good time, and I don't think I need to get in any big talks . . ."

"NONSENSE!" she screams like a drunken aristocrat as

she continues to drag on. "We just want to . . . clear everything up and make it nice before you leave . . ."

"Britney, I'm not sure I want to—OH HEY, GUYS."

Before I know it, I'm standing in front of a picnic table face-to-face with Jordan and Patrick. Their eyes are slits situated among bloated, slow-moving faces. Booze sweats out of their pores. The marijuana stench I used to love feels like hammers being thrown at me coming off of them. They look at me, then at each other, then back at me, mumbling and nodding in unison, idiot twin brothers separated at birth.

Jordan could have been a California beach bum in the late 70s, surfing twelve hours a day and then sleeping in a pile of trash on the beach at night. His dirty-blond hair matches his monochrome brown pants and sweater. He always looks like he's covered in a thin film of dirt.

Patrick has an unremarkable, clean-cut, bookish aspect to his face. His hair is straightforward and short on both sides, with only a touch of length and curliness on top. He always wears the same prescription glasses; they look like small bifocals. He also has a small overbite, which when put together with all the other elements, makes him look a bit like an English professor when he smokes, or at least someone who is less of an imbecile than Patrick actually is.

He tempers his scholarly face with a slow, moronic speaking delivery, and an unending supply of the same t-shirt, jacket, army camo pants, and combat boots, all of which he wears now. He's also really good at strangling people when they're high, if you're ever in a pinch.

"Sit down, Floyd-o!" Britney slobbers as she pulls me down onto the bench across from Jordan.

Jordan peers at me through his slits from across the table. He tilts his head upwards and looks over his nose for maximum accuracy. Patrick does the same. They look like old men trying to gauge the yardage on a golf course, or locate an ancient text in a library.

My fear juices start flowing again. I can't think of anything more uncomfortable for me to be doing right now. I get the feeling Patrick and Jordan are in a similar boat, and that Britney coaxed them into doing this, which I suppose is more decent than usual for her. My face does me no favors; I can't stop grinning like a fool.

I guess it's not really strange or explosive for us to see each other this way, though. A fair criticism to level at me is that after I was betrayed, mangled, and strangled by people who I thought were my friends, I continued to treat them like my friends. I don't know if I was thinking as much as I was just feeling desperate and lonely. I guess I thought of us like a gang. We all liked hanging out with each other, but there was a hierarchy. When a member of the gang steps out of line, he just needs to be taught a little lesson, then everyone knows their place and they can be friends again.

Jordan and Patrick seemed to embrace this unwritten narrative; if I acted up again, they could just destroy me physically and mentally again. Britney was mortified at first, but it never amounted to anything, unless you count this act. Alo remained clueless as always—no difference to him one way or the other. I briefly tried to go back to how things were. I may not have had trust with these people anymore, but at least I had familiarity. '*Hey, I get it guys, you say I was outta line. Okay . . .*' But in truth, I was like Andy Dufresne in *The Shawshank Redemption* after Tommy gets killed and he's finally released from the hole. Sure I went back to business as usual for a bit, but had already made up my mind to escape. I finally did about a month ago, cutting off communications completely. Or so I thought . . .

"Floyd-o, these guys just wanna talk some things out with you," Britney slurs. She'll make a great older alcoholic. Patrick starts.

"Listen, man. It's like, we used to hang out a lot, and like, it was cool, but like, I feel like things are a bit stressed between us now, you know?"

"Well yeah . . . You beat me up."

"Right, okay. I know that. That was . . . not . . . that was like a bad thing that happened that I did, right? I mean, I still think you mustn't talk shit loudly, but I . . . like maybe, that shouldn't have happened, right?"

"Definitely at least maybe."

"Right, okay. So like, I think I would like it if it could be like, cool again between us, you know?"

". . . I'm sorry, is that a question?"

"Well, yeah, I mean you're looking at me funny right now because I'm totally fucking drunk, and I know I am—I know I'm drunk. But you mustn't worry, because people always tell the truth when they're drunk."

Jordan nods in deep agreement. For years after, I will wonder if this is really true or not. They're satisfied it is, given their own extensive personal research.

"That's right," Patrick seconds his own point after seeing Jordan nod. "I only ever tell the truth when I'm drunk . . . And I want to be cool with you again if you want to be cool."

Britney nudges Jordan, who jumps.

"Ah! Yeah, I just want to add that, like, you're a . . . pretty cool guy, so I like, hope we can be cool again." He and Patrick are nodding and smiling dumbly now. I never noticed before how much they both look like hyenas.

"Yeah, let's be cool again," Patrick says with warmed-over enthusiasm. He holds out a dead-fish hand for me to shake.

Michael Corleone screams in my head: *"EVERY TIME I THINK I'M OUT, THEY KEEP PULLING ME BACK IN!"* Seriously, was this really necessary? I have to shake hands with my attacker, thank him for pissing in my face, and apologize for fucking up the shoes he kicked me with? I'm supposed to be able to change the ending, but they changed it on me, making it somehow even worse than it was before. Before, I was just beaten up, now it's been commemorated with a handshake.

I grip the cold, limp hand in mine. It's wet with sweat and just lies there in my palm. What else can I do? Refusing a handshake is an invitation to outright war. Britney nudges Jordan again and he offers his as well. Why not? Britney grins as if she has just brokered a Middle East peace accord.

I feel the screen around me. The lights and cameras are on me. And I'm blowing my lines. It can't end like this. They can't win everything all the time. *I can change the ending.* How does the underdog defeat the villain in a movie? Gimmicks. Misdirection. Confusion. The Jedi mind trick. Turning the enemy against itself by getting under their skin and in their head. So what are my resources? A drunk guy, his drunken girlfriend, and the drunken guy's drunken best friend. Time for this scene to write itself.

"Damn, Jordan. Have we never shook before? You've got strong hands! I bet you could arm-wrestle the shit out of someone."

Jordan shrugs and smiles coyly, as if no one has ever complimented him in such a way.

"Patrick, let me see your handshake again."

Patrick offers his dead fish again. I grip and palm at it like a doctor examining a patient.

"Oh yeah. That's not even close. You guys ever arm-wrestle?"

Patrick and Jordan look at each other with something that is half skepticism and half curiosity.

"I mean I just bring it up because I read somewhere that Tony Hawk and Stacy Peralta always used to arm-wrestle as a way to get fired up for skate competitions, and because it warmed up their muscles so they could better do tricks that they needed their hands for."

I have no idea if that's true or not. In fact, I know it's not true. Stacy Peralta and Tony Hawk are just skaters I've seen in one of Jordan's thirty thousand skateboard videos, and I made it up. I can tell Jordan is now considering this.

"Plus, I just think it would be interesting because Jordan's got that really strong grip, but as Patrick has mentioned before, Jordan is a much smaller guy than him."

Jordan's face turns to stone, much like it did the only other time Patrick mentioned Jordan's size. A late night at Alo's long ago, everybody drunk and high, Patrick made a really innocent joke about Jordan being small, which caused Jordan to blow up. Patrick immediately apologized and swore to never do it again. For the purposes of this experiment, though, it would really help if I could convince Jordan that Patrick thinks of him as a puny little shit often and out loud.

"Hey, come now, I don't say such rubbish . . ." Patrick begins, trying to cut it off immediately.

"Well I mean, not a lot, but surely we all remember at least one time (the only time) over at Alo's where you were talking about it. Right, Brit?"

Now when you're in a small clique of friends and one friend's girlfriend tells you off the record that she's just luke-warm on her boyfriend's best friend, well, you keep that to yourself. Unless they beat you up—then feel free to take the occasional modest distaste she has for the best friend and exploit into a full-blown hatred with the aid of alcohol and a little prodding.

"Yeah!" Britney blurts out. "I remember—you were starting shit for no reason."

"Oh come on now. I said I was sorry about that," Patrick dismisses the allegations, looking away. Jordan is still stewing over who might have called him small and when.

"I'll fucking arm-wrestle you right now, *China*."

"Yeah, do it, hon!" yells Britney.

"*Jassus* . . ." Patrick is getting uncomfortable.

Jordan and Britney have taken the bait, filling up with an anger that is probably ninety percent alcohol. Now just to stir a little more.

"Oh come on, Patrick! Just a little friendly arm-wrestle. No one is suggesting you guys fight or anything, right Brit?"

"I don't care," she sneers and crosses her arms.

"Whoa, what's going on *there*? Some secret shit I don't think we need to get into now that we've all made up—"

"Secret? What's a fucking secret?" Jordan demands.

"No, there's no secret. Please, Brit?" Patrick pleads with

Britney in an attempt to calm the situation while still not taking it completely seriously.

"Please yourself! I wanna see you fucking arm-wrestle Jordan!"

"The winner should get a kiss from you," I throw in, dancing around the edge.

"Yeah, sounds great!" Britney doesn't miss a beat. "I know he wants to kiss me all the time anyway, the way he looks at me! But he's not gonna get it, cuz Jordan's gonna pin him in a second, right honey?"

Jordan doesn't answer. His gaze is fixed on Patrick now, his face somehow even deader than before. I would always take the odds on Jordan in a fight. The guys who puff out their chest the most, yell the loudest, and talk the most shit usually fall the hardest. The guys who are real psychos become as quiet and still as a mouse before they explode.

"You fucking looking at Britney, hey?" Jordan asks, barely audible.

"Jordan . . . Look . . . I never."

The air is hot and tense. Someone is breathing very heavily. Out of the corner of my eye, I see Thibault come into view. His eyes bulge as he sees my company. He gives me a nervous thumbs-up to say the ride has been secured. I give him one back, and my motion breaks the standoff; Jordan pounces on Patrick over the table. I stand and step away from the table just as it collapses over where I was just sitting. Jordan and Patrick smash into two more tables while grappling with each other, knocking over various foods/drinks/drugs/people. They'll probably be best friends again in the morning. Just keeping the gang in order. A mob of party-goers swarms the action for a front-row seat.

Thibault and I are inadvertently still giving each other thumbs-up as we distractedly watch the mob and the center of the storm move further away from us. Lucille rushes up to me from behind the mess.

"There you are! What the bloody fuck hell is happening here?"

"Did you know that in the hyena kingdom, the female is dominant, and the status of the male is determined by his relationship to her?"

"Hyenas? Wot the fuck? I'm talking about this fight!"

"Oh. Patrick and Jordan got into an argument about something, no idea what."

I can't even see Patrick anymore. Jordan's sweater has been half-ripped from his torso and he's fighting two other guys now. Lucille looks at me as I still can't stop grinning, and we both bust out laughing. We hug.

"I gotta go, Lucille."

"I'm so sorry about tonight, Floyd. I don't what the dumbfuck I was thinking. I just wanted you to have a great time to remember, and I fucked it up . . ."

"Eh—it's actually not all that bad. I mean, I've had some moments of sheer terror, and I spent half an hour talking to Robby while he was unconscious on the bathroom floor, but it also changed my perspective around a bit. Maybe I had to go a little crazy to get some clarity. I feel like I'm back. Here—look me in the eyes."

Lucille squints from multiple angles.

"Oh! Yeah, there, I see it. That's quite nice."

"Yes. In the end, I think everything is ending as it should."

We are distracted by the sound of glass bottles breaking, shrieking, and debris flying out from the center of the mob.

Lucille and I hug again.

"Take care, Floyd. Maybe we'll see you again someday?"

"Maybe . . . If you ever get the hell out of here."

"*Jassus*, I know what you mean."

"Tell Kayla and Richard I had a great time at the party."

I wave to her as I head off to meet Thibault, Sebastian, Romuald, and Agnieska. She waves back until she sees me get into the car, then runs over to the edge of the mob, jumping up and down to try and get a glimpse of the action over someone's shoulders.

12
ROADS LESS TRAVELED

"We're on a mission from God."
- Elwood Blues, *The Blues Brothers*

*M*iami. South Africa. Japan. New York.

"*Jassus*, but how do I end up being the one who has to sit under the dash when I was the one who thought of asking for the ride?" asks Thibault, a scrunched ball of human in between Agnieska's legs.

Kim. Penelope. Kayla.

"Thibault, we've been through this," begins Romuald Pawlowski in a mock scholarly tone from behind the wheel. He also always refers to Thibault as 'TIE-bault' on purpose.

"Tih-bault," Thibault grunts back.

Martin Erasmus. Richard Koening.

"TIE-bault, we got to show our cousins Aleksi and Antoni from Poland a good time while they're in town, so we can't very well ask them to sit under the dash, and you are smaller than everybody else."

"Yes TIE-bault," Agnieska Pawlowski snarls over her bottle of liqueur, "don't be such a selfish bastard!" She kicks him with her feet. He groans and Aleksi and Antoni chuckle next to me.

Lucille's Patrick. Jordan's Patrick. Patrick Worsdale from 7th grade in Miami.

"I must say, for not having a license, not knowing how to drive a manual transmission, the sudden rain, *and* taking all that acid, I think I am driving quite well, if I do say so myself," says Romuald.

"I agree, Romuald," Sebastian agrees.

"Why thank you, Sebastian. I value your opinion."

The car groans as Romuald awkwardly grinds into another gear.

Woodmere. Woodridge Road where I grew up. James Woods.

"You're doing okay, Roma, but don't blow my clutch," says Agnieska, swigging from her bottle. She's the only one of us old enough to drive, and the only one old enough to drink. The latter choice prevailed.

Joburg. Randburg. Rosebank. Roburg. Jurjang. Rorung.

"*Jassus*, Aggi, must you drink while we're in the car? We're all already going to go to jail for a million years if we get pulled over, you need a million more?"

TIE-bault. Thibault. Tillery. Tympani.

A car horn blares as it screams by us in a haze of gray. The windows are almost completely fogged over. Romuald waves.

"Yes, thank you."

Japanese. Afrikaans. English. Spanglish. Liquorish.

The car endures another guttural scream as Romuald shifts again. Aleksi and Antoni stare out the window at the passing lights, pointing and giggling. They and Romuald purchased the rest of the acid Lucille didn't drop in my Coke.

Change your face. Change the ending. Change lanes.

"CHANGE LANES!!!" I scream in Romuald's ear and he swerves to avoid an oncoming truck. More horns blare.

"I swear I really did not see that coming," he says matter-of-factly.

"You were in the third lane of a two-lane highway, you git!" Agnieska screams at him. Their cousins laugh from the back seat. Romuald briefly snipes at them in Polish.

"I'd really rather not die like this," grunts out Thibault from underneath the dashboard. Gears scream in agreement.

The beginning. The end. The middle . . .

Ideas are coming too fast now, one for every streetlight that whizzes past overhead. Real life isn't a movie, and it's not based upon a written script. It's a slow-moving machine—grinding gears and clicking dead bolts—triggered by riddles and combination locks, with each part moving only after the last part has finished doing so. When it's finished, it may have the appearance of a well-constructed narrative—peaks and valleys, a beginning, middle, and end, the fluff and filler edited out—but getting there was all chaos. Nothing was written down beforehand. You can't tell the story unless it's already been told.

"Shut up, TIE-bault!" shouts Romuald.

"Yeah, shut up, TIE-bault!" doubles Agnieska, kicking him again.

"Ow, dammit! Knock that off!"

Aleksi and Antoni giggle again.

We feed the machine with variables: proper nouns, adjectives and adverbs—people, places, things. It's a Mad Lib waiting to be filled in. In the present, we fill in those variables with whatever looks good under the hot lights; better to just keep the machine going by plugging something in and finding out how it moves next. Only when the movie is over and everything is locked in can we lie and say it made sense at the time.

"*Jassus*, is that the giant walking thing from *Star Wars* coming at us?" asks Romuald. He emphasizes *Wars*. Sebastian tries to focus through the foggy windshield, hoping to corroborate this sighting.

"Maybe just another eighteen-wheeler," he says, dejected.

"Ah, right you are. Good answer. Good passing of the test. Glad everyone is staying sharp," says Romuald.

Each variable is determined by live audition. You audition the names and dates of people, places, and things for the variables in your life. Did you go to school in South Africa for two years at age fourteen? Or did you go to work in New Jersey, studying penguins for seven millennia at age thirty-four?

Executive 1: His name's Floyd. His girlfriend's name is Kim. They date for two weeks total.

Executive 2: I love it. Just change a few things. His name's Richard. His girlfriend's name is Kayla. They date for two months.

Executive 1: Even better. But just change a few more things. His name's Sizwe, he's black, has no girlfriend, and works in a movie theater . . .

And on it goes.

"I say, is it hailing now or has the rain just become a bit more forceful and demanding?" Romuald asks.

Chunks of ice slap down into the windshield and roof with cracks and thuds as horns continue to scream by at regular intervals.

"I do believe that's hail," says Sebastian.

"*Jas-sus.*"

A variable is only locked in after it's too late to change, after the next part of the machine is already moving. You can audition actors and actresses, sift through wardrobe choices, and scout locations for only so long until you just run out of time. Then that part is locked into place forever. I was born on July 17, 1981. CLICK! I lived in Miami, Florida until I was fourteen years old. CLICK! Then I lived in South Africa for (2 weeks?/ 2 years?/ 2 decades?). It was the most (miserable?/ joyous?/ enlightening?/ confusing?) experience of my life. After I moved away, I (often?/ seldom?/ never?) went back. We fill in the blanks with what we think makes the best story at the time. We are directing without a script, or rather, we reverse-engineer the script from the movie we end up with.

"I don't want to alarm anybody," says Romuald, "but I do believe a couple of the bad black demons from the movie *Ghost* are flying around the car right now."

Sebastian again looks to corroborate but finds nothing.

"That might just be exhaust from the truck you're tail-gating. At least it stopped hailing."

"Plus I think they only come when you have wronged the dead," I add.

The last variable to lock into place is when and where you died. The machine stops. The movie and script are finished. Some artful direction and editing can shape the narrative, sure, but as they say in the trade: 'garbage in, garbage out.' Who did you finally go with for the female lead? Where did you ultimately decide to shoot the bulk of the film? How much time and effort did you put into gathering the supporting cast? Every choice is an interchangeable variable affecting the arc of the story. It's like the ending of *Clue*: here's how it could have happened, here's how it should have happened, and here's what did happen. The big question is: when each variable finally locked into place, did you capture your best take on film? Did you make your best movie?

"Do you guys ever feel like your life is a slow-moving machine with gears and pieces that lock up?"

SCREEEEEKKKHHHHHH- KOW!

The car makes a vomiting sound as gears crunch together. This is followed by a gunshot-like sound, followed by gray smoke from the hood, followed by the car gradually slowing down and eventually ceasing to move. Romuald manages to turn down a side street before we come to a complete stop. The car is silent for a moment, the sound of rain on the roof and windshield the only thing audible.

"GODDAMMIT ROMA, YOU FUCK! I TOLD YOU NOT TO BURN THE CLUTCH OUT!" Agnieska yells as she smacks him with her non-booze holding hand. He blocks feebly.

"Well *jassus* Aggi, attacking me isn't going to make the bloody car start again! Also, I think I know where we are, and if my calculations are correct, I definitely drove a large majority of the way home."

"A large majority is very good," says Sebastian encouragingly.

"Yes it is, Sebastian. I value your opinion."

More silence.

"Say, do either of you have Nick Sutter's number?" I ask.

"Sutter?" asks Romuald, surprised. "Fuck no! Why?"

"We need him to give us a ride out to Woodmere."

"What the fuck d'you need at Woodmere at this hour?" asks Agnieska, her hand over her closed eyes.

"A Jimi Hendrix tape," grunts Thibault.

"Oh yes, he's very good, Jimi Hendrix is," Romuald almost whispers towards Sebastian.

"Very talented. Exceptionally talented," Sebastian concurs.

"Okay. But if you needed to go to Woodmere, why are you riding back with us? We were only about ten miles away at that party."

"FUCK!" shouts Thibault from under the dash.

"You see, I knew there was something wrong with that map." Sebastian shakes his head.

"Okay. Well we need to get back to Woodmere one way or another, and I think Nick's our guy to do it. Do you know where he'd be tonight?"

"Fuck! Probably at home wanking off!"

The Pawlowski clan laughs at this.

"He lives not too far from us, though, I know. Over in Rivonia. I rode on his bus once or twice. His stop was right by the SPAR supermarket there."

"Okay. So when the tow truck gets here, we'll have them take us all back to your place with the car since repair shops aren't open now. Then Thibault and Sebastian and I will hitch our way back up toward Nick and Woodmere and you guys can get your car looked at in the morning. Sound good?"

"Yes! And we can put the tow on Daddy's card," says Agnieska. "But wait. What tow truck are we talking about?"

"This one right here." I point to the tow truck just pulling past us. It stops in front of us. Romuald and Agnieska look at each other, confused.

"When did we call the tow truck?" Agnieska utters. She fingers her lip in contemplation.

"Come on guys, how could there be a tow truck here for us if we didn't call it," I reason as I open the door and get out.

"Yeah, who cares? Let's go. I think my neck is broken," grumbles Thibault.

"I say. This does feel a bit strange, doesn't it?" Romuald asks no one in particular.

The rain has stopped and the air is thick and fresh with it. Clouds still linger ominously overhead, and the sky is a strange chocolate brown color in the moonlight.

"It's okay." I lean back in to tell him, "I changed the ending. The original variable had us all just sitting here forever and dying of starvation."

– – —— – –

"I tell you—you let a *kaffir* get smart to you once, soon enough they start thinking they the boss of everything. Especially in the 'New South Africa'."

The grizzled old Afrikaans tow-truck driver rubs the stubble on his face. His fingernails are stained with nicotine. Or maybe it's blood. Years and years of blood.

"Uh . . ."

"Yah, they'll just take and take"—he squeezes something imaginary above his steering wheel—"until they've bled this country dry, hey."

Romuald spoke to the tow-truck driver initially. He could take us all back, but he needed one person—and only one—to ride in the cab of the truck with him. This was just 'the rule'. Thibault had suffered enough, we didn't want to break up the family, and I forget why Sebastian wasn't eligible. Either way, I ended up with the short straw. Everyone else is still riding in the car. Lucky me.

"They can have all the stuff we do, 'kay? Just keep it to themselves, right? Keep it in the townships and within themselves and leave folk like you and me alone."

"Ah . . . I'm sorry. I've lost the narrative thread here . . ."

He glances sideways at me skeptically for a few seconds before answering.

"Listen *China*, you come in my cab, you listen to what I have to say, 'kay? You don't like what I have to say, you have a problem with what I have to say, you wanna mess me around because of what I have to say?"

He reaches over and slowly pats the glove compartment in front of me.

"You want to mess me around, I introduce you to my fucking friend—"

"No problem. No problem," I mutter with my hand in front of my face.

He returns his gaze to the oncoming road and his posture to a more upright position.

"You know the only thing I hate more?"

"Do tell."

"The fucking yanks."

"What's that?"

"Fucking yankee bastards. All high and mighty, think they have the biggest dicks in the world. Think they're the world's police."

"Okay . . ."

"Oh come on, you can't tell me you've got a problem with *that* now? You love yanks or something?"

A response is problematic. If he hasn't noticed my accent by now, do I even bother to try and change it? Even if I attempt my best Afrikaans accent, will the change alone alert him to foul play? I decide to let it ride.

"No . . . I hate those . . . cocksuckers."

"Fuckin' a right you do! With their big fucking Hollywood movies and their *poofta* American football and their stupid *Friends* sitcoms—"

"Wait, you're angry at the sitcom *Friends*?"

"I just find it very unrealistic."

"I suppose that's actually a valid criticism."

"And fuck! The *kaffirs* there already think they own everything! The yanks let the animals out of the cages and now they run the zoo! And then they have the nerve to tell us we should do the same and look down on us until we do!"

"I don't . . . umm . . ."

"Fucking cunts. I tell you, *china*"—he points back at the glove compartment—"I'd do a yank worst of all. Maybe sing the American anthem while I do it, hey."

". . . yeah . . . uh, fuck those guys . . ."

"You know what's funny is that you sound a little bit like one of them."

"Ha! Me? That is funny . . ."

"Yah . . . something weird in your voice . . ."

"I just watch a lot of movies . . . Say listen, hate to change the subject, but do you know how close we are? And does my friend have all the correct info from you? Like, uh, if he needs to . . . follow up or something?"

"I'd say it's maybe another five to ten minutes. Your friends in the car have an invoice with all of the shop's info on it, but if you want to go home and look me up just for future reference—in case you get stuck sometime yourself— I'm under *Big Trouble, Little China Towing*."

"Wait, what's it called?"

"*Big. Trouble. Little. China. Towing.*"

"Like . . . like the *movie*?"

He slams on his horn in excitement.

"Fuck yes, like the movie! I can't believe you got it! I've been running this business for years, but no one ever gets it because no one has ever seen the movie! But you get it, right? Like—'*uh oh, your car broke down. Looks like you're in Big Trouble, Little China.*' This truck is called The Porkchop Express as well!"

"It's in my top five movies of all time."

"I fucking love that movie!"

"Wait, you? Why do you love that movie?"

"'Kay. First off: no blacks."

I open my mouth to dispute the ridiculousness of this claim, but in wracking my brain, I actually can't remember one. Christ.

"Okay. Let's say you were going to judge a movie on something other than the amount of black people in it. What's the next thing you like about that movie?"

"Man . . . The action . . . The battles . . . The fucking brilliant mystical shit."

"But it's all Chinese people and yanks."

"Eh, Kurt Russell seems like maybe he'd be the one good American oke. I like his attitude in that movie. And I've got nothing against the Chinese. I met some Chinese when I was in the military. They were good okes as well."

"But *not* blacks?"

"Listen *china*, don't make me repeat myself—"

"Nevermind. I like how they make him seem like kind of a screw-up for most of the movie, but then he finally becomes the big hero at the end."

"Fucking brilliant, right? 'It's all in the reflexes.' Ha!"

"And he's lost in this completely foreign culture the whole time, totally alienated, he even gets his shit stolen from him. But by the end, there's a mutual respect between him and that culture based on his actions when it mattered most."

"Haha, yeah. And how about those 'Three Storm' bad guys, eh? Kicking the fuck out of everybody else—"

"And like I mentioned, the hero—he's so clueless most of the time, but when he drinks that magic potion towards the end, he can—"

"'See things no one else can see. Do things no one else can do.'"

"Exactly! It's like—he had to take this completely weird magical drink in order to get the right perspective and energy. Only then could he do proper battle with the forces of evil and basically save the world."

"Yeah, the battles, right? Wicked fighting—"

"You could also say it's a story about friendship, too, I suppose. I mean, who are our real friends? The ones who are willing to follow us into the dark in the face of total uncertainty. That's what matters. Even if they come from different cultures."

"Yeah, *china* . . . uh . . ."

"The romance angle is really interesting, too, though. The hero jokingly flirts with the love interest the whole movie, but will they ever actually get together? Well they do, but it's not like 'happily ever after' because he's got to leave and they both know she's not going to be coming with him. And so they say goodbye . . . longing for each other in their eyes . . ."

The tires of the tow truck screech to a halt.

"We're here. Get out."

"Wha? Okay. Thanks."

He shakes his head as I open the door and start to get down from the cab.

"'Longing in their eyes'. *Jassus*. Fucking *poof*."

Romuald and Agnieska stumble up to the tow-truck driver to settle the final details while Sebastian and Thibault approach. We pow wow at the back of the truck.

"We lost a big chunk of time with that whole thing," Thibault begins.

"Thibault's worried we're not going to make it all the way back to The Khyber in time before it closes."

"We're going to make it. Remember you looked—"

"Right right, there's something wrong with your eyes, I remember." Thibault throws his hand up, not wanting to hear it.

"Hey!" shouts Romuald, peering up from some final paperwork. "This guy is based right up by where Nick Sutter lives. Maybe he knows him."

I see them talk for a few seconds more, ending with the tow-truck driver shaking his head 'no'. Thibault, Sebastian, and I meet silently with our eyes for a second, understanding the urgency.

"Hey Jack Burton!" I yell.

The tow-truck driver looks up.

"Any chance my friends and I can hitch a ride with you back to the neighborhood of your shop?"

"Are any of them fucking yanks?"

"No sir."

Sebastian turns to me. "But you—"

"Shh."

"I'll give you *chinas* a ride, Wang, but the rule is still the rule: only one in the cab with me."

"But then how do we get a ride? Where are the other two going to sit?"

"You're going to stand . . . here." He smacks the blue praying mantis of metal that is the truck's back, and laughs.

"No," says Thibault. "There's got to be a better way."

"There isn't. And you just said we were running out of time."

"Running out of time, *chinas*!" the tow-truck driver screams at our backs. "Leaving now."

"Sebastian, stay back with me. You're a bit better built for the back—no offense, Thibault. Plus you're too dark to be up front anyway."

"What?"

"Thibault, ride in the cab with him. Don't say anything to him at all but listen to everything he says and nod whenever you can. If you have to say something, use as many Afrikaans words as you can. Oh, and don't 'mess him around'. Ready?"

"Wait. 'Mess him around'? What the fuck does that mean?"

"I dunno what the fuck it means! Don't you? Afrikaners say that shit all the time!"

"Well yeah, I know what it's supposed to mean, but how do I know if anything I do is going to fucking 'mess him around' or not?"

"Just listen to the first couple of things I told you and it'll work out, trust me. Ready?"

"You owe me big for this," says Thibault, resigned.

"Me as well," seconds Sebastian. "More if we die."

"I promise I'll get you guys back next time I'm in town."

— — ———— — —

"OhfuckOhfuckOhfuckOhfuck."

"ShitShitShitShitShitSHIIIIIIIIIT!!!!!"

"AAAAAHHHHHHHH!!!!!!"

"HOOOOOOOOOOOOOOOAAAAAAGGGHHH-HHHH!!!!!!"

Roads pass by much faster when you're on the outside of a car than when you're on the inside.

"WE'REGONNADIEWE'REGONNADIEWE'REG ONNADIIIIIEEEEEEE!!!!"

"AH!AH!AH!AH!AH!AH!AH!"

My hands grip a metal rod attached to the large towing arm in front of me with all the might their white knuckles can muster as I stand with my back to the cab. My feet rest on a surface area about ten inches in diameter, the only flat one I could find. Through open cracks I can see the concrete below scream by at speeds I'd rather not think about.

Sebastian is in more of a reclined crouching position. He grips a bar similar to mine on the other side of the arm, but he rests almost parallel to the bed of the truck in a sort of cradle, with his feet braced in different points further down his side of the arm. He actually looks like Batman and Robin whenever they would rope climb the wall of a building in the old TV show.

Practically speaking, this would go better for both of us if we were wearing shoes.

"Oh god we're slowing down. Oh thank god."

I peer around my edge of the cab; we're inching up to a red light.

"Hang in there, Sebastian. Not so bad is it, ha?"

Sebastian gives me the dirtiest look I think he is capable of. Our driver yells something at us from the cab that I can't make out, and then screeches off again as the light turns green. He is clearly relishing this.

"FUUUUUCCCCKKK!!!!!!!!"

"NONONONONONONO!!!!"

We hit some large bumps and Sebastian begins to wobble in his cradle. I grab his shirt with one hand while keeping my other on the rod before we hit another bump, the biggest, and he nearly goes flying off the truck. He instinctively squeezes his hands around my wrist, and we both smile at each other hysterically, trying not to think about what almost happened. Sebastian decides my positioning is optimal and pulls himself up to stand the same way on his side of the truck. It's not often that you know the absolute dumbest thing you will ever do in your life while you are doing it. And at such a young age, too.

"Sebastian! I feel like we haven't talked enough since I've been here!"

"WHAT?"

"I SAID I FEEL LIKE WE HAVEN'T REALLY HUNG OUT ENOUGH SINCE I'VE BEEN HERE!"

"WHERE? ON THE BACK OF THIS TRUCK?"

"NO! IN SOUTH AFRICA! BUT I FEEL LIKE THAT'S BEEN MY MISTAKE! YOU'RE A PRETTY COOL GUY!"

"WELL . . . THANKS! I LIKE YOU AS WELL!"

"OH, THANKS! THAT'S COOL!"

We stop at another light. Sebastian opens his eyes and gulps. He closes them again and we both inhale deeply as the tires begin to peel out once more.

"So what kind of movies do you like?"

"WHAT???"

"I SAID WHAT KIND OF MOVIES DO YOU LIKE?"

"OH! I DON'T GET TO GO VERY OFTEN! THE FARM, YOU KNOW!"

"RIGHT! WELL LIKE HOW OFTEN?"

"WHAT?"

"WHEN'S THE LAST TIME YOU WENT TO THE MOVIES BEFORE TODAY?"

"OH . . . SEVEN YEARS AGO!"

"WHAT?"

"SEVEN! YEARS! AGO!"

"NO, I MEAN I KNOW I HEARD IT, BUT . . . SEVEN YEARS IS A LONG TIME!"

"I SUPPOSE!"

"WHAT DID YOU SEE?"

"I THINK IT WAS AN AFRIKAANS MOVIE . . . ABOUT FARMING!"

"A DOCUMENTARY?"

"NO IT HAD A STORY AND EVERYTHING!"

"OH! THAT'S NICE!"

"YEAH!"

"COOL!"

We stop at another light. Two girls pull up in a car next to us. They smile and wave. We wave back as coolly and as calmly as two barefoot teenagers on the back of a tow truck can. The light changes and we speed off again, but we only go a few hundred feet before screeching to a halt in the middle of the road. I try to peer into the cab as we idle but only a second or two passes before the passenger door opens, and Thibault climbs swiftly and nervously down.

"Go. Now. Go. RUUUUNNNNN!!!!!"

He takes off and Sebastian and I vault down after him as quickly and as ably as two barefoot guys jumping off the back of a tow truck can.

"COME BACK AND FUCK WITH THIS, *CHINAS*! HAHAHAHAHA!!!" our driver screams from behind us as we run. We hear the sound of the engine roaring back to life and the tires screeching up again, but we don't bother to look back to see which direction they're going in. Just run and run down side streets until everything is dark and undefined around us. If we don't know where we are, maybe he won't either. We finally stop in at an empty set of cross-streets.

"I told you not to mess him around!" I say, panting. Thibault kicks me in the shin.

"Oww! FUCK!"

"Mess him around?" Thibault pants. "I did exactly what you said to do! I was keeping my mouth shut while he was all '*kaffirs* this' and '*kaffirs* that'. Then he got angry I wasn't saying anything. He started shouting at me to answer him about something so I finally said that like, maybe, kind of, sort of, I wasn't in to hating *kaffirs* like he was and he slammed on the breaks."

"Holy shit, did he pull that gun on you?"

"Gun? It was a fucking dildo!"

Sebastian and I burst into laughter, as if it weren't already hard enough to breath.

"Oh yeah, very fucking funny, yes?"

"Did he threaten to 'mess you around' with it? HAHAHA!"

"Of course he fucking did!"

"HAHAHAHA!!!"

"AHAHAHAHA!!!"

"I can't believe that's what he wanted to do to all the people he hates."

"Oh yeah! And yanks, too! I should have offered you up as a sacrifice for Sebastian and me to go free!"

"I already dodged that bullet, buddy. Our guy isn't so good at picking up accents, and we bonded over a mutual love of *Big Trouble in Little China*."

"Congratulations. You're friends with a sexually deviant racist with good taste in movies."

"Hey man, there's friendship and there's self-interest. I only gave him enough to not get a dildo pulled on me."

"But who keeps a dildo in their glove box?" ponders Sebastian.

Tires screech in the distance and the man who keeps a dildo in his glove box and his tow truck turn onto our street, stopping a hundred yards away. He idles and shines his brights on us. We glare head-on into our fate, silent except for our panting. I think I hear a maniacal laugh but it's unlikely we'd hear that from here, and more likely I'm just on drugs and have seen too many movies. For a moment, I watch the scene from afar. I feel like I finally get the 'black comedy' now, and bust out into more laughter.

"Whooo! I did NOT see this end coming!" I throw my hands up.

Thibault and Sebastian stare over at me horrified, and I come back down quickly.

"Okay. Sorry. Still a little—you know."

The tow truck trembles as it revs up for confrontation.

Two lights blink at us from our left.

"What was that?"

"Looked like headlights."

The tow truck revs louder.

The headlights blink at us again, slower.

"Go. NOW."

We dash towards the headlights at Olympic speeds, screeching tires, dildos, and screaming motors in hot pursuit. The headlights continue blinking at us slowly as we run towards them. To me, they look like a smiling face, but then, I'm fucking high.

"Hey, if you guys had the time machine from *Back to the Future* right now, would you want to go back to earlier tonight when—"

"SHUT UP!" they yell in unison.

We're getting closer to our smiling headlights but I can hear our company getting closer, too. We can't turn back, lest we're turned to a pillar of dildo bait.

"It's a bus!" yells Sebastian.

"It's a Woodmere bus!" yells Thibault.

"IT'S MY BUS!!!" I yell.

The door is cranked open, and lo and behold, my bus driver sits in his usual seat, smoking a joint.

"*Eta, chanas.*" He eases out and smiles. The bus's engine is on and into gear in the span of about one second. We all grab the seats immediately behind my bus driver, going from zero to a game of chicken in another second. The tow truck speeds at us from about fifty feet away. Thibault, Sebastian, and I scream like girls. The bus driver laughs. He is still laughing when the tow truck swerves out of the way and crashes into a telephone pole.

Thibault and Sebastian flop back into their seats with sighs and closed eyes.

"How did you find us?" I ask the bus driver. He takes another hit off his joint and keeps laughing.

"I already tell you. You. Your friends—"

"I know I know. You see us. The corner. We *bemma* too much."

"You *bemma* too much."

— — —— — —

Thibault takes a hit and passes the joint to Sebastian.

"Okay"—he exhales—"so he's about my height."

"Well, actually he's a bit taller," says Sebastian just before taking a hit.

"Okay, well he's his height then." Thibault points at Sebastian, who passes the joint back to me. I abstain and pass back to the bus driver.

"Not really, perhaps a few centimeters taller than you and a few centimeters shorter than me."

"Okay. So however tall that is . . ." Thibault points at Sebastian again. "Got it so far?"

The bus driver takes another hit and stares at him blankly.

"Right . . . Let's see . . . His hair is brown," says Thibault as the joint is passed back to him.

"Well, shouldn't we specify if it's a light or dark brown?" asks Sebastian.

"Certainly that would help."

We are parked nowhere we can recognize, attempting to describe Nick Sutter's appearance to my bus driver. Every bus driver at Woodmere has driven every bus and every route and dropped off every kid on those busses at some point or another. They rotate semi-regularly for some reason. If my bus driver can remember Nick from a route, he'll remember where his stop was. It's a long shot. Good thing we're only working with certainties tonight.

Thibault inhales and makes wishy-washy gestures with his hands after passing the joint back on to Sebastian.

"So—lightish darkish brown hair."

"Kinda moppish cut," adds Sebastian before inhaling.

"Like a Beatle," adds Thibault.

"An early Paul maybe," says Sebastian.

"But not all the time," warns Thibault.

"Yes, he did cut it to something a little more contemporary in the middle of Standard 8," agrees Sebastian.

"Maybe like a Paul early and a solo John Lennon late," decides Thibault.

"Yes, that's right. Is this helping?" asks Sebastian.

The bus driver takes another hit and shakes his head slowly.

I would say there's a significant language barrier in our communications with my bus driver, but I would also say it doesn't seem to matter at all; he knows everything that's happening already anyway.

"It's not helping because you guys are possibly the worst two people on Earth at describing another person," I interject.

"Okay, well Mr. Smartee, why don't you try?"

"No. No, I'm not gonna try to describe Nick Sutter. I'm just gonna talk about *The Thing*."

"What?" Thibault and Sebastian both ask. I point to my cheek.

"*The Thing*!" I say in ghost-story tones.

"Oh yeah, *that* thing. Ugh," says Thibault.

"Oh, god." Sebastian winces.

"Yes. Our only chance of him remembering Nick is if he has seen or heard legends of *The Thing*, and that fateful two-week stretch in the beginning of Standard 8. A stretch in which Nick grew a pimple on his face, the scope and breadth of which will haunt my dreams till my dying day. At first it was just a blemish, a small whitehead—not uncommon for teenagers. But it grew. It grew larger and stronger. It conquered more land mass over time, changing colors like the chameleon as it matured, first white, then red, then a greenish tint."

"Oh god . . . stop . . ." Thibault insists, his hand over his eyes.

"No, Thibault. I've got to press on."

I turn to face my bus driver.

"It just kept growing and growing and nobody said anything. How could we? None of us had ever seen anything like it, even on our own worst faces. We were unprepared for the assault. Was he ill with something toxic? What could make a human produce something like that on their face? What was worse—he never did anything about it. Just pretended it wasn't there. It glared at and intimidated everyone it met, becoming the talk of school. Even though it looked like a wind-blown leaf could have punctured it and brought infinite relief to both Nick and the frightened townspeople, he refused . . .

"And then finally, Nick came back one Monday after a weekend and *The Thing* was gone, a large Band-Aid in its place. Nobody ever spoke of it to him and he never spoke of it to anybody. Little kids tell each other stories about it to scare themselves, not really knowing if they're true. But if you ever saw it . . ."

I move close to my bus driver's face. He eyes me skeptically while taking another hit.

". . . you would never forget . . ."

I put my hand up to my right cheek.

". . . the hideous, green and red, pulsing *Thiiiiiiinnngggggg*."

I pump my fingertips over my cheek slowly, adding a heart-pumping sound and my bus driver's eyes light up. He snaps his fingers, cranks the door closed, and starts the bus up into gear. I snap in response.

"He's got it. I'm heading to the back to chill."

"Mind if we come?" asks Sebastian.

"We don't usually get to sit at the back," says Thibault.

"I don't think it'll be an issue this time."

I sit in the last seat on the right and begin carving into the back of the seat in front of me with my house keys. Thibault and Sebastian each take seats in front of me, sitting on their knees so they can face me.

"So like—*something* is happening," whispers a smiling Thibault.

"Shh!" I continue carving.

"Yeeeaaahhh," enthuses Sebastian, "I think I'm starting to get what you mean about smoking and movies. I can feel it now, too. It's like . . . *something* is going on . . ."

"Shhhhh!!! Shut up you guys or you'll jinx it. They'll be time enough for sucking each other's dicks when we're all dead."

"What the fuck does that mean?" asks a befuddled Thibault.

"I don't know, actually. I just thought it sounded poetic."

"So why don't we just ask him to take us to Woodmere, though?"

"We need a package deal, Sebastian. Getting to Woodmere at this time of night isn't the biggest problem, but it will be completely deserted, and impossible to get out of, let alone for a straight shot to The Khyber. This guy won't chauffer us around that much, but Nick will, and in theory, he should already be close by."

"What are you carving?" asks Sebastian.

"I'm locking a variable into place, a piece of my history. This was my bus, so I want to mark the territory with a line in the historical sand: everything on one side has happened already and been printed to film, everything on the other side is yet to be determined and free. Now, when it's all said and done, you'll be able to trace back to this time period and refer to it in days/weeks/years 'ABC' for 'After Bus Carving'."

"That sounds deep," says Sebastian. "So what are you actually writing?"

"My name and the date."

"Hmm. I would hope for something a little more meaningful than that," says Thibault.

"Yes, but my keys are bad for this kind of work and this giant dick and balls someone drew on here in Sharpie takes up a lot of space."

The bus screeches to a halt and we all run up front to see the bright lights of a SPAR supermarket marquee stare back at us through the windshield.

"This is it. You guys head out and I'll be there in a second."

Thibault and Sebastian both slap five with the bus driver

as they exit. I sit down across from him and slightly behind in the first seat on the opposite side of the bus.

"You didn't tell me about the girl."

He laughs.

"Why tell you? There always more than one."

"I know that now. But what happens with this one? I did everything else you said so far. The last two were that I dance. I fly. Do I dance with the girl?"

"You already dancing, haha," he laughs and shakes his arms and hands above his head like a drunken Joburg club girl about to pass out at last call.

"But do I dance with the girl?"

"You go now, friend. If you too late, you no dance. You too late, you no fly. You too late, you still cry. Never stop less you change."

"Okay, friend. I hear you."

I shake his hand and hop down the steps of my bus for the last time. We all wave as he drives off into the night. He waves back with a light double-honk as a goodbye.

I always thought driving a bus was a lot harder than people make it look, which is funny, because the people who drive busses don't often seem to be rocket scientists. A school bus is an unwieldy chunk of long, heavy metal, sharing the same two-lane roads as compact cars and wagons, running on a schedule that stays more or less the same despite all of life's random imperfections, and filled with twenty to forty screaming seatbelt-less children. Now I know the only people who can handle that are guardian aliens.

13
DIVINING RODS

"Somewhere, somewhere close by is a man who can help us. I cannot find him alone. I need you. I need you to guide my sword. Please, guide my sword."

- Inigo Montoya, *The Princess Bride*

He's here. I can smell him."

I'm Al Pacino at the end of *Heat*; I've been tracking my prey for so long, I can just feel it in the air whether he's escaped or not. Thibault and Sebastian sit glumly on a curb while I look from one end of the parking lot to the other.

"Well he lives near here; it all adds up. But near doesn't help when trying to locate an exact person, and the leads have dried up," says Thibault.

"Yeah, we've just been sitting here with you looking up and down the lot for twenty minutes," adds Sebastian.

"I think we already did that today, too," says Thibault.

"Guys! Did you eat a bowl of quit soup a second ago while I wasn't looking? Have we learned nothing yet tonight?"

"I'm not slow-clapping for you," says Thibault. "I swear to fucking god—"

"I'm telling you I can feel it! He's here, or he'll be here later, or he's on his way here. Can't you feel his presence in the air? Can't you feel how far we've come?"

"Well, maybe that's it—you just think you feel it because we've invested so much and you don't want to give up, even though we have nothing else to go on right now," says Thibault.

"Yeah," seconds Sebastian. "Or like maybe we can abort one part of the mission and focus on the other more important one so we make sure we make it. It's getting late."

"We're not half-assing it, and this attitude sucks, guys. We're not as far as you think. It's not in time or distance. We're close out there." I wave my hand around in an imaginary aether to the side of me.

"The script is writing itself now. We pushed the wheel all the way up to the top of the mountain, and its momentum is taking over. We can ride it the rest of the way down if we just hop on top and hang on."

"Actually, in your analogy we'd be crushed and killed under its weight during the first revolution," counters Thibault.

"Well . . . we haven't been yet . . . So there."

"Touché."

"Look—let's just put our heads together, take a deep breath,"—I inhale deeply and close my eyes—"and think. I'm Nick Sutter. It's Saturday night. People like Martin Erasmus, who sometimes call me to hang out at night, probably won't do it tonight because they'll have *real* plans with *real* friends. The biggest party in town tonight ended in violence, but I wasn't there anyway, because I almost never get invited to parties. In short, I am lonesome tonight."

"So lonely," seconds Thibault.

"Very lonely," agrees Sebastian.

With my eyes still closed, I place my hands into the air in front of me, waiting for the universe to take them. I walk. Thibault and Sebastian don't follow until they hear tires screeching and a horn.

"What the fuck! You just walk in front of my car, moron?"

"Sorry, sir!" yells Thibault at my left, his hand now on my shoulder. "Our friend went blind very recently and he's still getting used to it!"

"This is really good progress, though!" Sebastian yells from my right, his hand on my other shoulder.

I continue to walk forward, but slower now. We stop.

"I need something," I say and turn left. The hands stay on my shoulders.

"I need a cheap yet reliable substitute for friendship since I don't have any real friends to hang out with."

I veer slightly to the right.

"People that will be good company the whole night without ever judging me."

A hard right now.

"I need fantasy because my life is based on it."

I stop. Back up three feet. Turn left.

"I need to escape reality to something a little more interesting. It's why I make so much shit up."

I speed up slightly. Thibault and Sebastian occasionally apologize to people in the parking lot I come close to inadvertently strangling.

"I need to fill up this evening with noise so I can't think about being alone. I need new exciting friends and new exciting stories so I can believe I am also an exciting person with an exciting story."

I stop and pivot ninety degrees to my right. We're very close now.

"I need to get all this easy, too, because I know it's not easy in real life. If it's going to be my fantasy, I might as well go all the way. I need to find my Saturday night friends and stories close by and accessible. I need to be able to experience them in the comfort of my own home, and accomplish this quickly and easily, with minimal fuss."

The hands drop from my shoulders as I walk what I know to be the last few feet alone.

"And if I can buy some candy, or ice cream, or soda or something while I'm getting it, even better."

I open my eyes. A sign proclaiming "LATE DROP" over a handled slot stares back at me. Of course—it's a video store.

— - ——— - —

"How's it guys? Welcome to MovieQuest. I'm happy to help you find something, but I do just want to let you know we'll be closing in ten minutes."

"We're looking for a guy a few centimeters shorter than me who may have a haircut like a young Paul McCartney or an older John Lennon," says Sebastian.

"No no, tell the *Thing* story again," says Thibault.

"Does a guy named Nick Sutter rent videos here?" I ask. "We were hoping we could maybe bribe you for his home address."

"Nick. Sutter . . ." He types the name into his computer.

"Ohhh, yeeeahh." A look of recognition appears on his face as he studies the screen. "Oh, but wait—are you guys just meeting him here then?"

"Wait. So he *does* rent here?"

"Why are we meeting him here?"

"Is he on his way?"

"Oh, well I'm just guessing you guys are friends of his. I didn't recognize the name at first, but looking at his rental history I know exactly who you're talking about. Now I can't give out anyone's address, but I don't have to, because he comes here almost every Saturday night about five minutes before close, picks two movies quickly and then goes. If you guys wanna wait here for the next minute or two I'm sure he'll—"

The video store clerk is interrupted by the ringing bell of the opening door behind us. We all turn to look.

"NICK!" we all shout.

Nick Sutter stands in the doorway of the video store in a green jacket, two videos in his hand and a confused look on his face.

"Hey guys," he says slowly, not sure what to make of the scene. "You guys rent here, too?"

I rush up to him.

"Nick, damn good to see you. Feels like it's been a while."

"Maybe six months."

"Wow, really? Since the uh—"

"Yeah."

"What did you rent there?"

Nick holds up the boxes of two videos for me to see: *The Rock* and *You've Got Mail*.

"*The Rock*—certainly over-the-top as action films go, but I like something about the color in the cinematography. I wouldn't recommend watching it while high, though. Now *You've Got Mail*—maybe it's just me but I think they went to the Tom Hanks-Meg Ryan well one too many times. Like it just isn't that fresh and quirky anymore, you know? What did you think of them?"

Nick eyes me suspiciously. "So why are you guys here?"

"Well I'm not gonna lie, Nick. We were looking for you specifically. I saw Martin Erasmus earlier today and he told me you're a guy a person can trust when the shit starts to go down; you don't lose your cool and you're a big help."

"Martin said that?" Nick forces out each word, uncertain.

"Yes . . . Slightly different wording, but yes. The point is, the shit is going down now and the three of us need your help in a big way. We need someone with your type of background to get us through this."

"My background?"

"Okay Nick," I whisper while looking around, "I don't want to talk too much about this *particular* subject because I know in your line of work you value discretion, but certainly we've all heard the stories . . ."

Nick all of a sudden remembers who he is supposed to be.

"Oh . . . Yes . . . Yes, of course . . . I appreciate that . . . Things could get hairy . . ."

"Yes, and nobody wants that, Nick. But the fact remains that we need your help. You might even be the only person who can help us."

"What's the mission?"

"We need you to drive us to Woodmere so I can get something from Kim Mercuri's house, then drive us back into town so we can crash a party at The Khyber restaurant and talk to Penelope Vermaak. Now I know this may not make a lot of sense up front, but you've got to believe me that—"

"Sure."

"What?"

"Yeah. I'll do that."

I stare at Nick blankly for a second. He doesn't seem to form individual expressions on one end of the emotional spectrum or the other. His is a face cut from construction paper.

"I mean . . . I'm going to have to call my lady friend and cancel our date for later tonight, but she'll understand," he reasons. "She knows things come up with me all the time because of the position I'm in."

"You'd really do that for us? I mean I wouldn't want to inconvenience—"

Nick waves me off with a smile and a headshake. "I understand when a mission is important."

"Excuse me," the clerk calls out from the counter, "we're closing up now." He motions to Nick. "Did you want to get anything quick, sir?"

"No, it's okay. I'm just dropping these and we're leaving."

"We're leaving?" Thibault perks up.

"We're leaving," I reaffirm.

"We're leaving!" Sebastian cheers.

The bells above the door ring again as we head out.

"Thanks for taking a MovieQuest, guys! Hope the rest of your night goes well!"

14

THE JIMI HENDRIX
EXPERIENCE
TAPE EXPERIENCE

"Mortimer! We're back!"

- Randolph Duke, *Coming to America*

Y ou boys are lucky you caught me with a little down time,
hey. Just got off something really heavy with a lot of heat
on it, and I'll have to head out again in another week or so.
Probably Morocco."

Thibault starts to snigger in the backseat and I punch
him in the kneecap.

"Oww!"

"Oh! Wow, Nick, we're even more appreciative of the help
then. Although, I'm sure our mission probably isn't nearly as
dangerous as the stuff you usually get into, right guys?"

We all guffaw at something that isn't particularly funny.

"Why are we heading to Woodmere and Kim's, though?"

"Well, frankly Nick I think I'm not at liberty to say. You know how things—"

"He's got to get a Jimi Hendrix tape from Kim's," answers Sebastian.

"Mmmm," Nick answers, perhaps not really listening. "Yeah, Kim and I . . ." He sighs and chuckles a single time. ". . . It's been a while."

"Wait, what?" I ask.

"Well look, I mean, it was long ago, we were both younger and more naïve. It was a fleeting thing, really. We knew it could never work given my lifestyle . . ."

"Oh, really?" My voice rises. "You and Kim—"

Thibault now punches me in the kneecap.

"Oww!"

"Oh, Nick! Come on, man!" says Thibault, pleading like a child. "You know the rest of us don't get around like you do—why are you just trying to make us jealous when you know we can't keep up?"

Nick smiles coyly, chuckling some more.

"Sorry, gents. Don't mean to rub it in. Like I said, it was a long time ago . . . Getting back, we head to The Khyber after Woodmere—what's the deal with that?"

"Well Floyd wants to see Pene—" Sebastian begins before I punch him in the kneecap.

"Ow! Why are we all doing this to each other?" Sebastian asks, rubbing his knee.

"I have to talk to the manager about a meal I ate there the other night," I say behind clenched teeth. "Very important."

"Cool, man. Let's do this, then."

Before long we pull into the dirt driveway of Woodmere

for my last time. Of course, I also thought we had pulled in for my last time this morning, much as I thought my bus had pulled in here for my last time yesterday morning. Like Bill Murray in *Groundhog Day*, I'm stuck in an infinite loop of recurring visits to Woodmere, each one seeming like it will be my last.

"Don't park too close to her house, maybe over by the basketball courts," I say.

"Not my first black ops mission, buddy," Nick counters without humor.

Campus is almost pitch black, not surprising given it's the middle of night and the school year is finished. Only the faint flickering of a few stray night-lights from exchange student housing can be seen. Forty feet in the distance, Kim's house sits like a black lump of volcanic rock in the dark, even more ominous than it was this morning.

"Okay. Nick—keep the engine running and ready to go. We should be out of here in less than ten minutes. If it takes longer, it's probably safe to assume we're being tortured and that we need your help."

"Affirmative," Nick answers.

"Sebastian—take a lookout position in that big tree just in between the edge of the basketball court and Kim's. If anything suspicious starts coming your way, give us a signal."

"What type of signal?"

"Er, I dunno—a birdcall or something."

"What species?"

"Sebastian, just make it loud enough that we can hear it, enough like a bird that if a person heard it randomly that's what they'd think it is, but enough like you that if we hear it, we'll know it's you and something's up."

"I'll do my best."

"Thibault—you're coming with me."

"Why am I going with you?"

"In case there's an ambush, or I get scared of the dark."

"*Jassus.*"

The three of us exit Nick's car and tiptoe slowly towards the black volcanic rock of Kim's house.

"Richard said they were gone all weekend, right?" whispers Thibault.

"Shhh!" I say.

Sebastian speed-tiptoes over to the tree and is up it and out of sight in seconds.

"Didn't Richard take off for the rest of the weekend after we left as well?"

"Shh!"

"I'm just wondering why we're tip-toeing and whispering."

"Shut up. You are a crappy spy," I scream-whisper at him.

"Whatever."

The front door is locked. This is somewhat unusual but not crazy considering everyone went out of town for the weekend. Some door or window is always unlocked in this house, though. The Mercuri women have never had any possessions of any significant value to protect, nor a fear to try and protect it. Of course, that was *before* they started hanging on to Jimi Hendrix tapes that didn't belong to them.

We tiptoe around to the other side of the house. Kim's bedroom window is cracked a few inches open, her white curtains still fluttering inside. A bright moon hangs in the now blue-black sky overhead, and the curtains glow with moonlight. I gently push the window further open. It creaks deafeningly with each inch. Thibault and I look around us frantically in every direction but nothing stirs. We step into the room from the window sill.

The house is deathly still. Somewhere outside of Kim's room I can hear that grandfather clock of hers ticking. The air is thick and stuffy despite the window being open. I breathe deep.

"Gosh, I can still smell her here."

"Well, she lives here, Sherlock. Not much of a surprise. Stay focused."

"Sorry. If I were a Jimi Hendrix tape, where would I be?"

"Just do that thing you did in the parking lot to find Nick."

"The room's not that big, Thibault. If I walk two feet in any direction without looking, I'll trip and crack my head open. It's quicker if we actually just look for it in a few places that seem likely."

Thibault and I hunt for my tape like dads trying not to wake a sleeping baby, picking up items, looking under them and placing them back down gently exactly where we found them. Briefly opening and closing boxes. I finally come across a box under her bed that reads "TAPES" on it. I pull it out into the moonlight.

"Cross your fingers," I tell Thibault.

I open the top of the box and Jimi's face from the cover of my tape stares back at me, the first tape on top.

"Bingo," I say.

"Hallelujah," says Thibault.

I hold the tape up in the moonlight like the sword of Excalibur, just pulled from the stone, righteous power coursing through my veins. Jimi's eyes flash twice as lights from outside hit it. Nick. Nick just flashed his headlights twice.

"CACAW! CACAW! HOOT! HOOT! HOOT! GNAH GNAH!" Sebastian screams from the tree.

"For fuck's sake, keep it down!" Thibault whisper-screams back out the window at him. "We're ten feet away. We can here you!"

"Right," Sebastian scream-whispers back from somewhere in the tree, "but there's a car coming this way!"

Thibault and I line up by the window and see two headlights moving slowly down the dirt driveway towards us. Nick kills his car and slinks down into his seat as the other car comes into view.

"Who the fuck is that?" Thibault asks.

"That's Ms. Mercuri's car," I say, swallowing hard.

We slink back down the wall in a panic, crouching beneath the sill. I pocket my tape and shove the box roughly back under the bed.

"Fuck, they're supposed to be gone all weekend!" curses Thibault.

"Why don't you go tell them that?" I whisper-ask sarcastically.

"Maybe I will!" he whisper-snarls back. Headlights shine brightly through the window above us before turning off as the car comes to a stop. The tree outside may be trembling, or maybe I'm just imagining it. The engine stops.

"What do we do now?" Thibault mouths in silence.

"They have to come around front before we jump out here," I mouth back, pointing.

"Good plan," Thibault mouths.

Car doors open and then slam shut a few seconds later to a soundtrack of the Mercuri women screaming and cursing at each other in Afrikaans. We hear the arguing move away from the window until it's almost inaudible from where we are. The lock of the front door begins to turn.

"Go."

I grab Thibault by the shirt and nearly throw him out of the window as he stumbles over its sill and is promptly tackled by Sebastian descending from the tree. They bump various body parts nastily, and hold their mouths to stifle screams while dancing away in pain. Mercuri curses can be heard getting closer from the living room. I vault out but am no more graceful, landing on my chest and getting a mouthful of dirt in the process. I'm about to use my highest gear of escape when I notice the tape has already fallen out of my pocket in my jump, *and* I forgot to close Kim's window back to where it was.

In one fluid super-maneuver I adapt from *American Ninja II*, I roll headfirst back to the window, snatch up my tape, and push the window back in as gently as I can. I duck away to the side of the window just as Kim's bedroom door opens and her voice becomes present and immediate. She turns on the light, and pushes the window back open, the curtains fluttering out. She stops yelling at her mother for a second. She's looking out the window, correctly feeling like something is amiss in the world around her. Thibault and Sebastian have made it back to Nick's car, and now they all hunker down out of view.

"Whose car is that out there?" she asks back to her mother in English.

Hearing her English speaking voice sends a shiver through me. I haven't heard it in days. A week even? That voice used to mean so much to me. I suppose there is some great metaphor about our relationship happening right now, something about us being so close to each other and yet so far, like the night we spent at Abe's after she dumped me. Or speaking different languages. Not seeing eye to eye. Hiding the truth rather than confronting it. I could go on like this all night. Or until I'm arrested and thrown in jail.

"What are you on about now?" Ms. Mercuri screams back from the living room.

"There's a car out there by the basketball court. Somebody parked their car there."

"So what?" Ms. Mercuri yells. "You gonna tell people where they can park their car now, too?"

Kim huffs and begins cursing at her mom in Afrikaans again. She turns away from the window and her voice decreases in volume as she heads back to her living room. I decide to make a break for it, clutching my Jimi Hendrix tape in white knuckles as I run. In my head, I see Jimi on The Dick Cavett Show in the late 60s.

Dick Cavett: "Jimi, can you talk a little bit about your music, what you're going for, what it means?"

Jimi: "Well you know it's all about cats coming together and digging what I call 'sky music'. And you know, you can listen to it, or if you're into something else, you can steal the record out of your ex-girlfriend's house in the middle of the night and run away with it."

"Go. Go. Go."

Nick guns the engine as I slide back in. Thibault and Sebastian join in the chorus of 'go' and we spin out into a donut of dirt and dust before screaming back up the dirt road and out of Woodmere, finally and forever, cheering and screaming like madmen. When we're finally minutes away, the air quiets and we settle into our seats. I stare at Jimi on the cover of my tape, a weird smile on my face. Jimi smiles and winks back. Thibault notices my look.

"What's up?" he asks.

"I still never saw her again, Thibault. I heard her voice. We were only a few feet apart. But I never saw her face again."

Robert DeNiro in *Raging Bull* pops into my head. His character, Jake Lamotta—the 'Raging Bull'—is fighting Sugar Ray Robinson and Robinson is pummeling him. It's bad. And brutal. Jake knows he's beaten. But when the ref finally stops the fight, he smiles at Robinson from a puffed-up bloody face, clinging to the last bit of pride he has left: Sugar Ray never knocked him down.

"You couldn't put me down, Ray," he says, laughing. "You couldn't put me down."

I stare at Jimi Hendrix again and chuckle.

"So long, K. You couldn't put me down."

15

STONE FREE

"Get on me, Burt. I can't lose."

- Fast Eddie Felson, *The Hustler*

In all the time I've lived here, Johannesburg has never looked so peaceful, so pretty. Industrialized areas set against a backdrop of mountains and dry brush fly by as we crest over hills and down into valleys of highway. A petrol station appears every few kilometers, looking noble in its well-lit loneliness. A sliver of screaming air slips through Nick's slightly cracked window, dissolving into an almost soothing white noise, like ocean waves.

The road around us is empty and quiet. I can't remember seeing a car for the last twenty minutes. Maybe it's too late. The pale strip of skin where my watch used to be still hasn't learned to tell time, and no one else has a watch. Perhaps The Khyber is closed and Penelope is gone. If it weren't still dark out, I would say it's possible I already missed my flight; all sense of time has deserted us. The only thing we know and can feel in our bones is that we're on borrowed time.

But it doesn't matter. Even if The Khyber is closed and Penelope is gone, it won't matter. Because we've finally found the moment. And we're locked into it. The one I dreamed up this morning in the dark with an aching head and dried blood in my nose. I am the proud phoenix rising from the ashes of shame. And we are finally following the moment all the way, without hesitation, even if it takes us over that final cliff into oblivion. Like One-Eyed Willy's rogue pirate ship sailing off into the sunrise: directionless and beautiful in its chaos.

The final variable of our African night waits poised to lock into place. The closer we get to it, the more a sense of inevitability takes over. The road shepherds us along like an airport walkway: our natural movement toward Destiny is doubled by movement underneath us.

"What's the plan for The Khyber?" asks Thibault.

"You guys distract everyone else while I talk to Penelope."

"That's a bit more of a goal than a plan," Sebastian comments as if it's a question.

"It's a plan. Just rough."

"Why do we have to distract anyone? Why can't you just go up and talk to her?"

"Well, for one she's working. For another, she's dancing at some private event there for some foreign dignitaries. Our presence is probably not welcome."

"Thanks for the heads up," sneers Thibault.

"Well, great. How do we distract them then?" asks Sebastian.

"Just have Nick make up a bullshit story—"

I punch Thibault in the kneecap again.

"Oww! You have *got* to stop doing that!"

"I'll quit tomorrow, I promise. Nick, what Thibault was trying to say is that perhaps someone with your—*specialized training*—might be able to provide some high-level subterfuge for us to work with."

"Consider it done."

"'Consider it done,' he says," I repeat and we all lean back into our seats, spanning a minute in silence as more countryside flies by. Nick finally speaks first.

"Hey, you said we went to Kim's to get a tape, right?"

"Yeah."

"And did you get it?"

"Oh yeah."

"Do you want to put it on?"

Thibault, Sebastian, and I look at each other in subtle confusion. Somehow this idea never occurred to any of us; the music on this tape was so supplanted by the *idea* of it. I pass the tape up to Nick and he puts it in, turning the volume way up before it's even audible.

The first slide guitar noodles of "May This Be Love" kick in immediately, as if the tape were cued to it. They descend over Mitch Mitchell's patient drum roll until a crash of cymbals announces Jimi's singing.

"*Waterfall . . . Nothing can harm me at all . . .*"

Jimi's liquid guitar and Noel Redding's bass saturate the air inside the car and soak into the upholstery. We roll down all the windows, breathing the smell of the smoky night air into our nostrils and mouths. The rest of the space is filled with Mitch's smooth and rolling tribal tom march. Could Mitch have made it as the musical director of the Maasai Mara tribe?

"Waterfall . . . Don't ever change your ways . . . Fall with me for a million days . . ."

I lean back into my seat and the upholstery wraps its arms around me. I close my eyes, but not all the way. Through slits, the streetlights pass by overhead like the perforated edges of celluloid film. Everything is in soft focus. This could be our final scene: the four of us in *Thelma & Louise II*, all holding hands as we careen off the edge of a peak in the Drakensburg mountain range. *'Let's just keep goin', Nick,'* I would say, teary-eyed, and a slow-mo of his hatchback plummeting into doom would fade out into white.

That might be an ending that resonates with audiences. People might not laugh at the box for the movie if they saw it in their local video store. But it would still be a story of tragedy and unfulfilled potential. And we've got one last act to complete.

The car slows down.

"We're here," Nick says.

The entire Khyber property is located within a large fenced-in enclosure, including the restaurant and parking lot. Around the restaurant itself is dense foliage of whatever locale the place is trying to represent. A sign on the main entrance reads: "The Khyber: A Feast for the Senses!" This refers to the fact that—in addition to having great cuisine—The Khyber also boasts a spectacular floorshow of belly dancing, highlighted by Penelope for as long as I've known her. Apparently the idea that young people can't have serious jobs is an American thing; Penelope has been dancing her whole life, and her skills are well-regarded by her professional peers and audiences alike. I've only seen her dance one other time but I know the girl is good.

"Can I help you gents?" A valet leans down to Nick's window.

"We're here for the party," Nick responds.

The valet eyes us each individually.

"Are you on the list?"

"Perhaps, but I doubt it. Our arrangements were made at the consulate very last minute," says Nick.

"I'm sorry, gents. It's a private party. I can't allow you in unless you're on this list." He pats a clipboard in front of his chest. Thibault opens his mouth to argue, but Nick cuts him off.

"Okay, we're just going to go make sure our reservation is sorted out and we'll be back."

Nick turns the car around and we head back out of the enclosure.

"What the fuck was that?" demands Thibault. "We barely put up a fight!"

Nick casually waves him off.

"He had the high ground, Thibault. Never go to war without the high ground. We'll have to get inside some other way, and then take it from there. And we'll need to be face-to-face with a higher-up. No leverage out here."

We park just outside the grounds of The Khyber.

"Oh," Thibault responds, actually surprised by the soundness of Nick's reasoning, "the high ground."

16

TWIST & SHOUT

"You can never go too far."

\- Ferris Bueller, *Ferris Bueller's Day Off*

Listen," Nick offers in more hushed tones, "neither of us wants an international incident here, do we?"

The three men in front of us begin shouting at us again, all in different languages. One even yells at the other one for how he is yelling at us.

"I'm telling you boys just one more time," one finally takes center stage, "this is a *private* party. If you are on the list to attend this *private* party, I will let you in. If you are not, I'll have to ask you to leave, and if you insist on arguing and you refuse to leave, I'll have to call the police."

"The police?" Nick asks incredulously. "I wouldn't be so hasty on that decision. I myself can call on my friend Captain Murtaugh from Joburg's 35th precinct, and let me tell you, he goes to bed early on his off nights, and would *not* appreciate a call from me this late."

Our main opposition waves his hand unimpressed, and the two men around him begin shouting at us again in different languages. Thibault and Sebastian respond in kind, angrily yelling gibberish back at them while brandishing handfuls of useless paperwork pulled from Nick's trunk.

". . . If he can't review this Sri-Lankan accord immediately, it won't be able to pass in tomorrow afternoon's legislative session!" Thibault argues.

". . . Two thousand underwater hotels off the coast of Dubai by the beginning of next year. We've got the backing. Now I'm supposed to meet my contact here to begin the paperwork . . ." Sebastian rambles.

Various kitchen and wait staff gather momentarily to witness the scene before moving on.

"Now I'm tired of this bureaucratic nonsense, here," says Nick. "I painstakingly describe our credentials to your guys out there so they can finally let us in, now you want to give us more trouble and make us do it all over again. That's not a way to treat your customers with respect."

This of course, is completely untrue. After parking outside, we were all able to hop the back fence and sneak in without the valet noticing. After all, it's a restaurant, not a fortress. It might have been nice to avoid this bit altogether, though. The maitre'd's nostrils flare and his eyes bulge at Nick's last suggestion of impropriety. The men all begin yelling again, while Thibault, Sebastian, Nick, and I all yell back in force.

". . . breaking ground on thirty thousand oil wells by dawn!"

". . . needed for a deposition at the consulate immediately!"

". . . never treated with such disrespect in all my life!"

This is getting us nowhere.

Amidst the cacophony, two drunken middle-eastern businessmen stumble their way to the bathroom laughing, arms wrapped around each other's shoulders. Nick sees his opportunity and takes it.

"Heeeeyyy!! My friends!"

The Siamese contraption turns in clumsy unison to look at us, confused looks between them. The rest of us pick up on Nick's lead quickly.

"Heeeeyyy!!" we all shout in various forms with arms wide.

"Heeeyyy!!" they shout back, and within moments we are all hugging and backslapping, Nick going for it most of all.

". . . haven't seen you in too long!"

". . . haha! Watch out for this guy, huh!!"

". . . oh the times we had!"

One of the two men talks to the maitre'd briefly, shrugging as he talks, something along the lines of 'yeah, I guess we know these schmucks somehow.' The maitre'd shakes his head and begrudgingly points us all back to the restaurant.

"See, I told you our friends were in there," Sebastian says defiantly.

"Yes, extremely disappointing this had to go on for so long," Nick says, his arm now wrapped around the shoulder of the other businessman like we first saw them. Nick slams down a hundred-rand note on the maitre'd's desk.

"I want a round of drinks for all my friends here, and I don't want to be disturbed with such nonsense again."

"Holy shit, he really is Abe Froman," Thibault whispers in my ear.

"*Now* something is happening, Thibault," I respond with a grin.

The maitre'd accepts the note with a dirty look and a "yes, sir." He turns his anger on a waitress, screaming at her in whatever language to get us to a damn table already. Our new businessmen friends have forgotten they needed to use the bathroom, and the one arm-in-arm with Nick is almost asleep standing up.

The rest of the restaurant doesn't fare much better. A private party makes sense when you plan on having a bunch of government officials, dignitaries, and businessmen losing their minds on alcohol. Men in varying degrees of dishevelment wrap more arms around more shoulders, sing off-key, flirt angrily with waitresses, and knock drinks over. Aside from the waitresses, there isn't a female in sight. The floor is empty.

"Is the dancing done?" I ask the waitress.

"This five minute break. Last dance coming now."

I turn to Thibault.

"Penelope must be in a backstage area somewhere. I'm going to find her. You guys stay here, have some drinks with our new friends, and enjoy the show."

"But we don't drink."

"You should start; it's Miller time." I pat him on the shoulder.

I creep along a back corridor looking for a dressing room. I pass the kitchen, hosts of skeptical eyes watching me. I finally find a room marked "ENTERTAINMENT" and knock on it.

"Yes?" a woman's voice calls from behind it.

I crack the door open and step inside to see myself surrounded by half-naked women.

"Ah! Ah!" they begin shrieking and covering up with hands or whatever clothes they have in those hands. I cover my eyes with my hands and begin rambling as fast as I can.

"I'm sorry! I'm sorry! I'm just here to see my friend Penelope! It's very important! You see I'm leaving tomorrow—"

"FLOYD?"

I look between a crack in my fingers, and I can make out Penelope at the back of the room in front of a makeup mirror, turned around and eyeing me incredulously.

"Hey Pineapple," I say sheepishly.

"WHAT THE FUCK ARE YOU DOING HERE? And why are you dressed like Richard Koening?"

"PENELOPE!" says an older dancer to her, shocked.

"Oh . . . Sorry, Claire. I know I don't usually use that kind of language but I'm just shocked to see him here!"

"Ah! Ah!" one girl continues to shriek, stretching a thin piece of beige cloth to try and cover both her bra and panties.

"Put a sock in it, Samantha," says Claire. "It's nothing people haven't seen before."

Samantha stops screaming with a shrug and goes back to getting ready.

Penelope rushes up, pushing me in the chest.

"SERIOUSLY. What are you doing here?"

I smile goofily.

"You said you wanted to see me again, right?"

"I said I *would* see you again, not that I *wanted* to, and certainly not right here right now! You're gonna get me fired!"

A knock comes at the door. It cracks imperceptibly and a voice comes through: "Fire dance in two minutes, girls!"

Penelope looks at me, exasperated.

"But you do . . . like . . . want to see me . . . right?"

She smiles in spite of herself, blushing slightly.

"AHA! I knew it! You want to see me!" I hop up and down briefly.

She punches me in the arm.

"Oww!"

"Yeah, so! You're here, trying to ruin my career over it."

"No, that's not it. I came here for a few reasons. Boy, you look really pretty in this makeup, by the way . . ."

"Penelope! Are you ready?" Claire yells at her.

Penelope runs back over to her makeup mirror and makes sure she's got everything.

"One minute, girls!" Claire yells to the room.

"WOOO!!" the girls yell back, a marine-like battle cry.

"Um . . . like I said . . . there were a few things . . ."

"Go on, I'm listening," Penelope says, adjusting a fake eyelash.

I look around at some of the girls who are now curious and staring.

"Well our goodbye earlier—"

"Stunk," Penelope says flatly.

"Yes. I wanted a better one."

"And?"

"Aaaaand of course I wanted to see you dance one last time . . ."

"That's not it. I've got thirty seconds so you better stop stalling."

"What are we going to do with 'im, Penny?" asks a girl in a rough Cockney accent. "When Aashiq comes to get us for da dance, 'e's going to see 'im."

Another girl tosses me a black cloth. She sits in a chair with her ankle wrapped.

"Let him play The Pole," she says.

"Grace!" Penelope turns to her.

"Oh come on, Penny! We done this a thousand times. The

Pole never does anything except shake her hips and ass in the center of the stage. They don't even see any other part of her except her eyes. You only gave it to me because of my ankle."

I put the cloth over me and—sure enough—it covers every part of me except my eyes and naked feet. Penelope looks down at them.

"I was going to tell you that you have to take your shoes off, but I see you came prepared to dance."

"Always. And it's a long story," I mumble through the cloth.

"Tell it to me afterward," Penelope says, and lights two torches in front of my face. She looks me in the eye over the flames for a moment. That's the look I came back for.

"You better dance your ass off."

The door is pounded on twice.

"Now, ladies!" yells Claire.

"WOOO!!" yell the ladies.

They begin to file out. Grace stays in her chair, handing me some gloves. "I'll make you proud, Grace."

"Break a leg, not an ankle. Nice to meet you."

"Nice to meet—"

Penelope pushes me in front of her out the door, past the glaring eyes of Aashiq. She brings up the rear, holding her lit torches with her free hand.

Showtime.

"Gentlemen! The Khyber is proud to present our fabulous dancers for the final time tonight!" Aashiq says into the microphone as he enters the room.

The crowd cheers and spouts out raucous catcalls. From my view just behind the stage I can make out Thibault, Sebastian, and Nick leading the charge, their fists pumped in the air, joined by several more new best friends. I'll be damned.

"Gentlemen! We present to you—the only place in Johannesburg you can see this, mind you—The Dance of Fire, featuring The Khyber's own jewel, Penelope Vermaak!"

The men cheer wildly again, while introductory music slowly begins and girls file onto stage. The cheers increase.

"Remember what Grace said. Center stage. Shake ass and hips," Penelope whispers in my ear.

"Okay, but can I just tell you one—"

Penelope elbows me in the back and I am in the middle of the stage. The men in the audience "oooh" and "aahh" for the man-woman in black while the girls up front eye me nervously. I can see Thibault and Sebastian slowly turn to each other with disbelieving looks on their faces. I wink at them and the music hits full blast.

The girls begin to dance around me, spinning and twirling with arms above heads, hips swaying from side to side in sharp motions. I start shaking my ass, slowly and without artistry at first, but then picking it up after a few seconds. I almost break into a cabbage-patch but remind myself to stay in character at the last minute. The girls all simultaneously produce multicolored scarves from their waistbands and continue to dance around me, fluttering them my way, before all laying them on me as they rotate. I now look like a multicolored barber pole. The men cheer as the music crescendos and Penelope enters the stage brandishing her fire.

The rest of the girls move to the edges of the stage as Penelope takes over, whirling and twirling her flaming batons in front, behind, and around her. I shake my money-maker in back of her and she turns to me smiling. Penelope always smiles, but especially when she dances. She moves closer to me, then around me in circles as part of her routine.

Flames whiz by my ears. She dances facing me for a moment. Our eyes lock and I feel the energy again. I know she does, too. She laughs and turns back to the crowd for her ending, her torches turning to spinning Tasmanian devils of flame moving at supersonic speeds. To me, they look like they are cutting a hole in the air, in the fabric of reality. The crowd screams and claps uncontrollably as she finishes on one knee. The girls all wave and blow kisses. I figure I should, too. A girl next to me pulls my hand down as deftly as she can.

"The Pole never waves."

"Sorry."

We all shuffle off stage and back into the dressing room.

I pull off the cloth and the girls cheer and clap. I fix my matted hair, wipe the sweat from my brow, and give a small wave and bow. Penelope plops down in her chair in front of her makeup mirror. She smiles and shakes her head at me, as if she can't believe what just happened. I almost can't believe it myself.

"Did I tell you that you look really pretty tonight?"

"Yes, but you can tell me again."

"You look very pretty tonight."

"Thank you. You too."

"Thank you," I say, and put my cloth back on for a last dance around the room, the girls all clapping out a rhythm and cheering.

17

ABOUT A GIRL

"And I'm thinking to myself, Jeez, I should stop ruining my life searching for answers I'm never gonna get, and just enjoy it while it lasts."

- Mickey, *Hannah and Her Sisters*

Y ou now have my undivided attention," Penelope says.

We stand on the back patio of The Khyber. She's changed into her street clothes and pulled her hair back, although her heavy makeup is still intact, glowing eyes bursting out of dark purple and black pools. In one corner of the patio, Thibault and Sebastian talk quietly at a table, sipping Shirley Temples, looking like old friends in their fifties talking politics. In the other corner of the patio, a group of ten or so businessmen smoke and drink while gathered around Nick, who is telling a yarn. He hits an important point, and they all bust into laughter, patting him on the back and throwing their arms around him again.

"*Jassus*, is that Nick Sutter?" Penelope looks over, distracted by the laughter.

"Yes. He's our facilitator for the evening. I thought I had your undivided attention, though."

"Yes. Sorry. You were going to tell me what was so important that you had to come here in the middle of the night on your last night here without telling me in order to almost get me fired."

"Oh, come on! I was good, wasn't I?"

"You were . . . passable."

"I'll take passable."

"TALK."

Everything tenses up.

"Okay . . . Well . . . Um . . . So, like . . . So like—have you seen that newer *Good Will Hunting*? The scene with Robin Williams—'I had to go see about a girl'?"

"No. I never saw it."

"Oh . . . Okay . . . What about *Pretty in Pink*? With Molly Ringwald? She's got this friend who she doesn't know—"

"Haven't seen it. I don't watch a lot of movies. You know that. Not realistic enough."

"Huh. Well. Okay. What about—"

She grabs me by my shirt and looks me in the eye, like an angry detective roughing up a snitch.

"No movies. You have something to say. SAY IT."

"I . . . I like you, Pineapple."

I shrink back off my toes with the weight and tension that's been lifted. Penelope lets go of my shirt and her mouth opens slowly.

"And . . . I think . . . you like me too."

She looks down, touching her face. I can only see the top of her head now but can tell by the little shiver in it that she's crying.

"Why do you do this now?"

"I know. I'm sorry. It's just . . . well, you know I made some bad decisions with who to spend all my time with . . ."

She doesn't answer or look up. Her head trembles more with each tear, though.

"And you know . . . I'm like really bad at picking up signals—"

She looks up at me instantly, her face now red and tear-stained and bleeding mascara, and punches me in the chest.

"YOU'RE A FUCKING IDIOT AT PICKING UP SIGNALS!" She wipes away the running makeup in one swift graceful motion, as if she had just expelled the demon.

I take her hands softly in mine.

"I know. I'm sorry. Why did you never say anything to me, though? I mean I get it if you were shy and formal like other girls, but you're not like other girls."

"No I'm not shy," she begins, looking down at our hands, "but I don't believe in forcing anything in this life. You do your best, but you never try to move faster than the world around you or take shortcuts because you end up paying for them.

"I knew there was something with us from the day I met you . . . I knew you knew it too, but you didn't *really* know it, and I couldn't tell it to you, especially when you were caught up in all that *other* crap with those other people. I knew you would have to figure it out on your own or not at all. And maybe you would and maybe you wouldn't. Either way, I was going to keep being your friend, because we started as friends, and I love being your friend, and friends who really care about each other stay friends."

I can hear in her tone a subtle jab at Kim.

"That said"—she plays with a thread of Richard's shirt as she moves closer to me—"I was pretty sure you would figure it out eventually, I just didn't think you would do it at the LAST. POSSIBLE. SECOND."

She points into my chest to emphasize each of the last three words.

"I figured it out. Better late than never. If your magical mystical stuff keeps coming true, I might have to start believing it."

"You should try it sometime. With all the time you spend watching made-up lives, you could stand to notice a little 'magical mysticism' in the real world around you."

"I think I did tonight. We needed a lot of it to get here."

My hands are on her hips now, and I feel the warmth of her body close to mine. Our energies dance in the heat together, holding each other tightly.

"Yeah. You never did tell me how you got here. Or why you're with all these guys. I thought you were going to that party."

"I did. But I did some thinking there, talked to a few people, and realized I wanted to spend my last few hours here with the people I actually care about. You were right, Penelope. I figured it out, but I figured out more than just how I feel about you. Up to now, I've let everything happen to me, and never fought for anything on my own. I always pre-emptively found reasons why everything couldn't work and I shouldn't do it, rather than ever thinking about why I should.

"There are a million reasons I shouldn't have come here to see you tonight, but I came with the one reason I should have—I wanted to see you. I wanted to talk to you. I wanted to feel what it's like to be near you one more time, and I'm not thinking about tomorrow. Plus our ending stunk, so I decided to change it."

Penelope wraps her arms around my waist and smiles.

"You knew what you were doing when you got up this morning."

"Wait, what?"

"You went for it."

"Do you realize you just said the line from——"

Penelope pulls me in to kiss her. Sparks explode inside me and I'm pretty sure I whimper like a dog. The heat pushes out from our pressed-together bodies. Our energies play Twister.

This would be a perfect ending, us burning up in flames of supernatural emotion, brighter than Penelope's torches. I'm not looking for perfect endings all the time anymore, though.

To our left, Thibault and Sebastian begin a slow clap. Nick and his audience notice and join in, adding hooting and hollering. Penelope and I pull apart, giggling. The business-men see she is the star of the show, and all rush over to fawn over her. They kneel at her feet, kissing her toes through her sandals. They kiss her hands and propose marriage. She laughs and blushes, still looking at me. Real magic.

The door opens and Aashiq brings out the trash.

"Good show tonight, Penelope," he says sternly, "but tell Grace she was a little weak."

"It's the ankle, Aashiq. She knows she was a little off tonight."

He nods and heads back inside.

"I told you," she says.

"Everyone's a critic."

18

GOODBYE WAVE

*"Well, all I'm saying is that I want to look back
and say that I did the best I could while I was
stuck in this place. Had as much fun as I could
while I was stuck in this place. Played as hard as
I could while I was stuck in this place."*

- Dawson, *Dazed and Confused*

And then Nick was all like—'don't make me call Sgt.
So-and-So at the police' and I damn near lost it!" says
Thibault.

"AHAHAHAHA!"

"HAHAHAHHA!"

"Sebastian is screaming about his forty thousand dildos
he needs to get a work order for or whatever!"

"HAHAHAHAHA!"

"HAAAAAHHH!"

"Oh god, don't mention dildos! The tow truck?" Sebastian
reminds us.

"Oh yeah, is your ass still sore from getting 'messed
around', Thibault?"

"AAAAAAHHHHHHHAAAAAHAHAHAA-HAHA!!"

"AHAHAHAHAHAHA!!"

"Shut up. At least I wasn't on stage in a dress."

"Oh, I thought I worked it rather well up there . . ."

"Nick, so you didn't know those guys at all then?" asks Sebastian.

"Of course not!"

"AHHAHAHAHAHA!"

"They were so drunk it didn't matter, though!"

"HAHAHAHAHA!"

"'This is an outrage!'" I pretend to imitate Nick, hoisting my finger in the air.

"Do you know who I am?" Sebastian adds with an even more theatrically raised finger.

"AHAHAHAHAHA!!!"

"HAHAHAHAHAHA!!"

Thibault is looking at a piece of paper pulled from his pocket. It's my list of *Ferris Bueller* plot points from earlier. He's examining the bullet points.

"You know . . . I think we ended up finishing your remake after all. We finally went back to Woodmere to 'rescue your love from school', Nick helped us 'impersonate a VIP in order to gain access into an elite establishment', then you 'participated in a parade' by dancing."

"Hot damn," I say. "World gets out of the way of a man with a plan, Thibault."

"I mean you totally failed on the 'inspires those around him' and the 'helps and is helped by friends to appreciate the joys of life' parts, but you can't win them all," says Thibault.

"Miserable crushing failure," adds Sebastian.

"Thanks guys. I love you too."

"We're here," Nick says as we pull into Thibault's driveway.

"Nick, fine work tonight and I don't mind saying so," says Thibault shaking Nick's hand. "Where will you be in school next year?"

"There's actually a chance I might get let back into Woodmere. My mom has been talking with Mrs. Van den Berg . . . I mean, unless I have another assignment out in the field—"

"Of course," says Thibault.

"Of course of course," seconds Sebastian, coughing. He says his goodbyes and he and Thibault both get out. I get out of the back seat and talk to Nick through his window.

"You know he's right, Nick. You really saved our ass tonight. You were a big help . . . in uh . . . more ways than we maybe thought you could be. Thank you. Seriously, thank you."

Nick smiles. "Not a problem. I always like a good adventure."

"Well I mean . . . we're hanging out for a bit inside before I call a taxi to go home . . . if you wanna keep hanging . . . you're welcome."

Nick considers this with a funny look on his face, like he hasn't gotten an invitation like it in some time.

"Well, thanks . . . it sounds cool . . . it's just—well, I have to write this report . . . and I'm getting an emergency message from the consulate . . . and, you know . . ."

I sigh and look down.

"I know, Nick. I know . . . Maybe if you change your mind . . . or I mean, if that 'emergency' dies down really quickly, you can just come in and hang with us like a buddy for a bit."

Nick thinks in silence for a bit more, and then shuts his engine off.

"You know, the rest of the team might be able to handle things for a few hours . . ."

"That's good, Nick."

Inside Thibault's room, he and Sebastian are still regaling each other with stories from earlier in the night.

"Hey guys, Nick's gonna hang out for a little bit."

"Heeeyyy!" Sebastian and Thibault whisper-cheer as we walk in, hoping not to wake anyone else in the house. I settle into the same beanbag chair I didn't sleep in last night. It feels much more comfortable now.

"Hey what time is it, anyway?" I ask. "I still have to make sure I leave this country on time."

Nick consults an alarm clock on Thibault's desk.

"3:29."

"Wait a minute," I say, grabbing Thibault's remote and flicking on his small television. I change a few channels until landing on the opening credits of *Dazed and Confused*.

"Let's put this on."

"Yeah," says Thibault, "feels like a movie we should be watching while high though, hey?"

"You guys wanna smoke?" Nick asks. He produces a bloated bag of weed from his jacket pocket.

"*Jassus*, Nick!" says Thibault.

"I don't smoke a whole lot, but I like to keep some on hand. You never know . . ."

"You never know, Nick. This guy . . ." I point to him while shaking my head in disbelief at Thibault and Sebastian.

Within minutes, Thibault passes a lit joint to me. Our movie is complete. Our war has been fought, and won. The war general will now smoke his green victory cigar. I inhale and sink back into the beanbag chair. I'm watching the actors on the TV in front of me pretend to be high school kids, hanging out with their friends, getting high on the last day of school. Everyone is smiling and laughing, in the movie and outside. I think of the blackness of Penelope's lips closing over mine, of the warmth of her body against mine. I drift away for a bit, dreaming of nothing, feeling light.

Thibault wakes me by tapping me on the shoulder.

"Thought you might like to see the end."

I look around in a brief daze. Sebastian is passed out. Nick is awake for a few seconds, then dozes, then wakes again.

"I've seen it before."

"I know."

The last shot of the movie comes into focus. An empty road with a single car speeding along. Early morning. Friends get high inside the car while the stereo pumps. No past behind them. Undetermined future ahead of them. Living in the moment, for the moment. Fade to black.

"Good scene," I say as the credits roll.

"Good ending," Thibault adds.

- - ———— - -

Nick's dashboard rattles from the blare of bass, drums, and guitar as we blast across the South African countryside, this side of the earth warming and brightening in anticipation of the sun's arrival. He bangs on his steering wheel (mostly) in time to the music and we sing in unison. Badly.

"*STONE FREE! TO DO WHAT I PLEASE! STONE FREE! TO RIIIIIIIDE THE BREEZE! STONE FREE!*

BABY, I CAN'T STAY! I GOT TO GOT TO GOT TO GET AWAAAAY!"

"*HUUUGGHH!*" Nick's yells echo Jimi's grunts.

"*HUUUAAA!*" I yell. "TURN RIGHT!"

Nick has picked up the lyrics pretty well considering this is only his third time hearing the song.

"*LISTEN TO ME BABY, YOU CAN'T HOLD ME DOWN,*" he starts.

"*BROWR BROWR BRANH BROWR!*" I do Jimi's response guitar part while making air guitar gestures to match. "NOW LEFT!"

"*I DON'T WANT TO BE TIED DOWN!*" he really belts it.

"*BROWR BROWR BRANH BROWR!*" I increase my air guitar intensity to match his.

"*I GOTTA MOVE ON!*"

"HEEYYY!" I yell. "TWO MORE QUICK RIGHTS!!"

"YEEAAHH!!"

We both return for the final choruses and wail and whine our way out with the solo.

"Nice," Nick says.

"Nice," I say. "Pull over here."

He slows down and turns off the car.

"Which one of these is your place?"

"I actually live down at the end of this block," I say, pointing.

"Well why don't I drop you there?"

"I actually want to walk down my block one last time. Take in the air."

"Suit yourself. Nice knowing you." Nick puts his hand out.

"Ha. Sure thing, Nick. You too. You ever find yourself in America on a mission, you be sure and look me up."

"Of course."

We shake and I get out with my tape. He pulls away and I am alone. Again.

I put my hands in my pockets and stroll down my street. The silence comforts me, my surroundings smiling and waving to me. Not literally, though, not since a few hours ago.

The air is crisp with that chill that seems to exist at this time of morning all year round, no matter the season. It pricks me up and gives me life. I start jogging, then running. I run as fast as I can. I run and burn my empty stomach and the chemicals fading from my brain. My eyes and mouth water. My lungs wheeze as I near the gate of my house.

I'm alive.

19

MORNING

"We really shook the pillars of heaven, didn't we, Wang?"

- Jack Burton, *Big Trouble in Little China*

6:15am, the last day.

The first rays of the new rising sun come through the windows in sharp needles of pink and yellow. The mist of early morning covers every plant outside, tiny creatures dancing across them. Floyd sits at his desk, watching the beginnings of the day's life unfold. His alarm goes off and he laughs at the new day's indifference to what came before it. He smacks the alarm off before it gets even one full ring in. "For once, I got *you*," he whispers to it, grinning.

His body feels singed and run-down like it did when he woke up the previous day, but this time there's a light, a heat, an energy coursing through him. He stands and walks to the window by the side of the bed where he can survey the early morning hour in its glory. The day is fresh. Life has begun anew. He is the first mate on One-Eyed Willy's ship, sailing off into the sunrise.

He plays with the water temperature in the shower for kicks, taking turns with hot and cold. The hot relaxes him, the cold jolts him awake. He shampoos his hair once, and then again for good measure, hoping to soak the smell of apples into it.

He reaches for a t-shirt from his drawer, suddenly remembering his vomit-stained shirt rotting in the trash of Richard Koening's bedroom. He waves his hand in front of himself like a magician, pushing the dust of the vision into nothing. Gone. Set free. Happy trails.

Clean and fresh, he greets his just-waking mother with hugs and kisses. She eyes him with skepticism. They eat breakfast together and he talks excitedly about the future, Japan and beyond. Life is full of opportunity, he says. He compliments his mother on the beauty of the garden she has kept. Maybe he's just excited to be going home, she figures.

They drive to the airport. The road is quiet and mostly empty, and they talk the whole way—of movies, family trips on safari, messages for his brother back home. She inevitably gets teary-eyed as they near the airport. He tells her not to feel bad about any of his time there. He tells her that in the end, he got everything he needed to out of it. They hug goodbye in the airport, and he finds he is crying, too.

He finishes his check-in with time to spare. Mothers always insist on getting to the airport far too early. He decides to make a last phone call to pass the time.

"Yes, Mrs. Simms, I'm sure he's asleep, I'm just at the airport and wanted to say goodbye."

He waits a few moments as the mother leaves the phone. He can hear his friend groaning awake in the background.

"Yeah, what?"

"We've got to go get the tape, remember? I'll pick you up in ten minutes."

"*Jassus*, hehe, don't start that again."

"I know. Just kidding. How you feel?"

"Tired as hell. You?"

"I know, me too. I'll let you get back to sleep in a second. But . . . I feel pretty good. I feel . . ."

He smiles. For a moment only the sound of their respective breaths can be heard.

"We did it, Thibault."

"We did, Floyd."

"We really did it . . ."

More silence. He can hear his friend smiling on the other end of the phone.

"Take care, man."

"Keep in touch, hey."

"Bye."

He hangs up, and walks leisurely to his gate, a permanent smile on his face.

Soon he is on a plane on the runway. It speeds up and lifts off into the air, and a weight comes out of his stomach and off his shoulders, perhaps never to return. He puts on a tape, one of his favorites, one he almost lost forever.

It clicks on and his favorite song comes on; it's a slower tune, peaceful and fluid. He thinks of friends. He thinks of girls—one who was hot and then cold, and another who always looked at him with warmth. He pictures her smiling at him while dancing with flames between them, a weird movie-like dream that happened in real life.

He leans back and closes his eyes, waiting for sleep to take him.

Fade out.

ACKNOWLEDGEMENTS

I offer my sincere thanks to T. Kira Madden, John Madden, Michele Malo, Chris Peck, Mallory Baker, Derek Aubert, Tricia Murphy-Madden, Michel Fiffe, Justin Colletti, William Beaty, Kyle Frankiewich, Zach Gore, Myra Wexler, Janielle Hedt, Lori Banzai, Tim Clarke, Ben Sutter, Jenny George, Richard Bennett, My Young, Nikhil Sarma, Tiffany L. Vergara, Hallie Kapner, Ann Allen, Jeffrey Smith, Steve Madden, Nancy Alfaro, Eric Reidar, Sherrie Madden, Daniel Sutter, Stephanie Rose, Jennifer Page, Lorraine Rotanelli, Shawn D. Madden, Tilly Rodina, and Tammie Anthony. Without your contributions and support, this book would not be possible.

Rebecca Agiewich gave me the tools to begin this book. Waverly Fitzgerald gave me the tools to finish it. Leigh-Anne Jenks and Eva Talmage were the earliest eyes on these words. Michael French pushed me to do more. Ben, Mallory, and Derek made me a better writer. Michelle Josette brought care and enthusiasm to the editing. Sarah Plein brought elegance to the layout, and was generous with her time and effort.

Finally, I always thought it'd be funny if someone won an Oscar or something like that, and in their acceptance speech they said, "This is dedicated to Scotty Marcus, who kicked the crap out of me and called me names in 4th grade. Who's laughing now?" Perhaps if I ever published a novel, I thought, it would be funny if *I* did that. I'm a bit older now and realize that using such a platform to call out people would not only be extremely bitter, but a tremendous waste of the positive energy and accompanying sense of accomplishment generated by the act of creation. Still, I think it's only fair to acknowledge—if not necessarily thank—all the bad people, who don't get half as much credit as the good people do for making us better.

CPSIA information can be obtained at www.ICGtesting.com
Printed in the USA
BVOW07s1633270215

389268BV00001B/1/P